TYRANNY

TYRANNY

WILLIAM W. JOHNSTONE
with J. A. Johnstone

PINNACLE BOOKS
Kensington Publishing Corp.

PINNACLE BOOKS are published by

Kensington Publishing Corp.
119 West 40th Street
New York, NY 10018

PUBLISHER'S NOTE
Following the death of William W. Johnstone, the Johnstone family is working with a carefully selected writer to organize and complete Mr. Johnstone's outlines and many unfinished manuscripts to create additional novels in all of his series like The Last Gunfighter, Mountain Man, and Eagles, among others. This novel was inspired by Mr. Johnstone's superb storytelling.

All Kensington titles, imprints, and distributed lines are available at special quantity discounts for bulk purchases for sales promotions, premiums, fundraising, educational, or institutional use.

Special book excerpts or customized printings can also be created to fit specific needs. For details, write or phone the office of the Kensington sales manager: Kensington Publishing Corp., 119 West 40th Street, New York, NY 10018, attn: Sales Department; phone 1-800-221-2647.

PINNACLE BOOKS and the Pinnacle logo are Reg. U.S. Pat. & TM Off.

ISBN-13: 978-0-7860-3607-3
ISBN-10: 0-7860-3607-9

First printing: July 2015

10 9 8 7 6 5 4 3 2 1

Printed in the United States of America

First electronic edition: July 2015

ISBN-13: 978-0-7860-3608-0
ISBN-10: 0-7860-3608-7

Tyranny *(noun):* Cruel and oppressive government rule; a nation under cruel and oppressive government; cruel, unreasonable, or arbitrary use of power or control. From the Latin *turannus*, referring to a tyrant.

The tree of liberty must be refreshed from time to time with the blood of patriots and tyrants.
—THOMAS JEFFERSON

Manila

Storm warnings were out across the South China Sea. The typhoon sweeping toward the Philippines was a severe one, expected to deliver apocalyptic winds and torrential downpours when it made landfall.

After a peaceful day, the winds in Manila were picking up this evening. The fronds on the palm trees on the hotel grounds whipped back and forth as Ben Gardner stood on the balcony of his room watching them.

He shouldn't be standing out here in the open like this, he told himself. It was too risky. But the lights in the room were off, so he wasn't silhouetted against them, and besides, nobody in Manila wanted to kill him . . . that he knew of.

Gardner was a compactly built man in his thirties with close-cropped dark hair. His passport gave his name as Benjamin Gardner, and that was as good a name as any, even though it was a lie. The documents he carried stated that he worked for a company called Trans-Pacific Shipping, but that was a useful lie as well.

The phone in his shirt pocket buzzed. Gardner frowned.

He wasn't expecting a call. This stopover in Manila wasn't exactly a vacation, but he'd thought he was between assignments for a few days.

He took the phone out, opened it, and said, "Hello?"

"Mr. Gardner?"

The voice was smooth, the English unaccented, but the years Gardner had spent in the region allowed him to make an instinctive guess that it was Chinese. He didn't recognize it at all and wasn't going to give away anything until he knew more.

"Who's calling?"

"My name is Pao Ling. Geoffrey Ramsden gave me your number."

Gardner stiffened. He said, "I hope you're talking on a secure line, friend."

"I am, as are you. I have reached the correct Benjamin Gardner, have I not? The one who works for Trans-Pacific Shipping?"

In Gardner's line of work, a man often had to make swift decisions in order to survive. In the past, he had trusted Geoff Ramsden with his life on more than one occasion. Now he would do so again.

"That's right. We haven't met, have we, Mr. Pao?"

"No, but our mutual friend speaks highly of you. He suggested that I look you up when I came to Manila the next time, and so I have done so. I am downstairs in the lobby. Shall we meet and have a drink?"

Gardner's brain worked lightning fast. Ramsden wouldn't have known that he was in Manila unless he'd gotten the information from Company headquarters back in Langley, and even though Ramsden was as highly placed in MI6 as Gardner was in the Company, nobody in Virginia would have passed along Gardner's location unless Ramsden had convinced them it was urgent.

Gardner dismissed the idea that somebody was trying to lure him into the open for an assassination attempt. He was confident that none of their common enemies could break Ramsden. The big Englishman was too stubborn for that.

"All right, I'll be down in a few minutes," Gardner said into the phone. "How will I know you?"

"I'll know you, Mr. Gardner," Pao said.

Well, that wasn't too reassuring, Gardner thought as he broke the connection. But he was curious, and there was only one way to find out what was going on here.

When he was working, he relied on local contacts for armament, so he didn't have any guns. He carried several extremely sharp knives, though, made out of hardened plastic so they wouldn't set off metal detectors and hidden around his body so they'd be handy.

Those and his own abilities would have to be enough if he was walking into trouble.

He left his room and got onto the elevator. A very attractive Filipino woman was already in the car and gave him a dazzling smile when he entered. Gardner nodded and returned the smile but didn't say anything to her.

He watched her from the corner of his eye as the car descended, though, just in case she wasn't what she appeared to be, which was an expensive prostitute on her way out of the hotel after meeting a client. High-class hotels equaled high-class hookers.

As the car reached the first floor and the door slid open, the woman turned to Gardner and held out a business card in slender fingers with long painted fingernails.

"My website," she said. "I hope you will visit it and call me if you require companionship."

"Thanks," he told her. He slipped the card into his breast pocket and followed her out of the car.

The hotel was one of Manila's best, opulent and quiet. Gardner walked out into the lobby and paused, giving Pao Ling a chance to spot him. A moment later, Gardner saw a Chinese man in his fifties walking toward him.

The man was several inches shorter than Gardner, and his habit of stooping slightly made him appear even shorter. His gray hair was cut in an old-fashioned crew cut. Lines of strain were etched into his face. He looked like a man beset by pain or worries—or both.

"Mr. Gardner," he said as he came up to the American. "I am so very happy to make your acquaintance."

He didn't *look* happy, Gardner thought.

"How's Geoff?"

"The same as always," Pao said. "You know how he misses England—not, as you Americans would say."

For a split second, alarm bells had gone off in Gardner's brain. Geoff Ramsden didn't miss England at all. He was too restless by nature, too addicted to danger and excitement to ever go back to a stifling life at home. Adding the qualifier, though, as Pao had, made Gardner think the man really did know Ramsden.

"Shall we have a drink?" Pao said as he inclined his head toward the French doors that led to an outdoor bar.

"Sure, why not," Gardner said.

As the two men went outside, Gardner heard the buzz of excited conversation from the people crowded around the tables. All the talk was of the typhoon. Soon everyone would have to go back inside as the hotel battened down the hatches, so to speak, and got ready to ride out the storm.

An air of desperation and urgency hung over the outdoor bar. The drinkers wanted to get in as much partying as they could before all hell broke loose.

"Beer?" Gardner asked Pao. The man shrugged, so Gardner said, "Two San Migs," to the bartender and took the squat, icy bottles from him. Condensation dripped from them.

There were no empty tables, but Gardner spotted a stone bench under one of the palms and nodded toward it.

They sat down, and Gardner handed one of the San Miguels to Pao. He swallowed some of his own beer and said, "We didn't really come out here to drink, did we?"

Pao didn't touch his beer. He shook his head and said, "No. My body will no longer tolerate alcohol. I am ill, Mr. Gardner. Cancer. I have a month, if I am fortunate. And luck has never run in my family."

"I'm sorry," Gardner said quietly. "What can I do for you?"

Casually, Pao rested his free hand on the bench between them for a moment, and when he lifted it, a tiny USB drive lay there, a little metal rectangle half an inch wide by three quarters of an inch long, with a thin plastic rim around one end so it could be removed from a computer port.

"There is information on there someone must know," Pao said, "information vital to your country." His lined face twisted in a grimace. "Though I betray my own homeland by giving it to you. Some things transcend borders, however. This is a matter of humanity, not nations."

"Why me?" Gardner asked. He hadn't picked up the drive yet.

"Because I am told you are not a creature of politics." Pao smiled faintly. "Because Ramsden said you would do what was right, and screw bloody all else."

That brought a chuckle from Gardner. Pao knew Geoff Ramsden, all right.

"I'll do what I can," Gardner said. "I—"

He stopped short and lifted his head. At first he thought what he heard was the wind picking up even more, but then he recognized the sound. He had heard it before, in other countries.

That was a drone, and it was headed in his direction.

Pao gasped something in Mandarin. Gardner knew enough of the language to understand that Pao had said, "They have found me!"

That couldn't be good.

"Get out of here, now!" Pao said in English.

"These people—"

"Too late! Too late for us all . . ."

Gardner dropped the beer and grabbed the USB drive. He surged to his feet and yelled, "Get out! Everybody move!"

In a world conditioned to a constant low level of fear and preparedness because of terrorist attacks, people reacted quickly. With screams and shouts, the crowd in the outdoor bar began to scatter. Most of them headed for the doors into the hotel, but Gardner went the other way, sprinting toward a low stone wall that enclosed the adjacent garden.

As he ran, from the corner of his eye he picked up a red streak flashing through the air toward the building. He glanced back, saw Pao sitting there on the stone bench in that last instant, the untouched bottle of beer beside him, hands folded in his lap as he waited almost serenely to die.

The missile fired from the drone homed in on him and struck, and man and bench disappeared in a blinding flash as Gardner put his hand on the stone wall and vaulted over it. The blast's concussion wave slapped him to the ground like a giant flyswatter. A ball of flame blossomed from the site of the explosion, swallowing the outdoor bar.

The roar was so loud it was several minutes before people in the area began to be able to hear anything again. When they could, the first things they heard were screams. . . .

Washington, D.C.

One of the Secret Service agents put his finger on the earplug he wore and pushed it a little tighter into his ear to shut out some of the noise from the state dinner going on. As he listened to the voice on the radio, his normally expressionless face took on a slightly grim cast, but that was the only way he betrayed his reaction to the news.

After a moment, the agent moved to the side of the President, who was flanked on one side by a dignitary from a country in the Middle East regarded by the administration as an ally, despite the fact that its ruling family quietly funneled millions of dollars in funding to organizations whose goal was the complete and utter destruction of Western culture and the domination of the world by their religion.

On the President's other side was an Academy Award–winning film director whose big-budget movies tended to blame America for everything bad that happened in the world, past, present, and future.

The Secret Service agent leaned down to whisper in the President's ear. The President sat up straighter, murmured, "Is this confirmed?"

"Yes, sir," the agent said.

"How many casualties?"

"Unknown at this time. A minimum of fifty. And extensive destruction to the hotel and surrounding buildings."

"Has any group stepped forward to claim credit?"

"Not so far."

With a frown creasing his forehead, the President considered for a moment and then slowly nodded.

"Well," he said, "I suppose it could have been worse."

Secretly, he was pleased. He couldn't allow that to show, of course. As the leader of the free world, he had to maintain an appearance of grave concern and resolve every time there was a terrorist attack.

Things had gone according to plan, though, and now he could stop worrying about this problem, anyway.

"So, tell me," he said with a smile as he turned to the Hollywood director, "what's your next project going to be about?"

West Texas

The TV was playing quietly in the living room, but George Washington Brannock wasn't paying much attention to it.

Nothin' on it but bad news anyway, he thought. Some special report about a terrorist attack somewhere on the other side of the world. One of the various bunches of lunatics who seemed to be everywhere these days had fired a missile into a hotel and killed a bunch of folks.

Brannock was sorry for what had happened in the Philippines, but like most people he had gotten a little numb to such things.

Seemed like over the past thirty or forty years, the world had gotten crazier and more dangerous all the time, until it barely resembled the place he had grown up in. That wasn't just being a reactionary curmudgeon, either. It was the truth.

Carrying a longneck, he stepped out onto the ranch house's back porch and gazed toward the mountains in the distance, even though he couldn't see them in the dark.

He stood a couple of inches over six feet, was barrel-chested and a little thicker through the waist than he'd been forty years earlier as a young man, and his eyes were surrounded by the permanent squint lines of a man who spent most of his time outdoors. He was a Texan, born, bred, and forever, and didn't care who knew it.

He lifted the longneck to his mouth and took a long swallow, finishing off the beer that was still in the bottle. He set the empty on the porch rail and then leaned on the railing himself.

Something had drawn him out here tonight, and he didn't know what it was.

Then lightning flickered in the distance, jagged fingers of blue-white brilliance clawing at the sky. The flash revealed the saw-toothed mountain peaks that marked the border of Brannock's sprawling ranch.

That was it, he thought. That was what his instincts had sensed.

There was a storm comin'.

Chapter 1

The bus pulled into Sierra Lobo right on schedule, five minutes before noon. It stopped at the gas station/ convenience store/fast food joint that also served as the bus depot. No one was waiting to get on and only one passenger got off, so the bus was gone in a matter of minutes.

It left behind a young man with tousled, sandy hair and blue eyes. He was slender in jeans and a T-shirt, but the muscles under the shirt were well-defined, like strands of cable. He slung the duffel bag he had carried off the bus over his shoulder and walked into the store.

Sierra Lobo wasn't a very big place. A little over 2,000 people lived in the city limits, according to the last census—although who knew how accurate that count was in this era of government manipulation of every possible statistic for the benefit of the Democratic Party. Maybe another 1,500 people lived in the immediate environs of the town, but outside the city limits.

It appeared that a good number of those citizens were packed into the fast food end of the building today. It was Saturday, and folks came to town to visit and shop and commemorate the fact that they'd made it through another week.

Some things never changed in Texas.

The young man who had gotten off the bus stayed in the convenience store part of the building, walking up and down the aisles and picking up a bag of chips, some beef jerky, and a candy bar.

Simple food for a simple man, he thought as he approached the counter.

Four men were in line at the register. The first one, a harried-looking youngster, was paying for a jug of milk and a box of diapers.

Better you than me, amigo, thought the man from the bus. Just about the last thing in the world he was cut out to be was a dad.

The second man had a cup of coffee to pay for, the third a couple of canned soft drinks. They conducted their transactions pretty quickly and departed.

That left the man right in front of the newcomer to Sierra Lobo. He wore a shirt that said he worked for the county road department, unbuttoned and untucked at the moment so the white T-shirt under it was visible.

The man had two twelve-packs of the store's least expensive beer stacked in his arms. He stepped up to the counter and set them down in front of the young, pretty Hispanic woman working the register.

"Hey, Stella," he said. "You're lookin' mighty good today. *Muy bonita.*"

He was about forty and balding, which made him twice as old as the woman at the register, so he shouldn't have been flirting with her. Not that it was any of his business, the man from the bus told himself. He just wanted to get his food, sit on one of the public benches on the sidewalk, look at the mountains, and figure out what the hell to do with his life next.

Or to be more accurate, he mused, how could he foul up his life again? Because given his track record, that was bound to happen.

The clerk didn't respond to the customer's compliment, but when the man pulled a battered old checkbook from the pocket of his work shirt, she said, "Uh-uh, Vern, you can't write a check for that beer."

"What?" Vern exclaimed with a frown. "Who says?"

"This says." Stella tapped a red-painted fingernail on a check taped to the side of a cardboard candy display sitting on the counter. Several checks were taped there, and all of them had been stamped *Insufficient Funds*.

"But those aren't all my checks," Vern protested. "Just that one."

"One and done, Mr. Charlton says," Stella told him. "Mr. Charlton says if you bounce one check on him, you don't write no more."

"What? That's crazy! That . . . that was just a misunderstanding. A glitch. A bank error. I got the money—"

"Mr. Charlton, he tried to put the check through three times, and it bounced every time. Sorry, Vern. I got to do what he says."

"But how am I supposed to pay for my beer?"

"Cash, credit, or debit. Preferably cash. But no checks from you. That's final."

"Well . . . well, hell!"

"Don't swear at me," Stella said. "It's not my fault."

The man from the bus knew he ought to curb his impatience, but he and waiting had never gotten along well. He leaned forward and said to Vern, "Why don't you move that beer and let the young lady wait on me, and then maybe you can figure out what to do."

He thought that was a reasonable suggestion and that it was phrased politely enough.

Vern turned his head to glare and said, "Why don't you butt the hell out of what ain't your business?"

The clerk looked past him at the newcomer, frowned, and then said in surprise, "Kyle? Kyle, is that you?"

He frowned, too, because he couldn't place her. He had spent quite a bit of time in Sierra Lobo in the past, though, and there was no point in denying that he'd always had an eye for a pretty girl, so it was possible he knew her.

She saw his puzzled look and went on. "It's me, Estellita Lopez. Most people call me Stella now."

Estellita, Kyle Brannock thought. *Muy bonita, Estellita . . .*

Chapter 2

The name made his mind flash back to an autumn night a few years earlier. Visiting for the weekend, he had gone to a football game at the high school stadium on the edge of town, and that had led to meeting Estellita and then some frenzied, clumsy groping in the backseat of a car afterward. . . .

They hadn't made any declarations of undying love. In that particular moment, neither of them had been looking for such a thing.

Instead, all they were interested in was sharing the wonderful thing they had discovered together. Although, to be honest, Kyle suspected that Estellita had stumbled upon the great secret before, with somebody else. Maybe a number of different somebody elses.

Not that he cared. He wasn't all that innocent himself, and he sure as hell wasn't a hypocrite.

"Oh," he said now as she smiled across the counter at him. "Estellita. Sure."

He wasn't lying. He actually did remember her, and fondly, at that. He also remembered that everything had gone to hell and he'd left town not long after that, without ever calling her. Some girls would hold a grudge about being treated like that, but it didn't seem like she did.

"I get it now," Vern said. "This kid is one of your old boyfriends. I'm not sure how you remember 'em all, Stella, there's been so many of them."

"Hey!" she exclaimed. "You don't have to be ugly, just 'cause you're mad about the beer."

"You were always runnin' around after boys, never had time for a real man," he sneered.

"For a real pervert, you mean! I remember the way you looked at me when I was still in high school. If you can't pay for the beer, put it back in the cooler."

"Damn it, I just want to write a check!"

"No checks from you!"

This was getting ridiculous, Kyle thought.

Not only that, he had just seen one of the local cops come into the building through the fast food entrance, stopping for lunch, no doubt. It was open between the two halves of the business, so people on the other side could hear what was going on in here.

If the cop heard Vern and Estellita—Stella—yelling at each other, he was liable to come over to see what the trouble was. Kyle didn't really want that.

He set his duffel bag down, reached past Vern, placed the items he had picked up on the counter, and took hold of the twelve-packs.

"I'll put these up for you," he told Stella.

Vern slapped a big left hand down on the top twelve-pack, put his anger-reddened face next to Kyle's, and said, "Get your hands off my beer, you lame-ass little punk."

"Hey!" Stella said. "You leave him alone, Vern. I'll call the cops."

Well, this was yet another situation that had spiraled almost out of control, thought Kyle. He wanted to end it as quickly as possible and get out of here. Under other circumstances it might have been fun catching up on old times with Stella, but he was in no mood for nostalgia today.

Instead, he turned toward Vern, moving fast without really seeming to hurry, and did a stiff-hand strike to the older man's solar plexus. The blow traveled less than a foot, but it caused Vern's eyes to bug out from their sockets and his face to turn pale under his sunburn. He hunched over the pain in his middle and leaned toward Kyle.

Taking hold of Vern's upper arms, Kyle sort of propped him against the counter. Vern's mouth opened and closed a couple of times, like a fish out of water. He stared at Kyle in confusion, as if he couldn't understand what had just happened.

"What did you *do* to him?" Stella asked.

"Tried to teach him he shouldn't be an asshole. I doubt if it'll do much good, though. Some people, that's just their natural state."

Kyle started to pick up the twelve-packs again.

"No, no, just leave 'em, I'll put them up," Stella said quickly. "You should go now. Lemme ring you up. . . ."

She gave Kyle his total and then put the food in a plastic bag while he was getting out his wallet. He paid her, took his change, then picked up the duffel bag in one hand and the food with the other.

All the while, Vern stood there leaning helplessly against the counter, gaping and trying to catch his breath.

As Kyle turned toward the door, he glanced into the fast food half of the building. The cop was still there, putting in his order now at the counter, talking and laughing with the high school kid working the register. Kyle was glad to see that the brief confrontation in the convenience store hadn't caught the officer's attention.

He had made it halfway to the door when Stella cried, "Kyle, look out!"

He heard shoe leather slapping against the floor as he swung around. Vern was still pale and gasping for air, but somewhere he had found the strength to come lumbering after Kyle like a charging buffalo.

The store aisle wasn't big enough. Kyle didn't have room or time to get out of the way.

Vern plowed into him and the impact drove Kyle backwards. Both men crashed into a stacked-up display of two-liter plastic jugs of cola that flew everywhere as they sprawled to the floor.

Chapter 3

The Sierra Lobo Inn was at the eastern edge of town on the state highway. The horseshoe shape in which it was built, curled around a fenced-in area with a swimming pool in it, betrayed its origins in the 1950s.

The pool hadn't had a fence around it in those more innocent, less litigious days, of course, but now, what with liability lawsuits, the insurance company demanded the enclosure. Several signs on the fence warned people that no lifeguard was on duty and they swam at their own risk.

People lived at their own risk, Barton Devlin thought as he parked the late-model sedan in front of the office and looked through the windshield at the signs on the fence. Nobody got any sort of guarantee when they woke up in the morning.

After all, nothing was certain in life except death and taxes.

Even after all this time, that corny old chestnut brought a smile to Devlin's lips.

He got out of the car, pushed his glasses up on his nose, and went into the motel office, grateful for the blast of air-conditioned coolness that greeted him.

Even though the walk had been only a few feet and the

temperature really wasn't bad for West Texas, he didn't like the heat and didn't see how people could live in this hell-hole. Some of them even spent their whole lives here, he reminded himself. He wouldn't be able to stand that.

There were much better uses for West Texas.

"Help you?" the man behind the counter asked. He was stocky, with graying fair hair, and wore jeans and a polo shirt. "Check-in time's not until three o'clock. Not officially, anyway. But if you need a place to stay, I've got a few units that are already cleaned and ready to go."

"I'll take one of them," Devlin said as he slid his credit card across the counter. It looked like a regular card, but actually it was issued by the federal government and billed back to Devlin's expense account. He had used it to pay for everything since he'd left Washington.

"All right, Mister . . ." He read the name on the credit card. "Devlin. If you'll just fill this out . . ." He gave Devlin a registration form and pen, then went on, saying, "Traveling on business?"

"What makes you think that?" Devlin asked as he began filling out the form.

"I know a rental car when I see one," the clerk said with a nod at the vehicle parked just outside the office window. "Enough of 'em come through here. I'll bet that's a corporate credit card, too. Nice suit, accent says you're from back East somewhere. . . . Easy enough to make the deduction." The man gave Devlin a toothy grin. "I like to think I'm sort of a detective, you know, like the guys you see on TV."

"Is that right?" Devlin cocked his head a little to the side as he looked across the counter at the man. "Let me have a try at this. You're not Middle Eastern, so I assume you don't own the hotel, you just work here. I haven't stayed at a motel in years that wasn't owned by a Pakistani or an Iranian or a Lebanese."

The clerk said with apparent satisfaction, "Well, you're wrong right off the bat. The Sierra Lobo Inn is mine, all right, and I'm a hundred percent American, born and bred. Lou Scarborough's my name."

"All right, let me try again," Devlin said. He looked around the small lobby. "Place is clean, but not *too* clean. You hire illegal immigrants as maids, right? And since they're illegal, they can't afford to complain about the lousy pay or the way you get a little handsy with them sometimes. The young and pretty ones, you might even take them into a vacant unit now and then and have a little fun with them, because what can they do about it, right? And since you pay them under the table, you need to have a ready supply of cash, so when any of the guests pay you that way you tear up the registration form and put the money in your pocket and don't declare it on your taxes, because that's just the kind of guy you are. Did I figure you out right, Lou, like one of those TV detectives?"

Scarborough had stared at him, eyes getting bigger and bigger, as Devlin talked. His face had turned a dull, angry red. He put both hands on the counter and said, "I don't think I need your business after all, Mr. Devlin. You should find somewhere else to stay."

"I believe this is the only motel in Sierra Lobo."

"Then drive on. Hell, you could make it most of the way to El Paso by night."

"My business is here," Devlin insisted. "And it's a funny thing . . . my business is deductions, too, just a different kind." He tapped a finger on the registration form he'd filled out. "Check what I wrote down for my employer. It says *Internal Revenue Service*."

The angry flush drained out of Scarborough's face like water from a bathtub, leaving his formerly beefy features washed out into a deathly pallor. He said, "The . . . the . . ."

"That's right, the IRS. And I'm here on official business, like you thought. But that business doesn't involve you, Mr. Scarborough, not yet anyway. So, do I get that room or not?"

Scarborough swallowed hard, reached under the counter, and brought out an old-fashioned room key attached to a red plastic fob in the shape of an elongated diamond. The number 12 was painted on the fob in gilt letters.

"Unit 12," he said in a hollow voice. He set the key on the counter. "Best one in the place."

"Thank you," Devlin said as he picked up the key. "Now, you'd better go ahead and run that credit card before you forget. Want to do everything on the up-and-up, you know. Keep a good record of everything in case somebody wants to check up on it."

"Yeah. I always do. I swear."

"None of my business," Devlin said with a smile. "This time."

He chuckled to himself a few minutes later as he went back out to his car. The look on Scarborough's face at the mention of the Internal Revenue Service . . . it was just priceless. That feeling of power never got old, either.

But he was here on serious business, Devlin reminded himself as his face grew solemn again. He paused to gaze toward the mountains west of town. Even though the blue-gray peaks were twenty miles away, they looked almost close enough to reach out and touch.

Between the town of Sierra Lobo and those mountains lay the property of the man he had come to see. The man who was the last obstacle in the path of progress.

The man Barton Devlin was going to destroy.

Chapter 4

G.W. Brannock saw the dust cloud rising from the car's tires when the vehicle was still a couple of miles away, as soon as it turned off the state highway onto the private road that led to his house.

The opening in the fence didn't have a gate in it, just a cattle guard to keep stock from straying through it. Red signs with black lettering that stated NO TRESPASSING were fastened to the fence on each side of the gap.

The road had enough ruts and rocks in it that nobody could drive very fast on it, no matter how good a vehicle they had. That was the way Brannock liked it. He had plenty of warning when visitors came to call.

Time to make sure the old lever-action .30-30 and both shotguns were loaded, the side-by-side Stoeger and the Mossberg 500 Tactical pump.

The Browning Hi-Power he carried tucked behind his belt at the small of his back had a full magazine in it, too, as he stood on the porch waiting for his visitor to arrive.

Even covered with road dust the way it was by the time it came in sight, the car was familiar to Brannock. It was one of those Japanese compacts, something that annoyed Brannock from time to time since his dad had been a POW in the war against the countrymen of the fellas who'd built that car.

He was willing to overlook the annoyance, though, since the owner was on his side in a war of his own.

The car came to a stop in front of the porch. The driver waited a minute for the dust cloud swirling around it to dissipate before she stepped out.

Miranda Stephens wasn't dressed for court today. She wore jeans, a white tank top, and a lightweight red over-shirt. Her shoulder-length blond hair was loose instead of pulled back severely like she wore it when she had to go in front of a judge. With her wholesome good looks, punc-tuated by a scattering of freckles and a little dimple in her chin, she looked more like a college sorority girl than a lawyer.

"You didn't have to come all the way out here," Bran-nock told her. "You could'a just returned my call."

"No, I want to see this letter you got," Miranda said as she came up onto the porch.

"Don't know why you would. It's just more o' the same old bull . . . crap."

"You can say bullshit in front of me, G.W. Some crude language isn't going to offend my ladylike sensibilities so much that I swoon or anything. If you'd heard the way we used to talk in law school—"

Brannock held up a hand to stop her.

"No, thanks," he said. "I know I'm a dang throwback, but I reckon I'd rather preserve some of my illusions."

"If being a gentleman means you're a throwback, there should be more like you." Miranda stuck out her hand. "Now, let me see it."

Brannock had figured she might drive out from town after she got the message he'd left her, so he had the certified letter sitting on the little table between the two rocking chairs, ready for her to look at.

The rural mail carrier had brought it up earlier and gotten him to sign for it. Brannock picked it up now and extended it toward the lawyer.

She frowned at it like he was trying to hand her a diamondback rattlesnake.

"Yeah, I reckon that's the way most people feel about a letter from the IRS sayin' they're gonna take everything you've got," he said.

Chapter 5

Vern's weight coming down on top of Kyle drove all the air out of the younger, smaller man's lungs. He gasped for breath, too, like his attacker.

As he landed, his head bounced off the floor, which was thin tile over concrete, so it didn't have any give to it. Red rockets blasted off behind his eyes and blinded him for several seconds.

When his vision cleared, he saw Vern looming over him. The big man's fists sledged into Kyle's ribs as he threw wild punch after wild punch.

Kyle was still half-stunned from the blow to the head, so his arms didn't want to work right now. He tried, but he couldn't block the punches.

He couldn't just lie there and allow Vern to beat him senseless, though. As feeling started to return to his muscles, he kicked high with his right leg and brought it around in front of Vern's neck, then used it to lever the bigger man off him.

Vern sprawled in the aisle and couldn't get up because the soda bottles kept rolling under him. All the caps had stayed on, preventing the drink from spilling. A triumph of modern consumer engineering, Kyle thought fleetingly as he rolled, got his hands under him, and pushed himself up to his knees.

At that same moment, Vern began to recover as well and kicked the plastic bottles aside so he could get to his feet. He grabbed one of the bottles by the neck and swung it at Kyle's head.

Full of drink like that, even a plastic bottle could deliver quite a wallop, and Kyle's skull had suffered enough punishment today. He ducked under the sweeping blow and launched himself at Vern in a diving tackle.

This time it was Kyle who landed on top as he caught Vern around the midsection and drove him over backwards.

Unlike Vern's wild, flailing blows, however, the punches Kyle threw while he had the advantage were short, sharp, and precise. He chopped away at Vern's face with his fists, and blood began to fly from the cuts his knuckles opened.

"Get off of him!" a man's voice shouted from somewhere nearby. "Get off of him now!"

The words barely registered on Kyle's brain, which was filled with the sort of blinding rage that had always been a problem for him. When he got caught up in a fight, he couldn't think straight and everything else in the world seemed to go away except the punishment he was handing out to his opponent.

But then he heard Stella scream, "Steve, no!" and turned his head enough to glance over his shoulder.

He spotted the cop who'd been at the fast food counter a few minutes earlier. The uniformed man stood about ten feet from him now, aiming something at him. It wasn't a service revolver, Kyle thought, but some other sort of weapon. . . .

The small part of his brain that was still rational recognized the thing in the cop's hands as a stun gun. He opened his mouth to tell the officer not to shoot, but it was too late.

The cop pressed the button on the top of the stun gun, and with a *whoosh!* of compressed air the two sharp prongs and the attached electrical wires trailing behind them exploded from the end of the weapon.

Kyle barely had time to feel the twin stings as the prongs penetrated his shirt and lodged in his skin before the surge of current hit him like the proverbial ton of bricks.

He went over backwards as his mouth opened to scream. No sound came from his throat, though, because his vocal cords were locked up like the rest of his muscles from the electrical charge flowing through his body. All he could do was lie there helplessly and twitch.

The shock didn't last all that long, but when it was over, Kyle couldn't move, couldn't put up any sort of fight as the cop rolled him over and jerked plastic restraints around his wrists. His vision was blurry, but he could make out Vern lying on the floor a few feet away, gasping and sobbing.

But Vern wasn't being arrested, Kyle thought. No, *he* was the one who'd been Tased, the one being taken into custody.

That wasn't too surprising, actually. Vern, at least, was a local. Kyle had visited Sierra Lobo many times in the past, but to this cop, at least, he was a total stranger.

No wonder he was going to be blamed for the trouble. No wonder he was going to jail for something that wasn't really his fault.

It wasn't like this would be the first time for that to happen, he thought bitterly as the officer hauled him upright and held him there as his rubbery legs tried to fold up underneath him.

Chapter 6

Miranda quickly scanned the letter that Brannock gave to her. She'd always had the ability to read quickly and comprehend and retain what she'd read, a skill that came in handy when she'd honed it even more during law school. She could wade through the assigned reading and make sense of it in half the time of most of her fellow students.

Now she saw that the old rancher was right. The tone of this letter from the government was definitely threatening.

"I don't understand this," she said. "Well, I *understand* it, of course, but I don't know why they sent it to you. We've appealed the auditor's decision, and they're supposed to allow time for that appeal to be considered before they take any further action against you."

Brannock pointed at the letter and said, "Yeah, but that says they're gonna take my ranch if they don't get their dadgum $380,000, doesn't it?"

"That's what it says, all right," Miranda replied with a sigh. "But it doesn't make any sense. We've demonstrated beyond a shadow of a doubt that you *don't* owe those back taxes. In fact, if anything the IRS probably owes you a small refund. All they have to do is look at all the documentation we assembled and it'll be obvious that they're in the wrong."

"You know that and I know that, but that auditor fella we talked to in El Paso was bound and determined not to admit it, wasn't he?"

Miranda shrugged and said, "Well, of course he was going to be stubborn about it. That's what they're trained to do: stonewall and deny doing anything wrong. The taxpayer is always presumed to be guilty, and you not only have to prove your innocence, you sometimes have to do it two or three different ways before you explain it to them in a way they're willing to admit might be right. So I fully expected that the audit would go against you. I'm confident you'll win on appeal, though."

"Not if they don't give me a chance to. And if they go ahead and take this ranch away from me, what do you reckon the chances are they'll ever admit they made a mistake and give it back to me?"

Miranda's face was grim as she said, "Slim to none. And they'd just tie the case up in court for so long that you'd bankrupt yourself trying to prove them wrong."

"That wouldn't take much." Brannock's face was equally bleak. "I've never had a lot of cash, just this ranch. Without it . . . well, I won't be able to put up much of a fight. It might take me years to pay off just what I owe you."

Miranda shook her head and said, "Don't worry about that right now. I'm certainly not going to." She paused. "There's no way you can come up with, say, ten percent of what they say you owe? That might be enough to put them off for a while, and you can always try to recover it later."

"Thirty-eight grand is just as impossible for me as the whole shootin' match would be," Brannock said. "I just don't have it. I might be able to raise it by sellin' off some of the spread. . . ." The pain in his voice made it clear just how much he didn't want to take that drastic step. "But they won't even let me do that. The whole property is frozen, accordin' to the letter."

"Yes, you wouldn't be allowed to dispose of any holdings. Why should they let you do that when they can just seize everything and have it all?"

"Bunch'a damn pirates, if you ask me."

"You won't get any argument from me, G.W. This is just about the most blatant thing I've ever seen, though, even from the IRS." Miranda drew in a deep breath. "Don't give up, though. I've got a few days to try to come up with a strategy to block this—"

Before she could say anything else, Brannock's phone rang inside the old ranch house, its shrill summons easily heard through the screen door.

"Hold on a minute," Brannock said. He disappeared inside as he waved a hand at the wicker rocking chairs and added, "Have a seat."

Miranda sat down in one of the rockers. In the shade of the porch, with a little breeze blowing, the temperature was warm but not uncomfortable.

Miranda had grown up in the Florida Panhandle, so she was used to heat. It had taken her a while to become accustomed to the low humidity out here in West Texas, though.

She had never figured she would wind up in a place like Sierra Lobo, but it was a long, long way from the painful breakup that had prompted her to leave Florida in the first place. She had started driving west and, except for sleeping in anonymous motels, had stayed on the road until she gave in to a whim and stopped in the little town.

The first thing she'd seen was a sign on a building that read OFFICE SPACE FOR RENT, and she had said to herself, why the hell not?

It had taken a while to get licensed to practice law in Texas, and, of course, any new practice was slow to get started, but she'd advertised in the local newspaper and gradually she had taken on a few clients, including G.W. Brannock.

It wasn't a bad life, and Sierra Lobo was as good a place to hide out from the world as any.

Unfortunately for G.W., there was no hiding from the federal government, especially the IRS.

The screen door banged behind the old rancher as he came out of the house looking upset.

"We'll have to talk about this later," he told Miranda. "I got to go into town."

"What's wrong?"

"That call was the police chief. They've got my grandson locked up, and I got to go get him out."

Chapter 7

As jails went, the one in Sierra Lobo wasn't too bad, Kyle thought as he sat on the bunk with its thin mattress and single blanket. He had certainly been in worse.

He rolled his shoulders and stretched his arms and massaged his legs. His muscles still ached from the spasming they'd done as a result of the stun gun charge, and he didn't want them to stiffen up.

He looked around the cell and reflected idly that whatever company manufactured the ugly, institutional green paint that covered the cinder block walls, they must be making a fortune, he reflected. Every jail cell he'd ever been in had been painted that same shade.

If that was true, it was probably one of the few companies in the country that was still vibrant and healthy, since the vaunted "economic recovery" a couple of presidential administrations earlier had turned out to be nothing but an apparently endless cycle of recessions that were propped up artificially by the government to give the lapdog pundits in the mainstream media something good to say about their Democrat masters before the inevitable spiral began again.

Each round left the country worse off than it had been

to start with, because no matter how hard they tried, no matter how many executive orders the President issued, no matter how many micromanaging regulations came from petty bureaucrats unaccountable to the public or anyone else, and no matter how many borderline unconstitutional laws were passed by the liberal-controlled Congress, the politicians just couldn't make two and two equal more than four.

"Math always wins in the end," a guy in Kyle's platoon had told him when they talked about the state of the world. "There's a famous science fiction story called 'The Cold Equations,' because emotions don't enter into math. Numbers add up to what they add up to, and sooner or later if you're taking resources away from a steadily decreasing group in order to give them to a steadily *increasing* group in order to solicit votes, the system is going to crash. It's not a sustainable equation, no matter how much some people think it *should* be."

"So what happens then?" Kyle had asked.

"Blood in the streets when people who have been dependent on the government for everything they have realize that the free ride has run out. A near-total breakdown of society that our enemies will try to exploit. Why do you think I've been studying Chinese? I want to be useful to our new masters. Maybe that way I can dodge the reeducation camps."

That whole scenario seemed pretty far-fetched to Kyle, but he couldn't discount the idea completely. Just in the time he had been alive, he had seen conditions in the country steadily worsen as the so-called "progressives" strengthened their stranglehold on government, media, culture, and education.

One reason he'd lasted only a single semester in college before joining the army was that he couldn't stomach all the liberal crap that the professors tried to feed their students.

The only reason he'd lasted less than a year in the army before being booted out was that he was an angry asshole with poor impulse control. Not exactly what you'd call a textbook soldier.

The holding cell where they'd put him was in a hallway with a couple of other similar cells. At least they hadn't thrown him in the tank. He was grateful for that. All he needed to get himself in even more trouble would be to get tossed in with some belligerent drunk who'd force him into a fight.

Footsteps in the corridor broke into his musing and made him lift his head. The cell had a solid door with a small barred window in it. If Kyle had bothered to stand up, he could have looked through that window and seen if whoever was coming this direction stopped at the door. He couldn't find the energy and enthusiasm to go to that much trouble.

Anyway, the lock mechanism buzzed a moment later, and he knew whoever it was had come for him.

The officer who'd arrested him stood there. The ID badge he wore on his shirt identified him as CHAPMAN. Stella had called him Steve, Kyle recalled. He wondered if she and the cop had dated. It was certainly possible. Officer Chapman was only about twenty-five. Hell, the two of them might even have something going on now, thought Kyle.

Chapman jerked his head toward the corridor and said, "All right, Brannock, come on out. Your grandfather and your sister are here to get you."

Chapter 8

Sister—?

That would be a neat trick, Kyle thought, since he didn't have a sister. He was an only child—or rather, an only orphan since his mother and father were both dead.

Evidently G.W. had some young woman with him, though, and Kyle couldn't help but wonder who she was. His grandfather, who had been a widower since before Kyle was born, was long past the age when he could attract a hot young girlfriend, even one with serious daddy issues.

One way to find out, Kyle told himself. He stood up and went to the door in his stocking feet. They had taken his shoes and his belt along with everything else.

He'd tried to tell them that he didn't need to be put on suicide watch. He was a stubborn jerk, sure, but he wasn't crazy. But as usual with cops, they hadn't listened.

Chapman pointed along the hall and said, "Back the way we came in."

"Gee, thanks, Officer Steve," Kyle said with exaggerated politeness.

"Don't push your luck, Brannock. You already caught enough breaks today."

"Oh, really?"

"Yeah. Vern Hummel decided not to press charges, and Ed Charlton told your grandfather that if he'd pay for the damages, he'd let it go, too."

Kyle frowned and said, "Damages? What damages? We knocked over some jugs of Coke. Stack 'em back up and they're good as new."

"Don't ask me, I don't have anything to do with that part of it. We could have charged you with assault and disturbing the peace whether Hummel and Charlton pressed charges or not, but the chief decided not to. Something about how he was friends with your dad?"

That was true. Ernie Rodriguez and Ted Brannock were friends from elementary school on and had played ball together in junior high and high school.

Ted, Kyle's father, had gone to college at UT in Austin, married a girl he met there, then gotten a job with a tech firm in the suburb of Dallas where Kyle had been born and raised.

Ernie had stayed in Sierra Lobo and joined the police force, and he was still here, only he had risen through the ranks to be the chief of the department now.

Several years earlier, Ted and Linda Brannock had been on Interstate 20, on their way to West Texas to visit Ted's father, when a drunk driver in an SUV had crossed the wide, grassy median and plowed head-on into their car.

According to the report of the state trooper who'd investigated the accident, tire marks showed that Ted had juked back and forth desperately as he tried to avoid the oncoming vehicle, but every time he'd zigged, the drunk had zagged, and they finally came together as if fate had aimed them squarely at each other. The drunk in the SUV had died, too, but that was no consolation.

That had happened during Kyle's one semester at college and was another reason he hadn't gone back after the break. There didn't seem to be any point anymore. G.W. had figured that Kyle would take a semester off and then return to school once the grief had eased some.

Instead, he'd joined the army, failed at that, too, and after being given a general discharge embarked on what seemed to be his true calling: being a drifting, homeless troublemaker.

Chapman opened another door that led out into the police station's small lobby. Kyle's grandfather stood in front of the counter, looking as stern and morally upright as ever. Behind the counter was the chunky figure of Chief Ernie Rodriguez.

Next to G.W. was the woman Chapman had mentioned. Kyle stopped short at the sight of her.

Even in casual clothes, she had the sort of classy beauty he wasn't used to seeing in Sierra Lobo. She pushed back a strand of blond hair that had fallen in front of her face, and he thought the gesture had plenty of grace and elegance to it.

"I'm obliged to you for seein' your way clear to doin' this, Ernie," G.W. said to the chief.

"It's fine, Mr. Brannock," Rodriguez said. "Kyle's just lucky no one else involved in the incident decided to press charges. If they had, I wouldn't have had any choice but to hold him until bail was set, and the judge wouldn't have come in for the hearing until Monday morning."

G.W. grunted and said, "Spendin' the weekend in jail might not have been a bad thing for the boy."

"It wouldn't have done any good," Kyle said. "I've spent weekends in jail before, and I'm still me."

"Listen," the chief said. "Keep your nose clean while you're in Sierra Lobo, kid. If you wind up in trouble again, it won't go so easy for you next time."

"I don't suppose it would do any good to mention that

the loudmouth in the convenience store was the one who actually started it."

"Vern Hummel? He told Officer Chapman that you threw the first punch, and the only witness agreed that that was true."

So Stella had thrown him under the bus, thought Kyle. He supposed, technically speaking, he *had* struck the first blow, but Vern had had it coming, and the fight would have been over after that if he'd had the sense to let it go.

Once Kyle's possessions had been returned to him and the three of them were outside on the sidewalk, G.W. said, "How come you to show up in Sierra Lobo right now, boy? You comin' to see me?"

"I thought I'd stop and visit for a while, yeah."

"Broke, are you?"

"Pretty much."

"Well . . . I was raised to never turn away family." Kyle's grandfather put a hand on his shoulder. "Come on. Throw that duffel bag in the back of the pickup and we'll head out to the ranch."

"In a minute." Kyle nodded toward the glamorous blonde. "Who's this?"

"I can speak for myself," she said. "I'm Miranda Stephens. I'm your grandfather's attorney."

"You brought a lawyer with you to get me out of a one-horse hoosegow like this?" Kyle asked G.W. with a frown.

"No, she was already out at my place when Ernie called, discussin' another problem I got." G.W. sighed. "When you hear what all's been goin' on around here, Kyle, you may want to head for the hills."

Chapter 9

Miranda had driven her own car back into town from the ranch, so Brannock didn't have to give her a ride. She said, "I'll call you later this afternoon or in the morning, G.W., after I've had time to look into things more."

"Thanks. I don't know what you can do, but I wasn't raised to just give up."

"Neither was I," Miranda said. She lifted a hand in farewell and turned to walk toward her car.

Kyle watched her go and muttered under her breath, "I can think of some things I'd like to look into right now."

Brannock resisted the urge to thump the boy on the back of the head. Instead, he snapped, "Quit oglin' that gal. Miranda's a nice girl."

"She does mighty nice things for a pair of jeans, that's for sure."

Brannock sighed and shook his head. He said, "Throw your duffel bag in the back of the pickup. Just because you don't have anything to do doesn't mean I don't."

"Sure, sure." Kyle reached over the pickup's side and deposited the bag just behind the cab. He opened the passenger door while Brannock went around the front of the vehicle.

"When are you gonna get a new ride?" Kyle asked as his grandfather slid behind the wheel. "I don't think this antique has power anything."

"I can still push down a door lock button and roll down a window just fine. Folks did that for years and years and never thought anything about it. Anyway, look at these little vent windows. Best thing the automotive industry ever invented. Turn 'em around so the air's blowin' on you while you're drivin', and you don't need any air conditionin'. So what did they do? They got rid of 'em and call it new and improved. Bunch o' damn *engineers*. They ought to have to live with and work on all the crap they design. That'd only be fair."

Brannock had started the engine, pulled away from the curb, and headed west along the street while he was talking. He glanced over at Kyle and saw that the boy was gazing out the window.

"You ain't listenin' to me, are you?"

"It's not like I've never heard that rant before," Kyle said. "And all the ones like it, too. Everything was better in the old days. The world today sucks. That about sums it up, right?"

"And the world tomorrow don't hold out much promise of bein' better," Brannock said. "So, you want to tell me your side of what happened back there?"

"No point in wastin' my breath. You'll just believe what the cops told you, no matter what I say."

"Ernie Rodriguez is a fine chief and runs a damn fine department," Brannock snapped.

"And I'm just the prodigal grandson."

Brannock's callused hands tightened on the steering wheel. Kyle was his own flesh and blood, all he had left of his own son, and he loved the boy. But Kyle sure as hell didn't make it easy sometimes.

"I'd still like to hear your side of it."

"All right, fine." Kyle launched into a recitation of the events that had taken place in the convenience store around noon, then concluded, "I was just trying to help out an old friend."

"Stella Lopez," Brannock said. "Nice girl. I didn't know the two of you were ever sweethearts."

Kyle scoffed and said, "I wouldn't go far as to call it that. We had a good time together once or twice."

Brannock felt his lips thinning in disapproval and couldn't help it. He said, "Well, it sounds like you remember her fondly."

"I suppose. And that guy Vern just rubbed me the wrong way."

"The whole world rubs you the wrong way most of the time, doesn't it?"

For a few seconds, Kyle didn't respond. Then he admitted, "Yeah, I guess it does. Don't think I'm trying to fool myself, G.W. I know what I'm like."

Brannock's foot pressed down harder on the accelerator as they reached the edge of town and the speed limit on the highway went up. The pickup surged ahead.

"You ever give any thought to callin' me Grandpa or Granddad or something like that?"

"Why? You've always been G.W. to me. That's what everybody calls you, including that sexy little lawyer of yours."

"She's smart as a whip."

"I don't doubt it. And she'd better be, if she's going to be taking on the IRS. Did I hear that right? Why are the Feds after you?"

"They say I figured my deductions wrong for the past ten years and I owe 'em a bunch of back taxes. To tell you the truth, 'most everything they say just sounds like a bunch o' gibberish to me. I can't follow it. That's why I got Miranda to give me a hand dealin' with 'em. She's pretty good at tax law."

"And pretty easy on the eyes, too."

"I don't reckon there's any disputin' that."

"So how much are you gonna owe them if they get their way?" Kyle asked. "A few thousand dollars?"

"They say I got to pay nearly four hundred grand."

Kyle's eyes widened and he let out a low whistle.

"That's a fortune," he exclaimed. "You don't have that much, do you?"

"Not hardly. And that's not the worst of it. They say if they don't get their money, they're gonna take the ranch. They've given me until next Friday to settle up with 'em."

"That's less than a week away!"

"Yeah, I know."

Kyle leaned forward with a solemn look on his face and asked, "What are you gonna do?"

At least the news had knocked some of the snottiness out of him, for the moment, anyway, Brannock thought. He said, "I don't know. Miranda's gonna try to figure out somethin'."

"Well, if there's anything I can do to help, I'd be glad to."

Brannock glanced over at his grandson and asked, "Are you sure you want to associate with an ornery old man who's liable to wind up in some federal prison . . . or dead?"

"Dead?" Kyle echoed in alarm. "G.W., what's going on in that stubborn old brain of yours?"

"Stubborn's right," Brannock said. "If those bastards come to put me off my land, they're gonna have a fight on their hands. They'll have to put me down before they put me off."

"Now, don't start talking crazy—"

"There ain't nothing crazy about it," Brannock insisted. "I'm right, they're wrong, and it don't matter how big and powerful they are, nothin's gonna change that."

"Do you really think right and wrong actually *mean* anything in this world anymore? How can you look around at what goes on and believe that?"

"They mean something to me," Brannock said softly.

Kyle sat back and shook his head.

"I hope that little blond hottie really is a good lawyer," he said. "I think you're gonna need one. But from the sound of it, what you really need is an army, if you want to keep the Feds off your land."

"Know where I can get one?" Brannock asked with a grin.

"If I did, I'm not sure I'd tell you. I get the feeling that you're spoiling for a fight, G.W."

Brannock shook his head and said, "No, I'm a peaceable man, as long as folks leave me alone."

"Yeah, that's what those movie cowboys you were always so fond of would say just before they beat the hell out of somebody."

"They never beat the hell of anybody who didn't have it comin'."

An uneasy silence fell between the two of them as Brannock drove on toward the ranch. Finally Kyle said, "I meant it, you know. If there's anything I can do to help, I will. I don't care if it gets me in trouble with the law, either." He snorted derisively. "Hell, I'm used to it."

"You never tangled with federal law, at least not that I know of."

"No," Kyle admitted. "I've steered clear of that sort of trouble. I've had my chances, too. Guys I knew in the army were mixed up in some sort of drug ring, and I could have thrown in with them. They promised me all kinds of money."

"How come you didn't take it?"

"Honestly?" Kyle laughed. "Because I knew that if you ever found out about it, you'd kick my ass six ways from Sunday."

"You got that right. Might even make it *seven* ways from Sunday."

Both of them chuckled as Brannock drove on. He'd been upset to get that call from Ernie Rodriguez and find out that Kyle was in trouble again, of course, but now that he'd talked to the boy, Brannock's instincts told him that Kyle could still make something of himself.

With all the trouble looming over his own head, Brannock didn't know if he was in any position to give Kyle a hand with that job, but he would do what he could.

One way or another, he thought, it was time his grandson started growin' up.

Chapter 10

The GPS on Barton Devlin's phone took him right where he needed to go. He brought the rental to a stop near the edge of a ridge that ran for more than twenty miles along a meandering path that followed a generally north-south orientation.

The rocky drop-off down to the flats was about forty feet. The slope was easy enough that a man could walk down it if he was careful, but a vehicle wouldn't be able to make it so the dirt road Devlin had been following—really just a barely discernible trace—ended here.

He didn't need to get any closer today. He was just here to indulge his curiosity.

He picked up the binoculars lying on the seat beside him and got out of the car to walk to the edge. He had already taken the binoculars out of their case, so all he had to do was lift them to his eyes and peer through them.

The valley spread out before him was several miles wide and greener with vegetation than much of the arid landscape around here. That was because it was watered by a clear, spring-fed stream that flowed down from the mountains on the other side of the valley.

The creek disappeared almost as soon as it left the mountains, swallowed up by the thirsty ground, but the moisture was still there, trickling under the surface and making it easier for grass and other plants to grow.

Because of that, this valley—designated Yucca Valley on official USGS topographical maps—was good ranch land and had been ever since one of G.W. Brannock's ancestors had settled here almost a hundred and fifty years earlier.

But there were other good uses to which Yucca Valley could be put, thought Devlin as he raised the binoculars and focused on the ranch house.

It was a rambling, two-story frame structure that had been built onto several times over the years, those additions to the original house being easy to see.

But that gave it a unique quality. There wasn't another house anywhere in the world exactly like it. Brannock probably liked that about it.

Several cottonwoods grew around the house and provided shade at various times of day. Again, the underground moisture allowed them to attain greater height than most of the rather scrubby trees in this area.

Set about fifty yards behind the house and off to the side a little was a large barn made out of sheet metal, even its roof. Devlin knew from studying Brannock's tax returns that the barn was six years old, having been built to replace the old wooden barn that had been there.

To the left of the barn was a large enclosure made from T-posts and horse panels. On the other side was an old-fashioned wooden pole corral. An open shed was also on that side of the barn, its roof overhanging metal water troughs.

Devlin swung the binoculars toward a row of small,

three- and four-room frame cottages. The ranch hands who worked for Brannock lived in those cottages, some with families, others single men who shared the cottages.

His workers were all Hispanic, but there were no illegals among them. In fact, all of them came from families that had been American citizens for several generations. The INS had no leverage to use against the rancher.

And they had searched high and low for just such leverage, Devlin knew.

He lifted the binoculars to look at the lower reaches of the mountains. At this time of year, most of Brannock's cattle would be up there on that higher range, although Devlin didn't spot any at the moment. Generally, winters were mild in this part of West Texas, but there could still be a considerable amount of snow, so during the fall the herd would be driven down into the valley.

Everything looked just about like he expected it to, thought Devlin as he lowered the glasses. He had never been here before, but he felt like he knew Brannock's ranch quite well despite that. He had spent a lot of time studying the place when he was given this assignment. He never went into a job unprepared.

This drive out here today had been just to get the lay of the land and make sure no one had overlooked anything. Satisfied, he started to turn back toward the rental car when something caught his eye.

A column of dust had appeared, moving slowly toward the ranch headquarters from the direction of the state highway. Curious, Devlin brought the binoculars to his eyes again and looked through them.

It took him a moment to locate the dust column through the lenses and then follow it down to the vehicle causing it. An old, dark blue pickup bounced along the rough dirt road leading from the highway.

That was Brannock's pickup, Devlin knew. He knew about everything the old rancher paid taxes on or registered with the state. He knew what was in all the e-mails Brannock retrieved once a week, his only use of the Internet. He knew what programs Brannock watched on his satellite dish, mostly sports and old movies and vintage sitcoms and variety shows. Brannock lived in the past as much as possible, no doubt about that.

That was going to be his undoing. A man had to look to the future to survive.

There was no garage, but a wooden carport sat to one side of the house. Brannock parked the pickup underneath it and climbed out.

To Devlin's surprise, the passenger door swung open as well and another man got out. This one was a lot younger, a slender, sandy-haired man in jeans and T-shirt.

The agent's forehead creased in a frown. As far as he was aware, Brannock lived out here alone except for the ranch hands. Maybe this guy was somebody the rancher had just hired.

Clearly, though, he wasn't Hispanic, which meant he didn't fit Brannock's pattern.

Devlin didn't like anything that didn't fit into a pattern.

But it didn't matter, he told himself. No matter who the man with Brannock was, he wouldn't have any effect on what was going to happen soon.

The plan had progressed too far for anything to stop it now. Satisfied, Devlin got into the car, backed it around, and started back the way he had come.

A couple of hundred yards away, hidden behind a rock spire, two men Devlin hadn't seen at all watched the IRS agent drive away.

Chapter 11

"Keep movin' and get in the house," G.W. said sharply as he and Kyle approached the porch steps.

"Something wrong?"

"Don't ask questions. Just get inside!"

The urgency in his grandfather's voice was plain, thought Kyle. He did what G.W. said and took the steps quickly, then crossed the porch to the screen door.

The wooden door was open. G.W. never locked up when he was leaving the house. Kyle pulled the screen open and stepped inside.

G.W. was right behind him. He reached over and took down a rifle from a wooden rack where it hung with several other long guns.

"What the hell?" Kyle asked.

"Stay in here," G.W. snapped. "Don't stand up close to the windows."

He pushed the screen door open with his foot and stepped back out onto the porch.

Kyle's confusion began to turn to alarm. He said, "Hey, if you're gonna shoot somebody—"

"I'm not plannin' to shoot," G.W. said as he nestled his

cheek against the smooth, polished wood of the rifle's stock. "I'm just usin' the sight."

It was true that the rifle had a telescopic sight attached to it. G.W. leveled the weapon and cupped the rear end of the sight against his right eye. For a long moment he didn't say anything and didn't move.

Kyle's nerves were taut as he waited for his grandfather to tell him what was going on here.

Finally, G.W. grunted, lowered the rifle, and said, "Looks like he's gone."

"Who?"

"Fella on the ridge over yonder who was watchin' us."

"What ridge?" Kyle asked. He recalled his days of exploring the ranch. "You mean that ridge all the way on the other side of the valley?"

"Yeah."

"That's miles away!"

"Air's clear out here," G.W. said. "A fella with good eyes can see a long way. But what I saw was the sun reflectin' off glass where there shouldn't be any."

"What does that mean?"

"Well, what I was worried about," G.W. said dryly, "was that there was somebody up there drawin' a bead on us with a high-powered rifle that'd shoot that far. Why'd you think I hustled you on into the house, anyway?" He rasped his fingertips over the beard stubble on his chin. "Of course, a bullet from a rifle powerful enough to shoot that far probably would've gone right through the wall. But at least the son of a buck wouldn't be able to see what he was aimin' at."

"Wait a minute," Kyle said as he tried to wrap his brain around what his grandfather had just told him. "You think somebody might have wanted to *kill* us?"

"Well, if they did, they left. More than likely, though, it was somebody with a pair of binoculars spyin' on us. Couldn't take a chance on the other, though. Shoot, you just got here. We ain't had a chance to visit much yet."

Kyle gave a little shake of his head as if what he'd just heard didn't make much sense. He said, "Why would you even think somebody might want to shoot you?"

"Like I said, I didn't, not really. I was just bein' careful. But there's been some strange things goin' on around here lately, Kyle. My hands have spotted fellas on the ranch who didn't have any business bein' here. So have I. We've never been able to catch any of 'em, though."

"Maybe they're smuggling drugs or undocumented immigrants over from Mexico," Kyle suggested.

"Yeah, I thought about that, but we're a little too far from the border to make that likely. Some of that sort of stuff goes on around here, of course, but my gut tells me this is somethin' different."

G.W. came in and hung the rifle on the gun rack again.

"Saw a little dust hangin' in the air, over on the ridge," he went on. "Like a car drove off. That makes me think somebody was watchin' us, too."

"Like maybe the IRS?"

"I can't see any reason why they would," G.W. said with a frown. "But at the same time, you can't really put anything past those ol' boys. They play fast and loose with the truth *and* the rules, and they've been doin' that ever since somebody decided workin' for the government means workin' for the Democratic Party."

"Still, skulking around a ranch doesn't seem like something the IRS would do," Kyle said. "Do you have any other enemies?"

"Not that I know of, but I've always been plainspoken

enough that there's no tellin' who might have me on a list somewhere."

Kyle knew that was true. Growing up in a suburb of Dallas, he'd been surrounded by liberal attitudes all his life, and naturally he had accepted most of them. When he was young, his grandfather's opinionated personality had rubbed him the wrong way on many occasions.

It had taken being out in the real world and seeing how things actually worked to open Kyle's eyes to the facts. He had worked construction during the summers while he was in high school, and that had taught him as much as any classroom ever could.

"You think it's safe for me to go back out and get my duffel bag from the truck?" he asked.

"Yeah, whoever it was, they're gone."

"But they'll be back?" Kyle guessed.

"More than likely." G.W. had a thoughtful look on his face as he went on. "But now that you're here, maybe whatever's goin' on, we can put a stop to it."

Chapter 12

The rest of the day passed uneventfully. G.W. didn't press Kyle for details about what he'd been doing since he'd seen him last, and Kyle didn't volunteer any. He just told his grandfather that he'd been drifting around, seeing the country.

Basically, that was the truth. When he was in a city big enough to have a day labor center, he picked up odd jobs that way, and when he had enough money for a bus ticket and to take care of his other needs for a while, he moved on.

Several times he had been approached by guys who wanted him to stand on a street corner with a sign saying he was a homeless veteran—which was technically true, Kyle supposed—and beg money from people who drove by.

Kyle had turned down every one of those invitations, and none too politely, as well. Whatever he had, even though it wasn't much, he worked for it. And when he couldn't get enough work, he did without.

He was perfectly willing to accept G.W.'s hospitality, though. Family was family, after all. And Kyle was willing to do whatever he could to help out around the place, too, and pay his grandfather back that way.

That evening G.W. fired up the grill on the back porch, and when he had the bed of coals the right shade of red, he wrapped two potatoes in aluminum foil and put them down in the coals, under the rack. Then two thick steaks from the refrigerator went on the grill, too.

Kyle thought it all smelled wonderful.

"I don't suppose we're going to have a salad with that," he said.

G.W. snorted and said, "If you want rabbit food, there's the makin's for it in the icebox. Help yourself."

Kyle had to laugh.

"You're a living, breathing time warp, you know that, G.W.?"

"Not sure what you mean by that, so I reckon I'll take it as a compliment."

"That's fine. That's pretty much the way I meant it."

When the food was ready, they sat on the back porch with their plates in their laps and longnecks on the floor beside them. The mountains rose before them, with a rosy glow from the fading sunset behind them.

The scene was such a peaceful one that it made Kyle angry to think that the government wanted to force G.W. off his land. His grandfather was happy here. The IRS had no right to do what they were doing.

"I don't suppose you want to go to church with me in the mornin'," G.W. said.

"I'm not much for singing hymns and listening to a preacher, you know that."

"It might do you some good."

"It probably would," Kyle agreed, "but if it's all right with you, I think I'll just sleep in."

"Fine. I'm not gonna argue with you."

"Maybe there are some chores around here I can do for you," Kyle suggested.

"I'll take care o' Sunday chores before I leave," G.W. said gruffly. "Don't worry about it."

Kyle nodded. He knew he had let his grandfather down, but there was only so much a guy could change at a time.

He changed the subject by saying, "Tell me about the people who have been sneaking around here. What did you mean when you said maybe we could put a stop to it?"

"Half a dozen times my hands have spotted a couple of fellas in a jeep out on the range where they shouldn't be. We still work the cattle mostly on horseback, so by the time my men rode out to where the jeep was, it was gone and so were the fellas in it. I've seen 'em myself. Not only that, I've heard their engine at night, up around that pool at the edge of the hills."

Kyle knew the pool his grandfather meant. The creek formed it by running into a basin in the rocks. It wasn't very big, maybe twenty feet across and five or six feet deep, and from there the stream trickled on out in the valley for another quarter mile before disappearing. Kyle had gone swimming in that natural pool when he was a kid, and he remembered how clear and cold the water was.

"What I was thinkin'," G.W. went on, saying, "is that you and me would stake ourselves out up there and wait for the varmints to show up."

"At night, you mean?"

"Yeah. We'll take our sleepin' bags and take turns standin' guard until they show up again."

"And what do we do then?" Kyle asked.

"Well, we'll take rifles, too," G.W. said. "That ought to help convince 'em to tell us who they are and what in blazes they're doing sneakin' around my ranch."

Kyle frowned and said, "You're going to throw down on

IRS agents? That's a good way to get your butt in a federal pen, G.W.—or shot off."

"Well, what do you think we ought to do?" G.W. demanded with a frown of his own.

"Having a stakeout and trying to catch them is a good idea, but maybe we'd better leave the guns at home. You've got a spotlight, don't you?"

"Sure."

"If we hit them with the spotlight, they won't be able to see us. They won't know whether we're armed or not. If they've got any sense they'll answer our questions. This is still your land, and you've got a right to know who's on it and why."

G.W. snorted and said, "Well, I'm glad we see eye to eye on that much, anyway."

"We'd better record the whole thing, too. If we can prove that the IRS has been trespassing, it might help your case in court."

"Maybe," G.W. said in grudging agreement. "I've got one of those fancy phones that'll record video."

"That's not fancy. They'll all do that now. They have for twenty years or more."

G.W. ignored that and said, "We'll start tomorrow night. Don't want to do it tonight because it might interfere with church in the mornin'—and with your sleepin' in."

Kyle let that little jab go on by unremarked and picked up the longneck from the porch planks beside his chair.

"To Operation Skulker," he said as he raised the bottle in a toast.

G.W. just made a slightly disgusted sound, lifted his own beer, and said, "To corralin' skunks—government and otherwise."

Chapter 13

Kyle spent the night in the room where his father had grown up. All of his dad's things were gone, and the bed and the rest of the furnishings were different. Even the paint on the walls wasn't the same as when Ted Brannock had lived here.

G.W. had changed all of that after the accident that took the lives of Kyle's parents. At the time, Kyle had thought that was pretty callous of the old man.

By now he had come to wonder, though, if his grandfather had done that more to shield himself from the pain of losing his only child. That certainly seemed possible, although Kyle wasn't going to ask him about it. For one thing, G.W. might have done it without even realizing that was the reason.

Despite his intention of staying in bed late, Kyle woke fairly early the next morning. His sleep had been restless, and he was vaguely aware that it had been disturbed by bad dreams, even though he didn't remember them.

He sat up and swung his feet out of bed, and as he stood up, he felt his muscles aching from the fight with Vern Hummel the day before, as well as having the stun gun used on him. He stretched his back, rolled his shoulders, and swung his arms around to loosen up a little as he went to the window.

When he pushed back the curtain, he saw that the sun was up, but he could tell by the quality of the light that the hour was early. As he turned away from the window, he caught a faint whiff of coffee brewing. For several seconds he stood there looking from the door to the bed as he pondered crawling under the covers again. He might be able to go back to sleep and get a couple more hours.

Then he muttered, "The hell with it," pulled on his jeans, and padded barefoot to the door.

When he walked into the kitchen, his grandfather was sitting at the table wearing shiny brown shoes, the pants from a brown suit, and a long-sleeved white shirt unbuttoned at the throat. He was eating a bowl of cornflakes with a banana cut up into them. A piece of toast lay on a saucer, and a cup of black coffee sat to one side. Kyle had never seen his grandfather eat anything else for breakfast.

"Coffee in the pot," G.W. said. "Help yourself to anything else you want to fix." He ate another bite of cereal, then added, "I didn't expect to see you up this early."

"I didn't expect to *be* up this early," Kyle said.

He got a cup from the cabinet and poured coffee in it, then added milk from the refrigerator and sugar from the old-fashioned sugar bowl on the table, ignoring the look of disdain G.W. gave him as he did so.

After he had sat down and taken a sip of the hot, strong brew, he went on. "I guess there's something about the air around here that makes it hard to sleep late. You never have."

"That's true enough. There's always too many things to do around a ranch to lay around in bed." G.W. finished the cereal and reached for the toast. "Since you're up—"

"I still haven't changed my mind about church."

G.W. grunted and said, "Suit yourself."

After he'd had more of the coffee, Kyle got up and put a couple of pieces of bread in the toaster.

"Get a saucer for that," G.W. said. "I don't want crumbs all over the place. Brings out the roaches."

"Sure, sure. I'll clean up after myself." When the toast was done, Kyle brought it back to the table and sat down again. "What about those chores?"

"Already done. The hands and I have been up for a couple of hours."

"How many men do you have working for you now?"

"Eight. Fella named Roberto Quinones bosses the crew. His wife cooks for the four unmarried hombres. They're good men. All of 'em been with me at least two years. They've all gone into town for mass."

"Why am I not surprised?" Kyle asked with a slight smile.

"You're gonna out here alone this mornin'," G.W. said. "Does that bother you?"

"Why should it? You're not expecting any trouble, are you?"

"I don't expect it, but that doesn't mean it won't show up unannounced."

"I know where the gun rack is with the rifles and shotguns. Are they loaded?"

"An unloaded gun's not much use for anything but a club, now is it?"

"I suppose not."

"Just be careful," G.W. advised. "Don't shoot at anything unless you're mighty sure it needs to be shot at."

Kyle nodded. G.W. lingered for a few moments over the rest of his coffee while Kyle ate both slices of toast with butter and strawberry jam spread on them. There had to be something in the air that gave a guy an appetite, too, he thought.

G.W. put his cup, bowl, saucer, and spoon in the white enamel sink. Kyle followed suit with his saucer, but he hadn't finished his coffee yet, so he took the cup with him. He stood in the open door of his grandfather's bedroom, propping a shoulder against the jamb, as G.W. selected a tie and put it on.

"I never quite mastered that art," Kyle said as G.W. tied the tie.

"I know. Your dad and I both tried to teach you, as I recall."

"Well, it's complicated. Anyway, I never had much need for wearing a tie."

G.W. got his suit coat from the closet and put it on. He said, "There's a time and a place for everything."

"I suppose."

G.W. picked up his Bible from the dresser. Church was just about the only place he went without wearing his straw cowboy hat. Kyle got out of the way and let him past.

"I'll be back after the service. Keep an eye on the place."

"I will," Kyle promised. He glanced at the gun rack and suddenly felt a little nervous. If the mysterious intruders showed up, his grandfather would expect him to deal with them.

Kyle had never had what anybody would consider a healthy respect for authority, but he didn't want to wind up in a shoot-out with federal agents. That was why he had told G.W. they ought to leave the guns at home when they staked out the pool.

G.W. drove off in the pickup. Kyle picked up the TV remote and turned it on, not surprised to find that the satellite receiver was tuned to a station that specialized in old movies. Randolph Scott was talking to some woman and looked worried.

Probably trying to figure out who he was going to have to shoot later, thought Kyle.

Despite his intention to change the channel, he sat down on the sofa and wound up watching the movie. He wasn't sure how long he had been there when he noticed movement outside. As he sat up straighter and looked through the front window, he saw a car coming along the dirt road toward the house.

He didn't know who drove what around here, except for his grandfather's pickup, so he had no idea who the visitor might be. Whoever it was, there was a good chance they weren't welcome.

Kyle stood up, went to the gun rack, and took down a lever-action .30-30. He worked the lever to be sure there was a cartridge in the chamber, caught the one that was ejected, and thumbed it back through the loading gate.

On the TV, Randolph Scott was making a solemn pronouncement about putting a stop to some badman's rampage. Kyle grabbed the remote and turned it off before he stepped out onto the porch.

When he got there, he realized he was still barefooted and shirtless and wished he had gotten fully dressed. He felt a little more defenseless than he should have, especially with a rifle in his hands.

But it was too late now, because the car came to a stop and the driver's door swung open as the dust settled quickly.

His grandfather's lawyer, Miranda Stephens, stepped out of the vehicle and looked at him. Her expression was serious, but he thought he saw amusement twinkling in her eyes.

He was sure of it when she said dryly, "Don't shoot."

Chapter 14

"I don't suppose your grandfather is here, is he?" Miranda said, her tone more businesslike now. She wasn't going to allow herself to be embarrassed about this. She was a grown woman. She had seen men without shirts before.

She had even seen men without shoes before.

Although none of them had been brandishing rifles at her.

Kyle lowered the weapon and shook his head. He said, "No, G.W.'s gone to church."

Miranda winced a little and said, "Oh, that's right. I should have remembered. He's a deacon at the First Baptist Church, isn't he?"

"I guess. I mean, he used to be. They don't have term limits on things like that, do they?"

"No, I don't think so. I'm a Methodist myself, so I don't really know for sure."

"You're not a big churchgoer, either, huh?"

"I got out of the habit in law school. There's always so much work to do."

"Speaking of work," Kyle said, "what brings you out here? Is there anything I can do for you?"

"I just had some news about your grandfather's case. Good news, I hope. I wanted to share it in person, but I didn't stop to think that he might not be here."

Kyle frowned slightly and asked, "Good news on a Sunday morning?"

"I heard back from an old friend of mine I reached out to. He works for a federal district court judge in El Paso. He thinks the judge might be willing to issue an injunction against the IRS to prevent them from seizing G.W.'s ranch until after his appeal has been heard."

Kyle looked skeptical about that.

"What federal judge is gonna go against his buddies in the IRS? That's liable to get him in trouble."

"One who was appointed by a Republican president."

Kyle let out a whistle of surprise and said, "Boy, he *has* been around for a long time, hasn't he?"

"And one who has terminal cancer," Miranda said solemnly. "*She* is a widow who has no children, so there's not really anybody the IRS can threaten to make her back off. All she's interested in is the law, and what's right and wrong."

"That's not always the same thing," Kyle observed.

"No, but in this case it is. My friend thinks we might have an injunction by the middle of the day tomorrow."

Kyle rested a shoulder against one of the porch posts at the top of the steps and said, "Boyfriend of yours?"

"No," Miranda replied. Her tone was sharper than she intended it to be. "We were in the same study group in law school."

"Oh. Okay." Kyle straightened from his casual pose and went on. "There might still be some hot coffee in the pot. You want to come in and wait for G.W.?"

Miranda hesitated.

"You could just tell him about the injunction," she said. "You know as much now as I do."

"Maybe, maybe not. But I'm sure he'd be glad to see you anyway." A grin tugged at the corners of Kyle's mouth. "I can put a shirt on, if that's what's worrying you."

"Who said I was worried?" Miranda asked, her voice sharp again. "Actually, I wouldn't mind some coffee. I was awake a lot of the night, trying to figure out what to do next."

Kyle pulled the screen door open and said, "Come on in, then."

"I know where the kitchen is, if you want to go get that shirt," Miranda said as she went into the house while he held the door.

Kyle hung the rifle on the gun rack and said, "All right. Be right back."

Miranda went into the kitchen, felt the side of the coffeepot and found it still warm, and filled a cup she took from the cabinet. As she took a sip from it, Kyle appeared in the doorway, buttoning up a faded blue work shirt. His feet were still bare.

"I can see why G.W. likes you," he said. "You drink that stuff black, no sugar, like he does."

"Another legacy from law school. The jolt of caffeine was all I was really interested in, not a bunch of frills."

"You don't care for mocha half-caff goat's milk lattes?"

Miranda sniffed in disdain.

"Sit down," Kyle said as he gestured at the table. "I'll get my cup from the living room."

When he came back, he added some coffee to his cup and sat down in the chair across from her.

"So you think you can get that injunction by the middle of the day tomorrow, eh?" he asked.

"Yes. I'll drive to El Paso early in the morning and see the judge in her chambers. My friend has already arranged the meeting."

Kyle quirked an eyebrow and said, "The guy must owe you some pretty big favors."

"Not really. He's just a good guy." Miranda paused, then added meaningfully, "His wife thinks so, too."

Kyle held up open hands and said, "Hey, I don't mean to pry in anybody's personal life. It's none of my business, counselor."

"That's right, it's not. What *is* your business, Mr. Brannock?"

"Oh, hell, don't call me that. I'm not sure I'll ever be old enough to answer to it. As long as G.W.'s around, he'll be the only Mr. Brannock around here. Or Señor Brannock, as the hands call him."

Miranda indulged her curiosity and asked, "Why do you call him G.W.? Shouldn't you call him Granddad or Gramps or something?"

"Yeah, he'd like that. But I heard somebody call him G.W. when I was barely old enough to talk, and when I started saying it, the way kids will, it stuck." Kyle shrugged. "Anything else just wouldn't seem right now."

"I suppose I can understand that." Then, feeling like she ought to, she said, "I'm sorry about what happened to your parents."

Kyle's mouth tightened into a grim line, and his fingers closed harder on the coffee cup.

"G.W. told you about that, did he?"

"It was a real tragedy. I know he was devastated by it."

"You couldn't really tell that by the way he acted."

Miranda thought she detected a trace of bitterness in Kyle's voice. She said, "Everybody deals with grief in their own way. G.W.'s just not a very . . . demonstrative . . . man, that's all."

"Yeah, I guess."

Miranda had been sipping on her coffee as they talked. It was cool enough that she was able to pick up the cup and drink the rest of it in a long swallow.

"I think I'll go," she said as she set the empty cup on the table.

"You don't have to leave on my account."

"I'm not. I just need to work on what I'm going to say to the judge in the morning." She got to her feet. "Please tell G.W. that if he has any questions, he should feel free to call me."

"I will."

Kyle walked her to the door and followed her out onto the porch. Miranda hadn't started down the steps yet when Kyle said, "Wait a minute."

Something about his voice made alarm bells go off in her brain. She looked around at him and asked, "What is it?"

He pointed toward the highway and said, "Somebody else is coming."

Miranda looked and saw the dust rising from the road. Kyle was right. She said, "It's probably G.W. on his way home from church."

Kyle shook his head and said, "It's too early for that. No Baptist preacher worth his salt preaches a sermon that short."

"Well, this is a popular place today, I guess."

"Why don't you go back inside?" Kyle suggested.

"You don't think this is trouble, do you?"

"I don't know, but if it is, I don't want you standing out here in the open."

Miranda was a little surprised that he would worry about her like that. From everything she had heard about Kyle Brannock, he was a pretty shiftless character. No-account, as some of the older West Texans would say. She wouldn't have expected him to have an outbreak of chivalry.

But maybe he knew something she didn't. She decided it would be a good idea not to argue with him. She pulled open the screen door and went back into the house. Kyle followed her.

He didn't stay inside, though. He took down the same rifle he'd been holding earlier and went back out onto the porch. Miranda stayed where she could watch through the screen.

The car that pulled up was similar to hers but at least ten years older, and it sounded like it wasn't running very well. When the door opened, Miranda wasn't expecting to see the person who stepped out.

Stella Lopez.

Chapter 15

Kyle drew in a sharp, surprised breath. Stella was just about the last person he'd thought he would see get out of that car.

Not that the sight of her bothered him. She looked spectacular today, wearing cut-off jeans and a sleeveless white shirt. She had tied the shirttails under her breasts, leaving her smooth, honey-colored midriff bare. Her long raven hair was loose today. It tumbled around her shoulders in dark waves.

She smiled and said, "You don't need that gun, Kyle. I'm not here to make trouble."

"You didn't bring your friend Vern with you, did you?"

Stella's smile disappeared as she made a face and said, "That jerk. He's not my friend. He's just a customer at the store."

"That didn't stop you from telling the cops I threw the first punch at him yesterday."

"Well, you did, didn't you?" Stella shot back. "I wasn't going to lie to the cops and get in trouble for that."

"He provoked me," Kyle said. Then he shrugged and went on. "But I guess I can't really hold it against you.

I wouldn't want you getting in trouble on my account, either."

"That didn't stop *you* from leaving town a few years ago when I might have been in trouble on your account, did it?"

Kyle's back stiffened as he thought about the import of her question as she used his own words against him. He said, "You weren't—"

"No, I wasn't," she broke in. "But that was no thanks to you."

Kyle glanced over his shoulder at the screen door. Miranda was right inside, and she had to be hearing all of this. For some reason that bothered him, even though he told himself that it shouldn't.

Under other circumstances he would have welcomed Stella's visit, even though he was still a little peeved with her for what she had told the police about the fight. Today, though, he found himself wishing she would just get back in her old clunker and head back to town.

"Why'd you come out here, Stella?" he asked. "Is there something I can do for you?"

She came toward him, her mouth set in a pretty little pout now, her movements naturally sensuous.

"I thought maybe we could catch up on old times," she said. "I figured your grandfather would be at church—"

"He is."

Stella leaned her head toward Miranda's car and went on, saying, "But I see you already have company."

The screen door's hinges squealed as Miranda pushed it open. Kyle grimaced, unsure whether he was reacting to the sound or to the fact that Miranda hadn't just stayed inside out of sight until Stella was gone.

"Don't worry, Ms. Lopez," Miranda said as she stepped out onto the porch. "I was just leaving."

Stella stopped short. The look she gave Miranda was almost but not quite a glare.

"I've seen you around town," she said. "You're that lawyer from back East somewhere."

"I'm Mr. Brannock's attorney, yes. And it's a legal matter that brought me out here today." Miranda looked coolly over at Kyle. "If you'll give your grandfather that information, I'd appreciate it."

"Sure," Kyle said. He added, "Thank you."

"Just doing my job," Miranda said. She took the porch steps down to the ground and headed for her car, circling to give Stella plenty of room as she did so. The two women watched each other warily as Miranda went past.

She got in her car, backed around, and drove off. Some of the dust drifted toward Stella. She waved a hand in front of her face to brush it away as she watched the car dwindle in the distance.

From the porch, Kyle said, "Come on in. I think there's a pitcher of iced tea in the refrigerator." He had seen it earlier when he got the strawberry jam.

"No, I should go. You're busy."

"I'm not the least bit busy," Kyle assured her. He was a little disappointed that Miranda had left so abruptly the way she did, but she was gone now and there was no reason for Stella to leave, too.

"You were talking to the lawyer lady."

"She was just telling me about some legal work she's doing for my grandfather."

"That's all?"

"That's it," Kyle said.

"She was kind of dressed up for a Sunday morning."

"Really? I didn't notice."

That wasn't strictly true. Kyle had noticed the way the jeans hugged Miranda's legs and hips. He had approved of the silk blouse and the lightweight jacket, too. But he had way too much sense to mention those things to Stella.

"Why'd you come out with a gun?" Stella asked, pointing at the rifle that Kyle still held with the barrel pointing toward the ground.

"I didn't know who was coming." Kyle decided it wouldn't hurt to tell her the truth. "G.W. said some guys have been sneaking around the ranch. I thought it might have been them."

Stella frowned and shook her head. She said, "Why would anybody sneak around the ranch? You think they're, like, rustlers or something?"

Obviously, Stella didn't know about the trouble G.W. had been having with the IRS. That was no surprise. G.W. kept things to himself. He wouldn't have gone all over town complaining. Chances were, the only one in Sierra Lobo who knew about the situation was Miranda, and G.W. would have told her about it only because he needed her help.

It must have rubbed his grandfather the wrong way to ask anyone for help, thought Kyle, especially a young woman. That was a good indication of just how serious the problem was.

G.W. wouldn't want him saying anything to Stella about it, so he replied, "I don't know what it's about. I just wanted to be ready in case it was anybody looking for trouble."

"Maybe I'm looking for trouble and you just don't know it."

She wore a flirtatious smile as she said it. Kyle had to grin back at her, glad that she had gotten over being miffed at him. He said, "I think I can handle that kind of trouble without a gun."

"You think so, do you?"

"Yeah, I—"

Her smile disappeared again as she snapped, "Maybe you better get some legal advice to be sure."

With that she turned and marched back to her car. Stella Lopez looked good leaving, no doubt about that—but Kyle didn't want her to go.

"Wait a minute!" he called after her. He started down the steps. "You don't have to leave—"

Too late. The slam of her car door cut off his words. With a rattle, the engine started. Stella didn't bother backing up. She just swung around in a wide circle and punched the gas as she started toward the highway, the car's tires spitting gravel and kicking up dust.

Kyle stood there on the porch watching her go and thought about how he'd two good-looking women come to see him this morning, and yet here he was, alone.

Yeah, that was about par for the course.

Chapter 16

Barton Devlin wasn't sure why he'd had to arrive in Sierra Lobo on Saturday. Monday was the earliest he could make his move against G.W. Brannock, so it seemed like he could have flown from Washington to Dallas and driven out here on Sunday just as easily.

But Devlin wasn't the sort of man to question orders, so he'd shown up on Saturday, as he'd been told to.

With nothing to do on Sunday, he had gone out for breakfast at one of the local cafés, gone back to the motel, and spent the morning double- and triple-checking everything in the documents he had brought with him. He didn't like to leave anything to chance.

That and his sheer love for what he did had enabled him to rise rapidly in his job.

While he was eating breakfast, he had been aware of the guarded, hostile glances directed at him by the café's other patrons. Word had gotten around town that he was an IRS agent, he thought. That meant the motel owner, Lou Scarborough, had spread the news.

The attention didn't bother Devlin. He figured he could probably charge Scarborough with hindering an official investigation. At the very least, one simple notation in the computer would ensure that Scarborough was audited every year for the foreseeable future, the same way many Republican business owners were.

Devlin thought about that several hours later as he was going over his paperwork, and it still brought a chuckle to his lips.

He wasn't nearly as amused when someone knocked on the door of his motel room that afternoon.

No one should be disturbing him. Maybe Scarborough was coming around to suck up and try to get back in Devlin's good graces. It wouldn't do him any good, but Devlin supposed it wouldn't hurt anything to let him make the attempt.

Devlin enjoyed a good grovel as much as the next federal employee.

But when Devlin opened the door, it wasn't Lou Scarborough who stood there. It was a man Devlin had never seen before, in a rumpled suit that was obviously expensive despite its wrinkles. The man's collar and tie were loosened, and sunglasses covered his eyes. A wooden toothpick stuck out of one corner of his mouth.

Devlin hated him on sight.

Without taking the toothpick out of his mouth, the man said, "Barton Devlin?"

Instead of answering the question, Devlin said, "Who are you?"

The man reached inside his coat. Devlin frowned and abruptly wondered if he should be scared. In all the years he'd been an IRS agent, despite all the lives he'd ruined, no one had ever pulled a gun on him or even taken a swing at him. The fear that the citizenry felt for the IRS—and it was only right and proper that they should feel that way, Devlin believed—was just too deep and ingrained for them to conceive of striking back.

The casual arrogance with which this stranger carried himself, though, said that he wasn't afraid of anyone.

And *that* made a chill go down Devlin's back.

But it wasn't a gun the man brought out. Instead it was a leather folder designed to hold a badge and an identification card. Devlin recognized it right away, because he carried the same type of folder.

The stranger flipped it open, held it out, and said, "Slade Grayson, BLM."

Devlin's first impulse was to say that he didn't believe it. He had known many men and women who worked for the Bureau of Land Management, and none of them had looked like the man standing at his door. They tended to be mild, peaceful sorts, the children and grandchildren of former hippies, unable to quite comprehend that they had become the unquestioning government drones their parents and grandparents had despised.

With his dark hair, sunglasses, and suit, the man who called himself Slade Grayson looked more like a Mafia hit man. Devlin wasn't sure such creatures existed anymore. He supposed organized crime was still around to some extent, but it had paled almost to insignificance in these days when the federal government thankfully controlled almost every aspect of every citizen's life from the cradle to the grave.

Grayson started to close the folder. Devlin said sharply, "Wait a minute. I want a better look at that."

With a grunt, Grayson opened the folder again and held it out farther. Devlin studied the badge and ID card for several seconds. Both of them certainly looked authentic enough, and there was no doubt that was Grayson's picture on the card.

"Satisfied, chief?" Grayson asked. The toothpick jumped up and down when he talked.

"Yes, I suppose so."

Grayson snapped the folder shut and put it away. With a cold smile, he said, "You gonna ask me in? You know, one of Uncle Sam's loyal servants to another?"

Devlin's hatred for the man deepened. No one had a right to make fun of the federal government, and he thought he heard mockery in Grayson's tone.

But he stepped back and said, "Come on in."

Grayson sauntered into the room and looked around.

"Not exactly fancy, is it?" he drawled.

"That doesn't matter. It's just a place to stay while I do my work."

"Nice utilitarian little bureaucrat, aren't you, Barton?"

Devlin bristled and said, "What are you doing here, Grayson? You obviously know who I am—"

"And I know why you're in Sierra Lobo, too," Grayson interrupted. "You're here to take G.W. Brannock's ranch away from him."

"He owes back taxes, fines, and penalties that he's refused to pay. He deserves everything that's going to happen to him."

"Maybe, maybe not. It doesn't matter anymore."

"Doesn't . . . doesn't matter anymore?" Devlin sputtered. He'd never heard anything so outrageous in all his life. Nothing was more important than collecting taxes so the government could continue to function.

Certainly nothing that had anything to do with the Bureau of Land Management!

"That's right," Grayson said with a smirk. "I'm heading up the government's dealings with Brannock now." His tone hardened as he went on. "I wouldn't have to be telling you that if you hadn't jumped the gun. You weren't supposed to seize the old guy's ranch until Friday. You shouldn't even be here yet."

Even though Devlin was angry, his keen brain still worked swiftly. Now it made sense why his superiors had moved the seizure up. They must have heard rumors that the BLM was interested in Brannock's ranch, too, and they wanted to bring the case to a conclusion before those rival bureaucrats could get their dirty paws on it.

"You're the one who shouldn't be here," Devlin snapped. "I don't know what you have in mind, but the IRS has a prior claim on Brannock's property. All the paperwork will be filed as soon as federal court opens in El Paso tomorrow."

"No, it won't," Grayson insisted. "That deal's dead. You can pack up and go home."

"I don't believe it!"

"Then call your bosses and ask them," Grayson suggested. "Or don't. It really doesn't matter to me. You see, Bart, ol' buddy, I don't care if you stay or go, as long as you do one thing."

"What's that?" Devlin demanded.

Grayson bared his teeth in another grin that sent chills down Devlin's spine.

"Stay the hell out of my way," said the man from the BLM.

Chapter 17

When G.W. got back from church, Kyle told him about Miranda's visit and the news she had brought with her.

He didn't mention anything about Stella showing up, too, figuring his grandfather didn't have any need to know about that. G.W. was old-fashioned enough not to want a girl with a reputation like Stella's hanging around the ranch.

With a frown, G.W. asked, "Miranda really thinks she can get an injunction from that judge to stop the IRS from takin' the place away from me?"

"That's what it sounded like to me," Kyle said. "She seemed really confident."

"Wish I could be," G.W. replied with a slow shake of his head. He looked solemn as he stood there in his Sunday suit and tie, still holding his Bible. "Even if she's right, though, I reckon some other judge higher up will just toss it out as soon as the Internal Revenue boys ask him to."

"Maybe. But hey, every day you can stall them is one more day something good can happen, right?"

G.W. gave him a surprised frown and said, "When did you turn into such a Pollyanna?"

"I have no idea what you're talking about," Kyle said.

"Never mind," G.W. said. "Lemme go put on some comfortable clothes, and then we'll see about grillin' some burgers for lunch."

"That sounds good to me."

It was a lazy, pleasant Sunday afternoon. G.W. didn't believe in working any more on the Sabbath than was absolutely necessary, so after lunch he and Kyle sat in the living room and watched a baseball game and a couple of old movies. Out in the cabins, the ranch hands were enjoying the time off with their families and friends.

Sunday supper in G.W.'s house was always fend-for-yourself and scrounge up whatever you could, so that was a pretty low-key affair, too.

Then night fell and G.W. took down a couple of rifles from the rack and started checking them.

"Hey, I thought we decided we weren't gonna take any guns with us," Kyle exclaimed when he saw what his grandfather was doing.

"You said that. I don't recall ever comin' right out and agreein' with it."

"You can't just start shooting at people—"

"Never said I was going to. If we can catch those fellas who've been sneakin' around, I want to ask 'em some questions, that's all. But two-legged trouble's not the only kind you might run into out there on the range after dark. There are snakes and coyotes and it's not unheard of for a panther or a bear to wander down out of the mountains. That's why we're takin' rifles with us."

"Oh." Kyle felt a little foolish now. "I guess I didn't think about that."

"That's because you didn't grow up out here. A man can't live close to nature for very long without realizin' that the world's got a whole heap of ways to kill you. The best way to survive is to never let your guard down."

"That gets pretty tiring, doesn't it?"

"Maybe," G.W. said with a shrug. "But it beats bein' a bunch of bleached bones picked clean and scattered by the scavengers."

Kyle couldn't argue with that.

They waited until it was good and dark, then went out and got into the pickup, taking the rifles and sleeping bags with them. G.W. didn't turn the headlights on as he pulled away, which prompted Kyle to ask him about it.

"Why would we need headlights?" G.W. asked. "There are plenty of stars up there, and besides, I know every foot o' this ranch. If somebody else is out and about, we don't want to announce that we're comin' by showin' any lights."

"Won't they hear the motor?"

"Maybe, but we can't avoid that. The pool's too far for us to walk."

"We could have taken horses."

"I thought about it," G.W. admitted. "But then I figured we might need to get back here in a hurry, if anything should happen to go wrong."

"You mean if one of us was hurt," Kyle said.

"I don't like to take foolish chances."

Kyle wondered if G.W. would have been so careful if he hadn't been coming along tonight. Maybe G.W. was just being protective of his grandson.

Or maybe he figured Kyle might foul things up somehow, and he'd need to be ready for that. Either version was possible, Kyle decided.

As G.W. had said, he didn't really need the headlights. He steered the pickup across the open range without any trouble, avoiding the arroyos that snaked across the valley here and there. The pickup's rugged suspension didn't care that there wasn't a road through here.

Instead of heading directly for the pool, G.W. drove to

a narrow canyon about half a mile from it. He ran the pickup into the thick shadows cast by the canyon's steep walls and brought it to a stop.

"We can hoof it from here," he said. "Don't slam that door when you get out. Just ease it shut. Then grab the sleepin' bags and follow me. Don't talk unless you have to. Voices carry out here at night."

Kyle did as he was told. He got the rolled-up sleeping bags from the back of the pickup and slung both of them over his shoulders.

That was the real reason G.W. wanted him to come along on this adventure, he thought wryly—to be a mule.

G.W. set off on foot with Kyle behind him. Kyle wore jeans, a black T-shirt, and boots thick enough and high enough to protect him from cactus and snakebites, if he was careful.

He carried the rifle with his finger outside the trigger guard and the barrel pointing down. Both G.W. and Kyle's dad had taught him at an early age how to handle a gun safely.

The breeze that swept through the valley had a hint of a chill to it, reminding Kyle they were at a fairly high altitude. The nights were cool here year-round.

The stars overhead were incredibly bright. Nobody in the eastern half of the state ever saw stars that bright, he thought. You had to get out here in West Texas, far from anywhere, and even here the air wasn't as clear as it once had been. Too much pollution drifting up from factories in northern Mexico.

G.W. led the way to the pool as if he were following a well-marked path. Kyle saw starlight rippling on the surface of the water, which was never completely still because the spring-fed stream never stopped flowing.

G.W. circled the pool and started climbing into the

rocks on the slope above it. He moved slowly and carefully, and Kyle knew why. There could easily be rattlesnakes in those rocks, and G.W. wanted to give them a chance to slither away once they sensed the humans approaching.

The two of them wound up stretched out on top of a huge slab of rock that had broken off the slope somewhere above and slid down here in millennia past. It was plenty big enough to accommodate both of them and their rifles.

G.W. took off his hat and set it beside him, along with his rifle and the handheld spotlight he had brought along. Kyle placed the sleeping bags behind them to be used later if they needed to stay out here overnight.

From up here they had a good view of the pool down below, as well as the approach to it. They would see anybody coming from the direction of the valley.

Lying on a big rock wasn't that comfortable, but Kyle tried to stay as still as he could. The rock still retained a little of the day's warmth, although that was fading fast in the dry air. Kyle moved his head closer to his grandfather's and whispered, "How long do we wait?"

"As long as it takes," G.W. said.

man who had walked away from the pool had come back. That way G.W. could catch them both in the beam.

That was what happened. The man finished his task and turned to rejoin his companion. In the starlight, Kyle couldn't be sure, but he thought the man had driven about two feet of the rod into the ground.

"How many more water samples do you need?" the man asked the other one. His voice came clearly to Kyle and G.W. on top of the big slab of rock.

"Just a couple," was the answer. "There are quite a few different tests that have to be run."

"Well, I've got the stake in the ground. I'll just hook up the equipment—"

That brief mention made Kyle think the man might be a seismologist and was about to use that metal rod to send waves of some sort through the ground so he could measure them.

Kyle didn't have time to ponder that any more, however, because that was when his grandfather squeezed the trigger on the spotlight and its brilliant beam shot out and speared both men.

Their reactions were almost identical. They both yelled startled curses, twisted toward the light, and threw up a hand to try to block the blinding glare.

"Don't move!" G.W. yelled. "You're both covered!"

That wasn't true, but there was no way the two men could know that. They stood there, each with a raised hand, as if they were frozen.

After a couple of seconds, the man kneeling beside the pool called, "Brannock! Is that you, G.W. Brannock?"

"I didn't tell you to talk," G.W. snapped. "When you say something, it'll be to answer my questions."

"Brannock, you're making a big mistake," the man said. "You're going to be in a lot of trouble."

"Damn right," the second man blustered. "You can't threaten us and get away with it."

"Looks like that's what I'm doin'," G.W. drawled. "Now, who are you boys and what're you doin' on my land?"

"It's not your land," the standing one said. "It belongs to—"

The other man made a sharp gesture to silence him.

"Look, Brannock, be reasonable. There's nothing you can do to change this. It's all out of your hands."

"The hell it is," G.W. said. "Stand up, mister." The man hesitated, and G.W. added, *"Now!"*

The tone of command in his voice was unmistakable. Most men didn't give an order like that unless they had the firepower to back it up.

The man by the pool stood up.

Kyle looked closely at the men. They didn't appear to be armed. In khaki trousers and work shirts they seemed harmless enough. Of course, they might have guns hidden somewhere on them.

"All right, both of you wade out into the water," G.W. told them.

"The hell with you!" the more argumentative of the two flared. "You don't know who you're dealing with, old man."

"Trespassers," G.W. said. "And since this whole range is posted, I got a right to shoot the two of you if I think you're threatenin' me. You're pretty damned close to it."

He turned his head toward Kyle and whispered, "Lever that rifle."

Kyle wasn't sure he ought to go along with that order. He didn't know who the strangers were, but they seemed confident in their right to be here.

On the other hand, Kyle had never exactly had much

respect for authority, either, and he didn't like these guys. Not one damned bit.

He picked up the rifle beside him and worked the lever to throw a cartridge into the chamber.

That metallic *clack-clack* sounded loud in the night. The man who had driven the rod into the ground muttered, "Crap, there's more than one of 'em up there."

"Take it easy, Brannock," the other man said. "Don't do anything you can't take back."

"Do what I tell you, then," G.W. said.

Both men sighed. Then, with obvious reluctance, they waded out into the pool.

"Keep goin' until I tell you to stop," G.W. said. He tracked them with the spotlight beam.

When they were up to mid-thigh, the more reasonable-sounding of the two asked, "Can we at least take out our wallets so everything in them won't get soaked?"

"Good idea. Take 'em out and throw 'em on the shore."

The two men looked at each other. Clearly, neither of them wanted to do that.

But G.W. still had the upper hand, and they knew it. One by one, they pulled their wallets from their hip pockets and tossed them on the ground near the edge of the pool.

"Go down and get 'em," G.W. told Kyle. "Let's see who we're dealin' with here." He added as Kyle started to stand up, "Just don't get in the line of fire."

Chapter 19

Kyle started to get up, then paused and asked quietly, "Do I take my rifle with me?"

G.W. didn't answer for a second. Kyle assumed he was thinking it over. Then he said, "No, leave it here. Wouldn't want one of those fellas jumpin' you and takin' it away from you."

Kyle felt a flash of annoyance. Both of the men revealed in the spotlight beam appeared to be in pretty good shape, but Kyle could take care of himself in a fight. In fact, he was pretty damned handy in one, he thought, as he had proven with Vern Hummel most recently and in any number of earlier scrapes.

But he wasn't going to argue with his grandfather, so he said, "Fine," and left the rifle lying on the rock beside G.W.

Kyle hadn't forgotten about the danger of rattlesnakes. He was careful to make some noise as he climbed down the slope. Once he was on the flat, he circled the pool and headed for the wallets lying on the ground.

The spotlight was focused on the men in the water, but the glare from it reached out to where Kyle was as he picked up the wallets. The man who had driven the rod into the ground said, "Hey, this one's just a kid."

"I'm older than you think, mister," Kyle snapped. "And I'm not afraid of you."

"Maybe you should be," the other man said. "Not of us, so much, but who we work for. And by the way, you're breaking the law here. You're just as guilty as that old man up there."

Kyle didn't volunteer that the old man was his grandfather. Instead he opened one of the wallets and looked at the contents, figuring that was what G.W. would want him to do. There was some cash, but he didn't disturb that. He was no thief. The driver's license was what interested him.

The picture on the license matched up with the man who'd been collecting water samples. Kyle nodded toward him and called to G.W., "This one's name is Warren Finley. Got a Virginia driver's license."

Another laminated card caught Kyle's attention and made him take a sharply indrawn breath.

"He works for the Bureau of Land Management." Kyle looked up at the rock where his grandfather was, even though he couldn't see G.W. because of the light. "That's the federal government."

"I know damned good and well what the BLM is," G.W. replied. "What about the other one?"

Kyle checked the other wallet and found the man's driver's license and ID card.

"Woodrow Todd, also from Virginia, also works for the Bureau of Land Management."

"All right." G.W.'s voice was flat and hard with anger. "Question is, what are a couple o' BLM flunkies doin' sneakin' around on my land?"

"As I tried to explain to you, Mr. Brannock," Warren Finley said, "this isn't actually your land."

"The hell it's not! This valley has been in my family for close to a hundred and fifty years. My great-grandfather bought it from some Mexican *hacendado* with a spread below the border. His family's original land grant from the King of Spain ran all the way up here."

"Yes, I'm aware of that, and that's the problem. It's been discovered recently that a clause in the original grant should have reverted ownership of the land to the Spanish government in Mexico following the death of the grantee. Therefore ownership of the property should have passed to Mexico when it won its independence from Spain, and following that to the Republic of Texas after 1836, and finally to the United States government after Texas was annexed in 1845."

"I didn't come out here for a damn history lesson in the middle of the night," G.W. snapped.

"Then let me boil it down for you," Finley said. "The man who sold this valley to your great-grandfather had no legal right to do so, because he didn't actually own it. By that time, the actual rights to the land belonged solely to the government of the United States. This ranch is federal property, Mr. Brannock."

Silence from the top of the rock. Kyle figured G.W. was stunned, because he was pretty thunderstruck himself.

Finally, G.W. said, "That's crazy. Like I told you, my family's owned this valley for more than a century."

"Your family was in illegal possession of it."

"Nobody ever told me anything about that! We've paid taxes on the land, worked it, turned it into something good. . . ."

"Indeed, you have," Finley said. "No one is claiming that you acted improperly, Mr. Brannock. You were only going by what you thought to be true. As I told you, the clause in the land grant was discovered only recently. Woody and I have been making some preliminary surveys—"

"Sneakin' around!"

Finley shrugged and said, "Call it whatever you'd like. We've simply been doing our job and gathering information before the BLM moves to take possession of the property."

"Take possession? You mean steal the valley from me?"

"It's hardly stealing," Finley said as he shook his head. "This is federal land, Mr. Brannock. Public land. And as soon as the proper paperwork is filed, that will be official. Someone will arrive to serve notice to you to vacate."

"Anybody who shows up tellin' me to get off my land is liable to get a hot lead welcome!"

Kyle winced. He understood that his grandfather was angry, and with good reason. But threatening federal agents with a shoot-out wasn't a very good idea. They had gotten more and more trigger-happy over the past few decades.

Finley said, "Now that you know who we are, is it all right for us to get out of this pool? The water from the springs that feed it is rather cold."

Again G.W. took his time about answering, but he finally said, "All right, you can get out."

"We'd like to have our wallets back, too."

"Fine. Then you can climb in that jeep and get the hell out of here."

"We were about to conduct some tests—"

"Well, now you're not goin' to. You're gonna leave and not come back, you understand me?"

Finley said, "We can leave, but we'll have to come back. Or someone else will. Nothing is going to change what's about to happen, Mr. Brannock. You can't stop the federal government. It would be like trying to hold back an avalanche with your bare hands."

"I've got more than my bare hands," G.W. snapped. "Keep pushin' me, and you'll find out."

With water streaming from their lower legs, Finley and Todd waded out of the pool.

"Kyle, put those billfolds down and back away," G.W. ordered.

Kyle dropped the wallets on the ground at his feet and started to back off to put some distance between himself and the two federal men. Todd stalked over to the wallets and bent down as if he were going to pick them up.

Then, while his head was lowered, he lunged forward and tackled Kyle around the waist, knocking him backwards off his feet.

Chapter 20

This was the second time in as many days that Kyle had been attacked like this, and he didn't like it.

He managed to twist some as he fell, so he didn't land flat on the ground with Todd's weight on top of him. His hip took the brunt of the painful impact, but that was better than risking broken ribs and having the breath knocked out of him.

Kyle whipped a punch to Todd's left ear and drew a howl of pain from the man, who was a couple of inches taller and probably outweighed him by forty pounds. Because of that, Kyle had no intention of fighting fair. He rammed his right knee into Todd's groin.

Todd really yelled about that. But even though he was hurt, he lashed out with a fist that caromed off Kyle's jaw and rocked his head back. For a second Kyle saw even more stars than there really were in the ebony sky overhead.

While Kyle was momentarily helpless, Todd grabbed the front of his shirt and jerked him forward. The government man tried to head butt him in the face, but Kyle writhed away just enough so that their heads scraped without any real impact. Kyle twisted his head and sunk his teeth into Todd's ear.

Todd screamed like a little girl.

Kyle didn't want to go full Tyson and rip the guy's ear off, so he let go and shot a punch into Todd's belly. While Todd was recovering from that, Kyle reared up on both knees, clubbed his hands together, and swung both arms in a roundhouse blow that crashed into Todd's jaw with devastating force. Todd sprawled on the ground and lay there trembling, unable to get up or continue the fight.

Kyle struggled to his feet and stood there with his chest heaving. From atop the giant slab of rock, G.W. said dryly, "If you two are through dancin' down there, you can come back up here, son."

Warren Finley still stood near the pool with his hands held out to the sides and raised to elbow height, so they were in plain sight. Clearly, he thought there might be guns trained on him.

It was possible, thought Kyle, although since G.W. still held the spotlight, he would have to fire the rifle one-handed if he needed to take a shot.

"For what it's worth," Finley said to Kyle, "I didn't tell Woody to attack you like that. I'd just as soon he hadn't. There's really no need for violence. The law is on the government's side, so the outcome of this whole matter is inevitable."

"Inevitable . . . to you . . . maybe," Kyle said, still a little breathless from the fight. "The British . . . probably felt the same way . . . back in 1776."

Finley's eyes narrowed, and his mouth tightened into a grim line. He said, "I wouldn't have taken you for a student of history, young man. Are you advocating violent revolution against the United States government?"

"Nope. Just saying people sometimes get tired of being

stepped on. Especially when the ones doing the stepping are supposed to be working *for* the people."

"Clearly you don't understand how things work in the modern world," Finley snapped.

"No, but I've read the Constitution. Figure that puts me one up on a lot of people in Washington these days."

G.W. sounded like he was trying not to chuckle as he said, "This ain't a debatin' society any more than it's a cotillion. Finley, gather up your buddy and get out of here. Don't let me catch you on my land again."

"It's not—" Finley stopped and sighed, evidently realizing the futility of his argument. "I'll need to get our equipment, too."

"Fine," G.W. said. "I don't want anything that belongs to the government on my ranch, anyway."

Finley helped Todd to his feet and led him, groaning, to the jeep. Todd slumped into the passenger seat and sat there glaring at Kyle while Finley went out to the half-buried rod, took hold of it, and worked it back and forth until he could pull it from the earth's grip. He stowed it in the backseat with the water samples and some other gear Kyle couldn't make out.

When Finley got behind the wheel, he paused and said, "You're making a big mistake, Mr. Brannock."

"So you keep tellin' me," G.W. said. "Now skedaddle."

Finley cranked the jeep's engine and backed away from the pool until he had room to turn around. This time he turned the vehicle's lights on as he drove away.

The spotlight shining from above went out.

The jeep's taillights were like the red eyes of some malevolent beast, Kyle thought as he stood at the edge of the pool and watched them dwindle into the darkness.

The scrape of boot leather on rock made him aware that G.W. had climbed down to join him. His eyes were starting to adjust now after the brilliance of the spotlight, and as he turned he saw his grandfather standing there with both rifles and sleeping bags. G.W. dumped the sleeping bags on the ground at his feet.

"Government men," Kyle said. "Were you expecting that, G.W.?"

"I didn't know what to expect. But I can't say as I'm surprised. When you need somebody from the government, they're nowhere to be found, but when there's trouble to be caused for honest folks, they pop up like ants at a picnic."

"They're crazy, right?" Kyle said. "There's no way this valley belongs to them."

"They claim it does, and in this day and age, when the average citizen doesn't have many rights anymore, that may be all that matters." G.W. turned his head and spat. "They find a way to get what they want, and even if it's not legal, more than half the country just flat doesn't give a damn. All that matters to those folks is that they get their government handout."

"What are you going to do?"

"Well, Miranda said she was going to El Paso first thing in the morning to get that injunction against the IRS. I reckon she'll let us know when she gets back."

Kyle hoped so. He found himself wanting to see Miranda Stephens again.

"And when she does," G.W. said, "we'll tell her about this. Maybe she'll have some idea what to do. She's a pretty smart little gal."

"Yeah," Kyle said. He moved to pick up the sleeping bags and slung them over his shoulders again. G.W. still carried both rifles as they started hiking back toward the canyon where they had left the pickup.

After they had gone a hundred yards or so, Kyle asked, "If that guy Todd had gotten the upper hand and looked like he was really going to hurt me . . . would you have shot him?"

"I'm not the sort of man who'd sit by and watch my grandson get hurt," G.W. said. "It looked like you were handlin' yourself pretty good, though, so I held off."

"I'm glad. We're probably in enough trouble already without any shots being fired." They walked on, and a minute later Kyle said, "You know, it's sort of odd, this business about the old Spanish land grant coming up at the same time the IRS is trying to take the ranch away from you."

"Yeah," G.W. said. "It is, isn't it?"

Chapter 21

Slade Grayson had taken a room at the motel, a few units down from that IRS rabbit Barton Devlin.

Grayson didn't have anything against the IRS. It was just another federal agency, and he had worked for several of them, bringing his own special expertise to whatever problem they had at the time.

He didn't have any use for all the faceless, nameless bureaucrats he had encountered over the years, though, toiling away at whatever boring, menial task they had so they could keep suckling at Uncle Sam's teat. Taking what little pleasure they could by making the lives of any citizens unfortunate enough to cross their path purely miserable.

That was their problem. They were small men and women. They thought small, and they settled for petty vindictiveness.

They had no idea how to rain down the holy hell of the federal government on any who transgressed. They didn't know how to deliver that fiery vengeance from on high with all the destructive fury of an angry God!

Not that there really was any god but the government, to Grayson's way of thinking.

No, men like Devlin didn't know how to do that . . . but Slade Grayson did.

Which made him a different sort of mortal than most, and so he was annoyed when someone knocked on the door of his motel room late that night just as he was getting ready to go to sleep.

Grayson picked up the small, thin, but lethal automatic from the dresser where he had set it earlier and tucked it into the holster at the small of his back. He went to the door and looked through the peephole.

Two men stood there, clearly visible in the light from the fixture mounted on the awning over the concrete walk. One was tall and rather burly, the other short and slender. Both were balding.

Grayson had never seen them in person, but he recognized them from pictures in the files he had studied when he was given this assignment.

He jerked the door open and snapped, "Finley, Todd, what the hell are you doing here?"

Both visitors looked surprised when he addressed them by name. Finley, the smaller of the two, said, "Mr. Grayson, we should introduce ourselves—"

"Not necessary. Come in."

Grayson stepped back. The two men came into the room and looked around nervously.

They had probably heard stories about him, thought Grayson. Rumors had spread through the various agencies in Washington. Nobody knew who Slade Grayson really worked for. He floated from job to job, showing up when there was a problem that couldn't be handled by regular methods.

As Grayson closed the door, he said, "I wasn't supposed to meet with you two until tomorrow. What are you doing here tonight?"

"Brannock knows," Finley said.

"Knows what? That he's screwed?"

"He knows that the BLM is going to take possession of his ranch."

Grayson leveled a cold stare at Finley and asked, "How did he find out about that?"

Todd, the big, dumb-looking one, burst out, "We were just doing our job, okay? We were supposed to be out there finishing up our observations."

Finley added, "We had orders to that effect, yes."

Grayson shook his head and blew out his breath in an annoyed sigh.

"You got caught, didn't you?" he asked. "That old man got the drop on you and you spilled the whole thing."

"What does it matter?" Todd said defensively. "He would have known as soon as you showed up out there tomorrow, anyway."

Grayson resisted the urge to shoot the stupid son of a bitch. Instead, he said, "Never give an enemy any more warning than you have to. When it comes to tactics, you can't get any more basic than that."

Finley said, "We're talking about twelve hours' difference. In circumstances like this, what effect could that have?"

"I guess we'll find out, won't we?"

Grayson walked over to the dresser, took the gun from its holster, and set it down again. There was a bottle of whiskey on the dresser, too, along with one of the squat glasses from the motel bathroom with a couple of half-melted ice cubes in it. He splashed some of the liquor into the glass, picked it up, and turned back to the two flunkies. He didn't offer them a drink.

"Tell me the whole thing."

For the next few minutes they did, with Finley doing most of the talking. Grayson found most of the story irritating—

he didn't like incompetence, and these two never should
have allowed themselves to be discovered that way—but
some of it was interesting.

"Who was the young man with Brannock?" he asked.

"We have no idea," Finley said. "Brannock called him
by name once. I believe it was Kyle."

"Kyle . . ." Grayson repeated. "Brannock's file says
that all the ranch hands working for him are Hispanic.
Immigration looked into it to see if any of them are undocumented, in case we needed to use that against him, but
amazingly, they're not. Maybe this man was one of his relatives." Grayson waved the hand that held the drink and
went on. "I'll find out, but it's not really important, I don't
imagine. Did you at least finish the readings you were
supposed to take?"

Both men seemed to squirm a little, even though they
didn't actually move. Finley said, "I have most of the water
samples I need. We weren't able to complete the seismo-
logical readings, however."

"I was just about to when Brannock and his buddy
jumped us," Todd added, sounding defensive again.

"You can finish up with all that once we've seized the
land," Grayson said. "It doesn't really matter what you
find. The project is going ahead anyway."

With a worried frown, Finley said, "I'm not sure it's a
good idea to proceed until we've nailed down all the pa-
rameters. There could be ecological damage. There could
even be a threat to the human population. If anything went
wrong, we could be talking about a disaster of catastrophic
proportions."

Grayson tossed back the rest of his drink and smirked.

"We're talking about Texas," he said. "After all this
time, the stubborn bastards still vote for Republicans. So
who gives a damn?"

Chapter 22

Kyle and G.W. were quiet as G.W. drove back to the ranch house. Kyle didn't know what his grandfather was thinking about, but his mind was full of a mixture of anger and worry.

The anger was because of the outrageous treatment G.W. was receiving at the hands of the federal government. The idea that they could just come in and take away the land that had been in the Brannock family for generations, first with phony tax charges and now with some crazy story about Spanish land grants, made Kyle furious.

At the same time, despite his own checkered past, he had never taken on the federal government. His scrapes had always been with local law enforcement agencies, like the cops in Sierra Lobo.

If you got the feds mad at you, there was a good chance you'd wind up disappearing in a black hole somewhere, never to be seen again, especially in these days of what was essentially one-party rule on the federal level.

The governor of Texas, Maria Delgado, was a Republican, Kyle recalled, and had clashed frequently with the Democratic administration in Washington. So far she seemed to be holding her own in that struggle. Kyle wondered if it would do any good to appeal to her.

He would have to bring up that possibility with G.W., he decided, and with Miranda, too, the next time he talked to her.

Thinking about Miranda made him realize that he was eager to see her again. He would be glad when she was back from El Paso, hopefully with the injunction that would stop the Internal Revenue Service in its tracks.

Of course, it might not matter. Even though everybody was afraid of the IRS—and rightfully so—in this case the Bureau of Land Management's planned seizure of the valley struck Kyle as an even bigger threat.

It was certainly more mysterious, that was for sure. And a little sinister . . .

G.W. broke into Kyle's gloomy musing by saying, "I'm glad you were out there with me tonight, son. When the odds are against you, it makes a difference, havin' somebody you can count on to back you up."

"I'm not sure anybody's ever thought of me as somebody they can count on."

G.W. looked over at him and said, "How you see yourself isn't necessarily the same way everybody else in the world sees you. Try to remember that."

Kyle nodded. He wished that what his grandfather had just said was true . . . but he couldn't quite bring himself to believe it.

Roberto Quinones, G.W.'s foreman, was waiting for them on the porch when they got back. The stocky, middle-aged man had a rifle across his knees. He stood up and came down the steps to meet them.

"Roberto, did you plan on sitting up all night?" G.W. asked him.

"If I needed to," Quinones said with a nod. "I knew there was a chance you and Kyle would not be back tonight, so I thought it best to stay alert. With as many enemies as you seem to have these days, señor . . ."

He left the statement unfinished.

"Did anything happen while we were gone?"

"No. Everything was quiet as could be, thank the Blessed Virgin."

"Good," G.W. said, "because it looks like we've got more enemies than we even knew about. More than just the dadgum IRS."

The moon had risen by now, and its silvery light revealed the frown that creased Roberto's forehead.

"What do you mean, señor?"

"The Bureau of Land Management is after the valley now, too."

"Madre de Dios," the foreman breathed.

G.W. told him about the encounter with the two BLM agents and the wild story Finley had spun about a clause in an old, forgotten Spanish land grant making the ranch federal property.

"That cannot be true, señor," Quinones declared emphatically. "If it were, surely someone would have found it before now."

"I've been thinking about that," Kyle said. His grandfather and Roberto turned to look at him, and both of them seemed a little surprised, as if they wouldn't have expected him to come up with any kind of theory to explain this sudden flurry of trouble.

"Well, get on with it," G.W. said.

"Those guys from the BLM have been around for a

while, right? You said you've spotted them sneaking around before."

G.W. nodded and said, "Yeah, Roberto and the boys saw 'em first, several weeks ago."

"So this effort to seize your ranch has been in the works for a while, by the BLM as well as the IRS. Sounds to me like some good, old-fashioned rivalry between the two bunches."

G.W. scratched his jaw as he frowned in thought.

"You mean they're competin' to see who's gonna ruin me first?"

"That's the way it looks to me."

"Yeah, but why?" G.W. swept an arm out to indicate their surroundings. "Just to get their hands on this ranch? I understand why it's so important to me, but how come it means enough to two different government agencies that they want to destroy me over it?"

Kyle could only shake his head and say, "Now that's one I can't answer, G.W."

San Francisco

Ben Gardner limped slightly as he crossed the airport terminal. He had wrenched his knee when he vaulted over that stone wall at the hotel in Manila. The blast from the rocket fired by the drone had collapsed the wall on top of him, too, fortunately not breaking any bones but leaving him bruised and sore.

Of course, this was hardly the first time he had been knocked around during the course of a mission for the Company.

This wasn't actually a mission, though. The terminally ill Chinese man had approached him with information. Gardner hadn't gone looking for it.

What he'd found on the tiny USB drive Pao Ling had

given him had come as more of a shock than it should have, Gardner supposed. He tried to be nonpartisan most of the time—domestic politics weren't really a concern in his job, or at least they shouldn't have been—but it would have taken a blind man not to see the way things had been going in Washington in recent years. Gardner's eyesight was just fine.

So he had laid low in a Company safe house in Manila for a few days while he tried to figure out what to do next.

Normally, he would have reported to his handler and sent the file from the drive through secure channels, but he wasn't sure that was the best idea this time. There was a question of whom he could trust.

He decided the best method for figuring that out was the old-fashioned way.

He wanted to look people in the eye while he was talking to them.

Because of that lack of trust, he figured he would be better off not reaching out to his usual sources of help. Manila was one of the many world capitals where he had stashed emergency caches of cash and documents over the years. Thinking that he would catch a flight from there to the States and fly with one of his phony passports, he left the safe house and started toward the emergency drop site, a shoe repair shop on a rather shabby side street.

The bell over the door rang as Gardner entered the shop. There were several pairs of shoes in the front window that were for sale, but they had a layer of dust on them showing that they hadn't been touched for quite a while.

No customers were in the place, and no one was behind the counter. But a moment later, an old Filipino man pushed past a curtain that hung over the entrance to a back room. His name was Ferdinand, Gardner recalled, just like the former dictator many years earlier—or the flower-sniffing bull.

Gardner had done a favor for Ferdinand one time, a favor involving the old man's grandson, drugs, and a smuggler who wanted the young man to work for him. Gardner had paid a visit to the smuggler, and since then the man hadn't come anywhere near Ferdinand's grandson.

Because of that, the old cobbler had been more than happy to agree to Gardner's request that he hang on to a sealed package until Gardner showed up to reclaim it. If more than five years went by without the American paying a visit to the shop, Ferdinand was supposed to open the package and do whatever he wanted with the contents.

The old man had sworn a solemn oath that he would protect the package with his life. Gardner had assured him that that level of devotion wasn't required to pay the debt. But Gardner was confident the money and the documents would still be there at the shop.

Ferdinand greeted him with a smile, as always.

"Benjamin," he said, speaking his native language, "I wondered when you would be coming by to visit with me again."

"My work keeps me busy," Gardner answered in fluent Tagalog. "Much to my regret. How is your grandson?"

"Doing well in school. No more troubles, thanks to you, my friend. He is thinking about becoming a doctor. Can you imagine that? The grandson of a humble cobbler, a doctor."

"I wish him the best," Gardner said. "Now—"

"You came for the package you left with me."

"That's right."

Ferdinand turned to a shelf on the wall behind the counter. It was crowded with shoeboxes with no lids. On the end of each box, a piece of paper with a number scribbled on it had been taped.

The old man didn't have to check the numbers. He knew exactly which box to reach for. He pulled it out from under several others that appeared identical and set it on the counter.

Inside was the package wrapped in brown paper and sealed with tape.

"No one has bothered it," Ferdinand told Gardner.

"I didn't think they would have." The American took the package out of the box and reached in his pocket for a knife to cut the tape.

That was when a taxi crashed into the front window, spraying shattered glass everywhere. The thin wood and plaster of the wall was no match for the speeding vehicle. Its front end surged toward Gardner.

Instinctively, he threw himself out of the way. The fender brushed his hip as the taxi went past.

The car hit the counter and splintered it. The only thing that saved Ferdinand was the fact that he had jumped back, tripped, and fallen through the doorway. The taxi lurched to a halt just short of where he lay.

Gardner had the package in his left hand. In his right was the knife he had planned to use to cut the tape.

Now he flicked the blade open with a practiced twist of his wrist as two men leaped from the taxi's front seat. Both were Filipino, squat, ugly, vicious-looking men. Hired killers, Gardner had no doubt. They both wore khaki trousers and golf shirts, but Gardner figured neither of them spent much time on the links.

They came at him from different angles. They might not be top pros, but they weren't amateurs, either. A swipe of the knife made one man retreat, but the other got close enough to land a brutal punch to Gardner's ribs.

Gardner grunted and stumbled to the side. He caught

his balance and slashed the blade at the man who had hit him. That allowed the other one to charge in as he flicked out a blade of his own.

Gardner felt cold steel burn a fiery line across his side. The wound wasn't deep, nothing more than a scratch, but it stung. Gardner feinted low, then speared the point of his knife into the man's upper arm. He tried to twist toward the second man, but he knew he might be too late. . . .

The would-be killers had forgotten about Ferdinand. The old man rose up behind the ruined counter clutching a big revolver in both hands. Gardner didn't know where Ferdinand had gotten such a hogleg or if he could aim it properly.

Ferdinand dispelled any doubt by squeezing the trigger. Flame licked from the revolver's muzzle. The second attacker went down like he had been punched in the chest by a giant fist.

That left just one man for Gardner to deal with. The thug was wounded, which slowed his responses enough for Gardner to slip past his defense and bury the knife in the man's throat. He ripped it to the side and leaped back to avoid the fountain of blood that spurted from the man's ruined throat.

The man collapsed and bled out in a matter of heartbeats.

The other man was dead, too, with a scorched bullet hole welling blood in the center of his shirt pocket.

Somewhere not too far away, police sirens clanged.

"Go out the back," Ferdinand told Gardner urgently. "When the police arrive I will tell them these men stole that taxi, crashed it into my shop, and tried to rob me. Such things are not uncommon in this neighborhood."

"And they'll think you killed both of them?" Gardner said.

"There will be none to claim otherwise."

The old cobbler had a point there. Gardner shrugged and said, "Thank you, Ferdinand."

"Our accounts are square now . . . almost. If you ever need help again . . ."

"I know who to call," Gardner said. He shoved the package inside his coat, put away the knife, and clambered through the wreckage until he could make his way through Ferdinand's back room and out into a filthy alley.

He knew the attack was no attempted robbery. Somebody had sent those two men after him. Whoever had sent in that drone to kill Pao Ling had figured out that Gardner was still alive and might have the information Pao had given him. They had picked up his trail, probably when he left the safe house, and organized this hasty attempt on his life.

He was going to have to drop out of sight and stay that way as much as possible until he got home and turned everything over to somebody who would know what to do with it. If they picked him up again and had time to make the proper preparations, it might be him they sent a drone after next time.

Knowing that, Gardner had called on every bit of tradecraft he possessed. He had changed his appearance as much as he could, shaving his head and subtly altering his features with makeup and a couple of rubber prosthetics he carried for just such a problem. The picture on one of the fake passports matched that look. With that and the cash, he'd been able to buy a ticket on a nonstop flight to San Francisco. . . .

Which was where he found himself now, unsure of his next move. Normally, he would be glad to be home again.

Unfortunately, as sickening as the thought might be, there was a good chance home was now where his deadliest enemies lurked. . . .

Chapter 23

For somebody like Kyle who didn't work at a job with regular hours, Monday was just another day of the week.

This one was a little different, though, because on this particular Monday there was a chance he might see Miranda Stephens again.

It was crazy for him to feel that way, he told himself sternly as he ate breakfast by himself in the kitchen. Despite their late night the previous evening, Kyle's grandfather was long since up and out somewhere on the ranch, tending to whatever needed doing.

Kyle had meant to get up early, have breakfast with G.W., and find out what he could do to help. But not surprisingly, he had overslept.

At least he could clean up after himself, he decided. G.W.'s breakfast dishes were in the sink. Kyle washed them, along with his own, and put them in the drainer.

Then he went outside to see if he could find something else that needed to be done.

Years ago, G.W. had put in a vegetable garden near the barn by making half a dozen sets of rectangular wooden frameworks that were four feet by six feet on the sides, as

well as six inches deep. He had filled those frameworks
with topsoil to form raised beds in which were planted
tomatoes, green beans, red and yellow peppers, two different kinds of squash, and corn. Those vegetables grew
better in the topsoil than they would in the more sandy soil
found here in the valley.

That sandy soil supported two large beds of watermelon
and cantaloupe, though. When Kyle was a kid, nothing had
tasted much better to him than a good yellow meat or black
diamond watermelon fresh out of the patch.

Now he saw several of the women who were married to
some of G.W.'s ranch hands picking vegetables from the
raised beds. Kyle walked over to them and asked, "Can I
give you a hand, ladies?"

One of the women made a shooing motion and said,
"No, señor, you have more important things to do."

"As far as I know, I don't have *anything* to do."

"Señor Brannock said you were looking after the place
today, in case more men from the government came to take
it away."

So G.W. wasn't keeping his problems secret from the
people who worked for him, thought Kyle. That came as
no surprise. His grandfather wasn't the sort to sit around
bitching and moaning, but he wouldn't conceal the truth
from his friends, either. G.W. could be a stern taskmaster,
but he had a lot of affection for his hands and their families and would feel like he needed to shoot straight with
them about the problems facing the ranch. That unfailing
honesty was one reason they were so loyal to him.

Kyle sighed. G.W. was trusting him to handle things,
but if half a dozen SUVs filled with federal agents showed
up, he didn't know what in the world he could do. There
were plenty of guns and ammunition in the house, but

he couldn't stand off a full-scale government assault by himself.

Of course, neither could he and G.W., and Kyle knew his grandfather wouldn't ask Roberto Quinones and the other hands to risk getting thrown in prison—or killed—on his account.

Still, maybe a show of force might do some good. He went back into the house and took one of the lever-action repeaters down from the gun rack. He carried it out onto the porch and sat down with it.

If G.W. wanted him to stand guard, that's what he was going to do.

Despite his determination to stay vigilant, and even though he hadn't really been awake that long, he began to get drowsy almost right away. The heat and the lack of anything to do made it difficult to remain alert.

His head drooped forward, and he dozed off. He didn't know how long he'd been asleep when the sudden shrill ring of the telephone in the house jolted him upright.

Kyle's neck ached from the position it had been in, and he felt a little dizzy and light-headed, not to mention disoriented, as he stood up quickly. The phone continued ringing, so he muttered, "Hold your horses," as he turned toward the door.

G.W. had a cell phone—he wasn't a complete Luddite—but he was also one of the few people around who had kept his landline. He probably wouldn't give it up until the phone company discontinued that type of service, as it inevitably would.

At least it was a normal digital cordless phone, not one of those old black rotary dial units with a curl cord running from the receiver to the base. Kyle had seen pictures of those, but he had never seen one in real life.

The menu screen on the phone displayed a number but

didn't say whom it belonged to. G.W. probably hadn't even gotten around to programming that feature, or else he had tried, failed, and given up.

G.W. Brannock wasn't the type who threw up his hands in surrender . . . unless it was to modern technology.

The phone was still ringing, so Kyle thumbed the Talk button and said, "Hello?"

"Kyle? This is Miranda Stephens."

He felt a little thrill go through him when she spoke his name. She sounded excited. Not excited to be talking to him, surely, but maybe that meant she had good news.

"Is G.W. there?" she asked. "I tried calling his cell, but it went to his voice mail."

"He's probably just out of reach of a tower," Kyle said. "This ranch is pretty big. There are places out on the range where there's no coverage."

"So he's not there?"

"Nope, afraid not."

She laughed, and he could almost see her shaking her head.

"I thought he might stay close to home this morning and wait to hear from me, but I guess I should have known better. If there's work to be done, he's going to be out doing it, isn't he?"

"You're right about that," Kyle said. "Is there anything I can do for you?"

"I'm still in El Paso. I just wanted to tell him about my meeting with the judge." Miranda paused, then went on. "I don't see any reason I can't tell you. She granted the injunction, Kyle. The IRS can't move to seize your grandfather's ranch until after his appeal has been heard. And I've got so much documentation lined up, I just know he's going to win that appeal."

It was Kyle's turn to hesitate. He didn't want to spoil her sense of victory at getting the injunction by letting her know that it might be moot. The BLM might wind up crowding the IRS aside.

On the other hand, Miranda *was* G.W.'s attorney, and she couldn't do her job properly if she didn't have all the information about her client's problems.

"That's good," Kyle told her, "but you'd better brace yourself. It looks like this whole mess is a long way from being over."

Chapter 24

For a long moment, there was silence from Miranda on the other end of the line. Then she said, "Something else has happened, hasn't it?" Quickly, she added, "Are you all right? Is G.W. all right?"

She asked about his welfare first, thought Kyle, but he put that out of his mind as he replied, "Yeah, we caught those guys who have been sneaking around the ranch for a while. They were from the Bureau of Land Management."

"The BLM?" Miranda sounded surprised. "Why would the BLM be . . . wait . . . no, you don't mean . . ."

"They claim the ranch actually belongs to the federal government," Kyle said. "They're going to take it away from him."

"That's insane! The ranch has been in the Brannock family for well over a hundred years."

"You're not telling me anything I don't already know," Kyle replied heavily.

"But how can they even *make* such a claim?"

He told her what Finley and Todd had said about the Spanish land grant.

"I guess they're bound to have a copy of it," he concluded. "Otherwise, they wouldn't come waltzing in saying they're gonna take over."

"I'll have to see it," Miranda said. Her voice fairly crackled with anger. "It has to be a fake. We'll find experts to examine it. This is blatant, outright theft they're trying to pull off, Kyle."

"Again, I'm not the one you have to convince."

She heaved a sigh over the phone line.

"I know, I know. I'm sorry if I yelled in your ear. You're not the one I'm mad at."

"I know that," he said.

"So, where is G.W. this morning?"

"I don't know. He was gone when I got up. I suppose he's out on the range somewhere, checking on the stock or doing something else that needs doing."

"Listen, I'm on my way. I'm leaving El Paso now. I'll be there in a couple of hours, so if he comes in, keep him there until I get there."

"That might be easier said than done," Kyle told her.

"Well, try. We've got to sit down and discuss our strategy. We're not going to let those bastards get away with this."

She hung up without saying good-bye. Kyle looked at the phone in his hand for a second before ending the connection on his end and replacing the phone in its base.

Miranda had sounded even more furious than he'd expected her to, as if the government's latest assault on G.W. was a personal attack on her, too. That thought put a faint smile on Kyle's face.

"She loves the old coot like he was *her* grandfather, too," he said softly.

As long as that didn't make her regard him as a brother,

because the feelings he was having for her weren't exactly brotherly.

He went back out onto the front porch and sat down in one of the rocking chairs again with the rifle across his knees. The women had finished picking vegetables and gone back inside the cabins. The ranch headquarters lay quiet and peaceful in the growing heat as the sun rose toward midday.

Naturally, that couldn't last very long.

Kyle's eyes narrowed as he spotted dust rising in the distance. The highway lay in that direction, and he knew from experience that such a dust cloud meant someone had turned off the pavement and was headed here on the narrow dirt road. The dust shimmered a little in the heat waves radiating from the ground.

Kyle supposed it could be G.W. coming in. His grandfather could have gone to town for some reason.

As the vehicle at the base of the dust cloud came into view, however, he saw that it wasn't G.W.'s pickup. It was a silver, late model sedan. A rental car, maybe?

That thought put a frown on Kyle's forehead. It wasn't a jeep this time, but this could be those two BLM agents coming back to try to throw their weight around some more.

Kyle stood up and moved to the top of the steps. He had the rifle tucked under his left arm where it was handy but not threatening.

He knew that if he had to, he could get his finger on the trigger pretty damn quick.

The car drove up in front of the ranch house and stopped. The engine continued to run, as if the driver didn't want to cut off the air-conditioning.

The man behind the wheel appeared to be alone. The

car's windows were tinted, so Kyle couldn't see him very well. About all he could tell was that the man wore dark glasses.

Finally, the driver's door opened. The man left the car running as he stepped out. He was tall and wiry, Kyle saw, and wore an expensive suit. His hair was dark and sleek. He moved around the open door and smiled, revealing brilliant white teeth as he said, "Good morning!"

Kyle didn't think that smile was the least bit genuine or friendly. Somehow, it reminded him more of a shark than anything else.

He gave the stranger a curt nod and said, "Morning."

He didn't add "Good," because there was nothing good about this visit that he could see.

"I'm looking for G.W. Brannock," the man said. "And I know you're not him."

"I'm his grandson, Kyle. What can I do for you?"

"Grandson, eh? My name is Slade Grayson, Kyle. Maybe you wouldn't mind setting that rifle down? It's making me a little nervous."

"It's not pointed at you, is it?"

"Well, no—"

"Then you don't have anything to worry about." Kyle paused, then added, "Until it *is* pointed at you."

"That would be worrisome indeed, for both of us. You see, Kyle— You don't mind if I call you Kyle, do you?"

Kyle shrugged. He didn't care what this man who reeked of trouble called him.

"You see, Kyle," Grayson went on. "I work for the United States government. If you'll let me reach in my pocket, I have identification—"

Kyle interrupted him, saying, "I don't need to see any ID. I believe you're who you say you are, mister. What line of bullshit are you gonna throw out there next, that you're from the government and you're here to help us?"

Slade Grayson's sharklike smile never budged. In fact, he laughed, then said, "Oh, hell, no, kid. I'm here to kick your grandpappy's ancient ass off the government's land."

Chapter 25

The laugh, the smirk, the bald-faced arrogance of Slade Grayson made anger boil up inside Kyle. This might all be a joke to Grayson, just another instance of an all-powerful government running roughshod over its citizens, but to Kyle it was deadly serious.

"I reckon you'd better turn around and leave, Mr. Grayson," he said, making an effort to keep his voice from trembling because of the depth of the outrage he felt. "You don't have any business here."

"On the contrary," Grayson said, and now a note of self-righteousness entered his voice as he went on. "I'm here on the people's business."

Kyle let out a short, gruff bark of disdainful laughter.

"As far as I can see, it's been quite a while since the government of this country really represented the people's interests. Not since your party discovered how to buy votes and get dead people to show up at the polling places."

Grayson shook his head and said, "See, there you're making a mistake. You're assuming that I'm a Democrat. I don't follow any party line. I'm just interested in getting the job done. If the Republicans were running things and told me to come out here and take this ranch, I'd do it."

"So you're just vicious and power-hungry, is that it?"

Grayson took off his sunglasses, and for the first time Kyle saw how narrow and unfriendly the man's eyes were.

"You're starting to piss me off, kid," Grayson said. He leaned over to reach back into the car.

Without hardly seeming to move, Kyle shifted his grip on the rifle so that the barrel pointed toward Grayson and his finger curled through the trigger guard.

"Unless you're getting back in there to leave, I think you'd better stay where I can see you, Mr. Grayson," Kyle said quietly.

"Are you *threatening* me, Kyle?" Grayson asked, and now his voice was soft with menace, too.

"I'm just saying that as far as I know, you're trespassing on my grandfather's property, and I have a right to protect it however I see fit."

"I told you—"

"You *told* me," Kyle interrupted. "Those other two BLM flunkies told us a lot of bull, too. But so far I haven't *seen* anything that supports what any of you are saying."

Grayson didn't like being referred to as a flunky. Kyle could tell that from the way the man's features tightened even more.

Kyle's heart was hammering now. He was well aware that he was pointing a gun at a federal agent, and that was a good way to wind up in deep, deep trouble.

But he was also convinced that he was in the right here—for whatever *that* was worth these days.

"That's what I was about to do," Grayson said. "I have a copy of the land grant, as well as a duly authorized notice of seizure and forfeiture that gives me the right to claim your grandfather's ranch for the Bureau of Land Management. If you'll just look at them, you'll see that there's no point in putting up a fight. That won't accomplish anything except to get you hurt, and for no good reason." Grayson

Now, I need to give you this document and get you to sign for it—"

The sound of a rifle's lever being worked interrupted Grayson. Kyle hadn't done that. His rifle already had a bullet in the chamber. He looked over at the corner of the house and saw G.W. standing there pointing a Winchester at Grayson.

The old rancher said, "No, what you need to do, mister, is get the hell off my land before I blow a hole right through you."

Chapter 26

Kyle hadn't heard G.W.'s pickup come in. He supposed his grandfather could have been out on horseback. G.W. might have spotted Grayson's car as he approached the ranch headquarters and traveled the rest of the way on foot to avoid letting anyone know he was around until he found out what was going on.

And when he'd found out, he hadn't liked it.

If it bothered Grayson to have a rifle pointed at him, he didn't show it any more now than he had when Kyle threatened him. In fact, he looked almost unnaturally cool in the midday heat. He had put his sunglasses back on, and his face showed no emotion.

"George Washington Brannock," he said as he looked at G.W. "I've heard a lot about you. It's nice to make your acquaintance at last."

"Can't say the same for you," G.W. snapped. "I don't know your name, and I don't want to know. You're just another government toady as far as I'm concerned."

Kyle thought Grayson stiffened a little at that jab. The man said, "You're wrong, Brannock. I'm not the sort of run-of-the-mill bureaucrats you've been dealing with. I'm not the *IRS*." The scorn Grayson felt for that agency was evident in his voice. "I'm the man they call in to get things done."

"A mercenary, in other words," Kyle said.

"Call it what you will," Grayson replied with a slight shrug. "I don't care. I don't care about anything except the job. That's why you shouldn't mess with me."

"So far all I've heard is a bunch of hot air," G.W. said. "Kyle, what's that paper he showed you?"

"It's supposed to be a copy of that stupid land grant."

"What's it look like to you?"

"Who can tell?" Kyle said. "It's just a bunch of fancy old Spanish handwriting."

Grayson said, "The land grant itself is genuine, I assure you."

"You'll have to prove that," Kyle said. He thought about what Miranda had told him earlier. "You'll have to prove it in a court of law."

"No, *you'll* have to prove that it's *not* genuine," Grayson said. "I work for the government, remember. You bear the burden of proof."

"Funny thing," G.W. said. "The way this country was founded, the way it used to work, that ought to be the other way around."

Grayson just grunted. He said, "I need that copy back."

"If that'll get you to leave, then take it," Kyle said. He came down the steps, still holding the rifle one-handed, and held out the document toward Grayson in his other hand.

With G.W. still covering them, Kyle didn't expect Grayson to try anything. The government man came closer, still holding the folder in one hand while he reached for the copy of the land grant with the other.

Then Grayson moved fast. The hand holding the folder shot out, hooked under the barrel of Kyle's rifle, and shoved it toward the sky. In a continuation of the same motion he slapped the folder across Kyle's face. The impact was stunning, and Kyle realized that the folder was weighted somehow to make it function as a weapon in an emergency.

As G.W. yelled an angry curse, Grayson dropped the folder, caught hold of the rifle, and jerked it out of Kyle's grip. Grayson's other hand came down on Kyle's shoulder and spun him around. Almost before Kyle knew what was happening, he found himself with Grayson holding him from behind, the rifle barrel gripped in both of the federal agent's hands and pressed tightly across Kyle's throat.

Grayson had Kyle in front of him, so G.W. couldn't fire without shooting his own grandson.

"I tried to tell you people it wasn't smart to interfere with government business," Grayson said. His voice was tight with anger. "Now put that rifle down, old man, if you don't want me to crush this kid's windpipe."

Grayson was right about not being just another government bureaucrat, thought Kyle. Clearly, he had some combat training. He was probably ex-military, although he could have been a private contractor.

But despite his skill and training, he was overconfident. Kyle sensed that and acted on it.

He drove his right elbow back into Grayson's midsection with explosive force. Grayson wasn't expecting that any more than Kyle had been expecting what the government man had done. The blow made Grayson hunch over for a second and gasp for breath. That brought the rifle away from Kyle's throat. Kyle lowered his chin to protect his larynx and slammed the heel of his left boot into Grayson's shin.

The pain from that blow made Grayson's leg try to collapse underneath him. As he struggled to maintain his balance and not fall, Kyle was able to twist away from him. He slashed a sidehand blow at Grayson's neck, but Grayson swayed aside just enough to take the impact on his left shoulder.

Kyle knew that must have made Grayson's whole left arm go numb. The rifle slipped out of his hands and thudded to the ground between them.

Kyle snapped a punch to Grayson's sternum. That would have been enough to paralyze most men. Grayson shook it off, though. He had regained his footing and struck at Kyle's head with his good right arm.

Kyle blocked that blow, but Grayson landed a blinding fast kick to his side. The impact knocked Kyle spinning off his feet.

Grayson pounced after him and tried another kick. Kyle grabbed his foot and heaved, though, and Grayson went over backwards. Crashing to the ground like that should have knocked even more of the breath out of him, thought Kyle.

Why didn't the guy just pass out already?

Unfortunately, Grayson was built of tougher stuff than that. He whipped his legs around and tried to scissor them around Kyle's neck. Kyle barely got his left arm up in time to counter that move. He caught hold of one of Grayson's legs and levered himself off the ground. Grayson had no choice but to roll over and go with him. Kyle tightened the wrestling hold and twisted. Bones creaked and tendons stretched painfully.

Grayson had made the same mistake other men had made in the past. Kyle looked slender, but he was incredibly strong. Corded muscles played under his skin like bundles of steel cable. If he kept up the pressure for much longer, there was a good chance he would dislocate

Grayson's thighbone from the hip and quite possibly tear some of those tendons.

The government man yelled in pain. Filthy curses spewed from his mouth.

"Kyle, that's enough!" G.W. called. "Let go of him and back away. You don't want to cripple the son of a bitch."

"I wouldn't count on that," Kyle said grimly.

Grayson's sunglasses had come off during the fight. He stared up at Kyle with dark eyes that reminded Kyle of a snake's eyes.

"You'll be . . . sorry you did this," he grated.

"That's what guys like you always say," Kyle replied.

"Kyle!"

Kyle knew G.W. was right. Grayson had attacked him. He might be able to get away with claiming self-defense, although it was more likely Grayson would call it resisting a federal officer and probably make the charge stick.

If he tore Grayson's leg from its socket, though, there was no doubt he would go to prison for it. He let go of the man's leg and stepped back quickly. Grayson lay there, pale and panting for breath.

"I reckon we've made our position clear, mister," G.W. said. "We're not gonna cooperate with your phony take-over of this ranch. This is Brannock land! Always has been, always will be."

"You're . . . wrong about . . . that," Grayson said as he pushed himself to hands and knees. He struggled upright. He was none too steady on his feet and had to lay a hand on the car to brace himself. "You've made a big mistake today, both of you. We're not going to do this . . . the easy way anymore. When I come back—"

"When you come back," G.W. said, "*if* you come back . . . you better be ready to duck, if you know what I mean."

Chapter 27

Slade Grayson was seething as he drove away from the Brannock ranch. His left arm throbbed, but at least feeling had come back into it. His left leg twinged every time he moved it, and he was glad he didn't have to use it to drive. He had assorted other aches and pains from the fight with Kyle Brannock as well.

None of that really bothered him all that much. He didn't mind hurting.

What really gnawed at him was the fact that both of the Brannocks had dared to stand up to him. To defy the government. That couldn't be allowed.

If such defiance went on often enough, long enough, people might start to think that the government *wasn't* all powerful. They might get the crazy idea that their so-called rights really amounted to something important and ought to be honored.

As he glared through his sunglasses and the windshield at the two-lane highway leading back into Sierra Lobo, he pushed the button on the onboard computer that opened the VoIP phone connection over the government's own high-speed network. Grayson said, "Call Finley."

Only one ring sounded over the speaker before Warren Finley answered.

"Mr. Grayson," the scientist said. "How did it go with Brannock?"

"Never mind that," Grayson snapped. "You were going to do some research on Kyle Brannock for me. What did you find?"

"Well, he's G.W. Brannock's grandson—"

"I know that. What's his background?"

"He's twenty-four years old. Both parents were killed in an auto accident when he was eighteen, during his first semester of college at the University of Texas. He dropped out after that and joined the army, but he received a general discharge less than a year later. Since then he hasn't had any fixed place of residence, or any steady employment. From time to time he's visited his grandfather, but never stayed more than a few weeks."

"So he washed out of the army and can't hold a job," Grayson said. "What about any criminal record?"

"He's been arrested numerous times for simple assault and disturbing the peace. Bar fights, for the most part."

"Not drunk and disorderly?"

"Well, no," Finley said. "It appears that he can hold his liquor all right, but he's naturally short-tempered."

Grayson rolled his left shoulder and thought that he had proof of Finley's supposition.

"He's paid fines and served time in local jails," Finley went on, saying, "but he's never been sentenced to a state or federal penitentiary. He's wandered around enough so that most of his offenses took place in different states, so he hasn't run afoul of any three-strike laws."

"So he's pretty much just a homeless bum," Grayson said. That didn't make sense. Kyle Brannock shouldn't have lasted a minute in a fight with him, let alone inflicted any damage on him. Instead he had handled himself almost like a professional. . . .

A thought occurred to Grayson and he went on, asking "Does his military record go into any detail?"

"No, just that he was given a general discharge and separated from the service," Finley replied.

"No reason given?"

"Not that I see."

"And you're sure it was a general discharge, not any other than honorable conditions discharge?"

There was a trace of impatience in Finley's voice as he said, "I'm reading it right off his DD-214. Which I shouldn't have any right to look at, by the way. That code you gave me got me right into the DOD database, though."

"Of course," Grayson said. "I want you to dig deeper, Warren. Find out why the army gave Kyle Brannock the boot."

Finley sighed and said, "All right. Did the elder Brannock agree to vacate the ranch in sixty days or less?"

Grayson still didn't answer that. He said, "I'll talk to you when I get back in a little while."

He broke the connection.

There was one good thing about West Texas with its flat, straight roads and general disregard for speed limits: It didn't take long to get from Point A to Point B . . . unless, of course, there were several hundred miles between those points, which was not only possible but likely.

But Grayson made it back to town pretty quickly. He parked at the motel, which he despised because of its throwback appearance. There was nothing good about the middle twentieh century as far as Grayson was concerned.

He limped to the door of the room Finley and Todd

were sharing and opened it without knocking. Todd was stretched out on the bed. He didn't have any shoes on and his legs were crossed at the ankles. An open can of beer perched on his chest. He was watching the motel TV with the sound turned off.

Finley sat in an armchair holding his tablet. He looked up at Grayson and said, "I've found out more about Kyle Brannock."

Grayson put his sunglasses on the dresser, opened the mini-fridge, and took out a bottle of water. He opened it, swallowed half the water, and then said, "Let's hear it."

"I managed to get his personnel file from the DOD. He made it through basic training without any trouble. In fact, he was considered an exceptional recruit by all his instructors. When he completed basic and then airborne school, he volunteered for the Rangers. He was transferred to Fort Benning and entered the Ranger Assessment and Selection Program."

There was a straight-back chair at the small table. Grayson turned it around and straddled it. He had never bought into a lot of the military hoopla, having seen firsthand that soldiers were no better or worse than anybody else, but he knew the army didn't let just anybody into the Rangers.

"He went through RASP with flying colors and continued into Ranger School," Finley continued. "There are three phases to that training, and Brannock was in the middle of the second phase, the mountaineering phase, when something happened."

"Don't drag it out," Grayson snapped. "What did he do?"

Finley swiped a finger on the screen of his tablet and said, "Gave another Ranger candidate a severe beating. Put him in the hospital, in fact."

Grayson raised an eyebrow and said, "They didn't put

him in prison and give him a dishonorable discharge for that? Or at least a bad conduct discharge?"

"That was the initial recommendation. But then several of the sergeants involved in the training program spoke up in Brannock's defense. It seems the other soldier involved in the fight was a troublemaker and had, in fact, attacked a third soldier, who was a friend of Brannock's. It was a messy situation, and ultimately, the easiest, cleanest way out was to give both Brannock and the man he put in the hospital general discharges." Finley looked up. "Everything after that is like I told you before."

Grayson drank the rest of the water and said, "So we've got a guy who lost his parents, couldn't stick it out in college, couldn't hack it in the army, and hasn't been able to settle down or hold a job since. He doesn't sound like that much of a problem."

"Kyle Brannock won't be a pushover, Mr. Grayson," Finley said, shaking his head. "Even though he didn't last in the army, his record while he was there is impressive. He doesn't shy away from trouble."

Grayson gestured with the empty water bottle as he said, "But he's hotheaded. He can't control himself. There's always a way to handle a guy like that. You make him do something reckless and stupid."

"How do you do that?"

"You don't waste your time by threatening him." Grayson thought about the pain he had suffered at Kyle Brannock's hands and smiled as he considered his response. "You threaten somebody he loves."

Chapter 28

"You all right, boy?" G.W. asked as he walked over to join Kyle. The dust cloud kicked up by the wheels of Grayson's car as the government man drove away was starting to dissipate. As fast and angrily as Grayson was driving, he would be back to the highway in no time.

"I'm fine," Kyle said. "I've been knocked around a lot worse." He pressed a hand on his side where Grayson had kicked him. The place was a little tender, but he could tell he didn't have any cracked ribs.

But the kick had glanced off a little, too, Kyle knew. If Grayson had landed it squarely, the fight might have ended differently.

The guy was pretty good, and it would be a mistake to deny that.

"Who was that, exactly?" G.W. asked. "Another fella from the BLM, right?"

"Yeah. He said his name was Slade Grayson."

G.W. snorted disgustedly.

"Sounds like somebody who ought to be workin' for those varmints," he said.

"He had a copy of that old land grant and another paper he said was an official order giving possession of the ranch to the feds and telling you that you've got sixty days to get off the place. He said you could take your personal belongings and the stock, but the house and all the other buildings and improvements are government property, too."

"That'll be the day." G.W. frowned. "But it proves something that we suspected. If they don't want the cattle, they're not interested in operatin' it as a ranch. They want the land for some other reason."

"You're sure the mineral rights aren't worth anything?"

"Not a blessed thing, and they've been checked out half a dozen times by oil and gas companies. And I'm *dang* sure there's no lost gold mine or anything crazy like that on it."

"Well, it beats me," Kyle said with a shake of his head. "Where were you this morning?"

"I rode out to take a look at one of the waterholes. Been a while since it's rained, and I wanted to make sure it hadn't dried up."

"I didn't see your pickup around anywhere."

"That's because Roberto took it to town this mornin' to have the brakes worked on. I noticed last night they were startin' to squeal a little."

"I thought you fixed things like that yourself."

G.W. shook his head and said, "Nah, I'm gettin' too old for mechanic work. Better to let somebody who knows what they're doin' handle it."

That attitude came as a bit of surprise to Kyle. G.W. had always been the sort who believed that a man ought to be able to fix anything mechanical or electrical, a legacy of his own father, Kyle's great-grandfather, who had grown up during the Depression when folks did for themselves.

Even a hidebound old dinosaur like G.W. Brannock could evolve, Kyle supposed.

"What are you smilin' about?" G.W. asked sharply. "You just got in a fight with a government man. I reckon the US Marshals are liable to show up after a while and drag you away."

"I don't think so," Kyle said. "Grayson struck me as the sort of man who'd want to handle his own problems. He bragged that he's the guy they call in for the difficult jobs. He's not gonna want to admit that he got his butt handed to him by an old geezer and a young bum."

"I'm not so sure about that geezer part," G.W. said, his voice dry now. "Come on inside. What've you been doin' all day?"

"I almost forgot! Miranda called. She got that injunction against the IRS, just like she said she would."

"It's probably not gonna matter now. We've got bigger problems."

"Yeah," Kyle said as he and G.W. went up onto the porch. He was grateful for the shade. "I told her about those two guys from the BLM we ran into last night. Grayson hadn't gotten here yet when I talked to her. I wish she'd been here to take a look at that land grant."

"She'll see it soon enough. I expect her first move will be to haul those sons o' bitches into court. She'll make 'em *prove* that land grant is the real thing."

"What if it is?" Kyle asked.

G.W. gazed off into the distance and sighed as he looked at his range.

"I sort of wish you hadn't asked me that, Kyle," he said. "Because it doesn't really matter if that land grant's genuine or not. The only way the government's gonna put me off this ranch is to carry me off, feet first."

Miranda got there about one o'clock. Kyle and G.W. were just sitting down for lunch, which consisted of ham sandwiches. G.W. led her into the kitchen and gestured toward the third plate on the table, saying, "I made one for you, too. Figured you'd be showin' up about now."

"Thank you," she said. She wore a sleeveless, light blue top and a darker blue skirt. Kyle thought she'd probably had a matching jacket on earlier for her meeting with the judge in El Paso.

He also thought she looked really good, although she was obviously angry and upset about the newest development in G.W.'s case.

Miranda sat down, took a drink from the tall glass of iced tea G.W. had poured for her, and said, "Tell me about what happened last night."

"I already told you on the phone," Kyle said.

"Tell me again," she said. "I want to know the story as well as if I were there with you."

Kyle looked at G.W., but his grandfather waved a hand and said, "You tell it. My throat gets tired if I talk too much."

Kyle went over the encounter with Finley and Todd while Miranda took small bites from her sandwich and chewed slowly and deliberately. Despite what G.W. had said, he added a comment now and then.

When Kyle was finished, he told her, "That's not the end of it, though. Something else has happened since I talked to you earlier."

"Oh, no," Miranda said. "What now?"

"Another man from the BLM showed up. He had a copy of the land grant with him, and an order for G.W. to pack up and move."

"Unpleasant son of a gun, too," G.W. drawled. "He and Kyle got into a little fracas."

Miranda's eyes widened. She stared at Kyle and demanded, "You got into a fight with a federal agent?"

"He jumped me first," Kyle said.

"That doesn't matter! He's a federal agent!"

"Well, it ought to matter," Kyle said stubbornly. "The government shouldn't have any right to come onto private property and attack somebody who hasn't done anything wrong."

"Damn straight," G.W. muttered. "But those people runnin' things in Washington, they've got it in their heads that there really isn't such a thing as private property. Deep down, they think that everything belongs to the state, and they're the state. That's why it seems right to them that they can take away more and more of somebody's money in taxes, because that money never belonged to the taxpayers in the first place. The government—the state—was just lettin' 'em use it. And since they think they're smarter'n everybody else, they ought to have the right to give that money to whoever they want to, mainly folks who'll then turn around and keep votin' for them. Same thing with property, like this ranch. There's one thing they haven't considered, though."

Kyle was almost afraid to ask his grandfather what he meant by that, but he did anyway.

"What haven't they considered, G.W.?"

"That there are still some folks in this world who'll put up a fight when you try to do 'em wrong."

Chapter 29

The three of them spent the rest of lunch discussing strategy. Miranda didn't want to approach the judge in El Paso again right away to ask for another injunction, this time against the BLM. But she would if she had to, she said.

"The first thing I'm going to do is request a meeting with the BLM so I can examine that land grant," she told Kyle and G.W. "I'm going to try to line up an expert to take a look at it as well."

"Where do you find somebody like that?" Kyle asked.

"I'll start at the University of Texas. If no one there can help me, maybe they can suggest someone I can talk to. We need an expert who's very fluent in Spanish, who also has a strong knowledge of history and antiquities. Maybe a forensic archeologist who can determine the age of the paper the actual land grant is written on."

"Like Indiana Jones," G.W. said.

"Well"—Miranda smiled—"he doesn't have to wear a fedora and carry a bullwhip, but yeah, somebody like that who specializes in Spanish antiquities."

After they had finished eating, Kyle and Miranda went out onto the front porch. Kyle perched a hip on the railing and asked, "What do we do if that fella Grayson shows up again?"

"Try not to get in another fight with him," Miranda answered without hesitation. "Violence isn't going to accomplish anything."

Kyle grunted. Sometimes violence was the *only* method that accomplished anything. But trained in the law as she was, Miranda wasn't likely to understand that.

What people often forgot was that violence was at the very heart of the legal system. The thing that made it work was the idea that people would be reasonable and follow the law, but what made them do that was the ever-present threat of force by the state. That was legally sanctioned violence, of course . . . but it was still violence.

When the state was in the wrong, as Kyle was convinced it was in his grandfather's case, there were only two responses: surrender or resistance. Surrender meant letting the wrongdoers win, but resistance might result in a different sort of evil as the state tried to impose its will by force. So which was the greater evil?

Kyle didn't have an answer for that.

"What if somebody comes to arrest me for what happened with Grayson earlier?"

"Cooperate with them," Miranda said. "But don't say anything. Don't answer any questions or make any statements. Just don't even open your mouth unless I'm there."

He grinned and asked, "So I guess you're my lawyer now, too? Are G.W. and I on the family plan?"

"You should probably pay me a retainer, just to make it official."

She smiled back at him as she said it, and that kindled a warmth in him that had nothing to do with the day's heat.

"Well, I don't have much money. . . ."

He thought about asking her if a kiss would be enough

for a retainer, then decided it was too soon for that sort of flirtatious banter.

"I'll draw up the paperwork and you can pay me later," she said. She started down the steps and added over her shoulder, "Just remember . . . cooperate and say nothing."

"All right."

Kyle lifted a hand in farewell as she got into her car and drove off.

The hinges on the screen door rasped as G.W. opened it and came out onto the porch. He stood beside Kyle and both of them watched the dust cloud moving toward the highway.

"She's a pistol, isn't she?" G.W. said.

"What? Oh, you mean Miranda?"

"That's right. You're a mite fond of her, aren't you?"

Kyle shrugged and said, "She's helping us fight the government. That makes her an ally."

"Seems to me this started out bein' *my* fight, not *ours*."

"Yeah, well, that's changed now, hasn't it? After last night and especially this morning, I'm in it up to my neck."

"I reckon that's true," G.W. admitted. "That fella Grayson's got personal reasons now for wantin' to come after you. With me it's just business for him. Although pointin' a rifle at him might've made that a little personal, too." G.W. paused. "You didn't really answer what I asked you about Miranda. What you're feelin' isn't just about her bein' on our side."

"She's smart. I like that in a woman."

"And easy on the eyes."

"Definitely," Kyle said.

"And ambitious."

"Which I'm not. Is that what you're getting at? The fact that we wouldn't be a good match because she wants to make something of herself and I don't?"

"Don't go puttin' words in my mouth, boy," G.W. said. "I don't plan on buttin' into your personal life." He shook his head and went on. "Anyway, the way things are goin', this may not end well for either of us, so there's no point in worryin' about whether or not you hook up with Miranda."

Kyle stared at his grandfather, cocked an eyebrow, and laughed.

"'Hook up'?" he repeated.

"Hey, just because I like the older movies doesn't mean I haven't seen any newer ones."

"All right, G.W.," Kyle said, still smiling. "Just do me a favor . . . Don't ever say 'hook up' again, okay?"

Chapter 30

Barton Devlin's cell phone buzzed in his pocket as he stood on the ridge focusing his binoculars on G.W. Brannock's ranch house. He grimaced, lowered the binoculars, and reached into his pocket for the phone.

The number on the screen was a familiar one. Devlin had been expecting this call.

"Hello, Charles," he said as he thumbed the button to answer.

"Barton, where are you?" Charles Pierce asked. "I thought you were supposed to be back here this morning."

"I know, but I'm still in Texas."

Devlin waited for an angry explosion from his boss. It didn't come. After a moment, Pierce said, "The Brannock file has been closed, Barton."

"I know."

"So there's no reason for you to be there. You need to get back here."

"No offense, Charles, but since when does a piddling little agency like the Bureau of Land Management get to tell us what to do?"

Again there was a heavy silence on the other end of the connection.

Finally, Pierce said, "The orders came from higher up. You should have been able to figure that out."

"How high?"

"As high as it gets."

Devlin frowned and said, "Wait a minute. Do you mean—"

"What I mean is that you should get back here," Pierce interrupted. "I'm not going to say anything else."

"But what about all the money Brannock owes? All the back taxes, the fines, the penalties—"

"Forget about it, Barton. It's . . . Washington."

Devlin knew what his friend and supervisor meant. The capital city operated by its own rules, unlike any other place in the country.

And anyone who violated those rules usually paid a high price for doing so.

Devlin knew he had already pushed his luck by staying in Sierra Lobo after Slade Grayson had told him to go home. Grayson had a reputation as a bad man to cross, and everyone in Washington knew he wielded a lot of influence no matter which agency he was working for at the time.

But the *BLM*? A bunch of damned dirt diggers?

Something wasn't right here. Devlin wasn't going to allow the IRS to lose anything it rightfully had coming to it. That was why he had decided not to leave. Why he had driven around Sierra Lobo until he found a private home with a ROOM FOR RENT sign in the window. Why he had moved in with the elderly widow who was looking for company as much as for rent money.

And why he had been lurking here around G.W. Brannock's ranch for the past couple of days as he tried to figure out what the hell was going on.

"Barton?" Charles Pierce said in his ear. "Are you still there?"

Devlin heaved a sigh and said, "I'm still here. Are you sure about this, Charlie?"

"I'm certain."

"We're going to just forget about everything that Brannock owes?"

"Damn it!"

Ah, there was the explosion Devlin had been expecting.

After a moment, as if the words were being dragged out of him, Pierce went on. "I'm not sure the old bastard owes anything."

Devlin wasn't the sort of man who staggered when he heard unexpected news, but if he had been, Pierce's comment surely would have thrown him for a loop.

"What do you mean, Brannock might not owe anything? You've seen the results of the audit, Charlie. You know he's been cheating the government!"

"I know what the audit said. What I don't know . . . is how accurate the results were."

Now Devlin was absolutely thunderstruck. He said, "The audit process doesn't make mistakes. It's just not possible. If the results are inaccurate, then it means . . . it means . . ."

Devlin couldn't go on. He couldn't express the thought in words. He could barely comprehend it.

If an audit was incorrect, it could only be because someone at the agency had made a mistake, which he had just said, and firmly believed, was impossible.

Or else they had falsified data on purpose to get the result they wanted.

For a second, Devlin's surroundings seemed to vanish. Instead, he found himself staring into an endless black abyss. Something lurked in that darkness, something horrible and insatiable that was always on the move like a

William W. Johnstone

giant prehistoric shark devouring everything in its path. Such a monster would do anything, stoop to any level, to keep stuffing whatever it wanted into its greedy, fang-toothed maw.

That couldn't be the government he had devoted his life to . . . could it?

With a sharp shake of his head, Devlin broke out of that terrible daydream. Charles Pierce was talking on the phone again, saying, "I don't know how soon you can get back to where you can catch a flight to Washington, Barton, so I'm going to cut you a little slack. But only a little. If you're not back here by the day after tomorrow . . . well, I hate to say it, but if you're not back by then, you're fired."

"You can't do that," Devlin said hollowly. "The union—"

"The union takes orders from the same people we do," Pierce said. "If you do anything to gum up the works, don't think the union can protect you. You'll be hung out to dry so fast you won't know what hit you. You'll be lucky if you're just fired, if you know what I mean."

Devlin knew, all right. Like everyone else, he had heard plenty of rumors about what might happen to people who didn't play the game or who stumbled over information they weren't supposed to uncover. He had known several agents personally who had just . . . disappeared. Their families apparently didn't know what had happened to them. They were just gone with no warning.

The same thing could happen to him, thought Devlin. If he persisted in trying to find out why he'd been shunted aside in favor of the BLM, he could be risking his life.

But how could he turn his back on a case? That would go against everything he had ever stood for. That would mean, when things were boiled down to their basic components, he was actually powerless.

He sighed into the phone and tried to make it sound full of despair and defeat. He didn't have to try very hard to accomplish that.

But there was still steel at his core as he said, "All right, Charlie. I'll see you in a couple of days."

That was a lie, he thought as he broke the connection.

He knew how risky the course of action he was contemplating really was. The idea of making an enemy out of Slade Grayson caused a chill to travel along his spine. And there could be people higher up who were even more dangerous than Grayson.

But he had to take that chance. He couldn't do anything else and still be the man he believed himself to be.

Barton Devlin wasn't going to leave Texas until he got to the bottom of this.

Chapter 31

Roberto Quinones got back to the ranch with the pickup in the middle of the afternoon. He gave the bill for the brake repair to G.W., who would send a check to the garage where the work was done.

"I hear there was some trouble earlier," Roberto said as he, G.W., and Kyle stood on the porch.

"How'd you find out about that?" G.W. asked with a frown.

"My wife called my cell phone. She said young Señor Brannock was fighting with a government man. She was afraid there might be shooting. I kept her on the phone with me until the man left and the trouble was over."

G.W. massaged his temples for a moment and then shook his head.

"That's just it," he said. "The trouble's not over. That fella left, but he'll be back. And as for the shootin' . . . well, I can't guarantee there won't be any." G.W. looked squarely at his foreman and gave Roberto a curt nod, as if he had reached a decision. "That's why I want you and the rest of the boys and your families to pack up and leave."

That surprised Kyle, but Roberto seemed even more shocked. He said in a tone of disbelief, "You are firing us?"

"What?" G.W. said. "Hell, no! I'm givin' you all paid vacations. Go see your relatives. Take a trip somewhere you've always wanted to visit. I don't care where you go, as long as you're not stayin' around here."

Roberto looked aghast at the very idea. He shook his head and said, "That's loco, señor. You cannot run the ranch without us."

"The cows have plenty of graze, and the waterholes are in good enough shape not to worry about them for a while. The ranch can get by just fine for a few weeks. I've got a hunch that by then, all this trouble actually will be over . . . one way or another."

"You would have us turn tail and run like cowards?" Roberto's voice was tight with anger as he asked the question.

"A man's first duty is to his family," G.W. said stubbornly. "You have to keep them safe."

"You are like family to all of us, señor, and you know it."

"I appreciate that, but I'm not gonna budge from this."

Roberto folded his arms across his chest and glared back at G.W. as he said, "Neither are we. It appears that we have . . ."

Don't say it, thought Kyle.

"A Mexican standoff," Roberto finished.

The tense tableau on the porch lasted about five more seconds before both G.W. and his foreman exploded in laughter. G.W. slapped Roberto on the back.

"All right," he said. "I know when I'm beat. But how about this? You'll send your wives and kids to stay with relatives for a while?"

Roberto nodded and said, "That we can do, señor. Our

wives are stubborn and will argue, too, but in the end they will do what we say." He added under his breath, "I hope."

Ernie Rodriguez showed up at the ranch house late that afternoon, driving one of the Sierra Lobo Police Department's SUVs.

G.W. and Kyle went out onto the porch to greet the stocky police chief. Ernie had a look of concern on his face as he shook hands with G.W. and then turned to Kyle.

"I hear you had some trouble out here this morning," he said.

"Word of that really got around, didn't it? With all due respect, chief, if you've come to arrest me, you don't have any jurisdiction out here. That ends at the city limits, doesn't it?"

"Yeah, out here in the county it's the sheriff's job to handle criminal offenses. But I hear things, you know. Sheriff Jacobs and I have a good relationship, and he knows that I'm an old friend of your family. He called to ask me about you, Kyle."

"What did he want to know?" Kyle asked tensely.

"If you were really the type of guy who would attack a government agent without provocation."

"Damn it!" Kyle burst out. "Is that what Grayson is claiming? Because it's not true. He started the whole thing."

"That would be more believable if you didn't have a record as long as my arm."

"Now hold on," G.W. said. "Kyle's never been in any really bad trouble with the law."

"His record says he's quick to throw a punch, though. Shoot, we saw that the other day when he mixed it up with

Vern Hummel. I had you in my jail, Kyle, and now it looks like you'll be seeing the inside of the county lockup."

"Grayson really filed a complaint against me?" Kyle asked. "He's pressing charges?"

Ernie shrugged and said, "That's what it sounds like to me."

Kyle was surprised. He had thought that Slade Grayson's pride wouldn't let him do such a thing. He'd believed that Grayson would want to settle the score personally.

Maybe, though, this was just one more way for him to harass the Brannock family and pressure them into giving up the fight against the BLM.

"What'd you tell Bill Jacobs?" G.W. asked Ernie.

"The truth. That I think Kyle is a good kid who's gotten into a lot of scrapes through no fault—or very little fault—of his own. But if this man Grayson insists on pressing charges . . ." Ernie shrugged. "There won't be much the sheriff can do except arrest you and let the system take over, Kyle."

"Fine," Kyle said bitterly. "I've got a lawyer. We'll fight this in court if we have to."

"All right. I'm going to head back to town. I don't want Sheriff Jacobs thinking I went behind his back . . . even though that's exactly what I just did."

The chief shook hands with them again and then left. Kyle sighed and said, "I guess I'd better call Miranda and tell her to get ready to arrange bail for me."

Despite everything, his heart jumped a little at the prospect of talking to her—and seeing her—again.

Chapter 32

It was another half hour before three cars from the sheriff's department arrived at the ranch house. As Kyle and G.W. stood on the porch and watched them pull up, Kyle commented dryly, "It looks like they thought I might put up a fight when they try to arrest me."

"I didn't vote for Bill Jacobs," G.W. said, "but he's been a decent sheriff so far. He's just bein' careful."

The men who got out of the cars wore bulletproof vests over their short-sleeved gray uniform shirts. They all had their hands on the butts of their service weapons except for one man who approached the porch and said, "Kyle Brannock?"

"That's me, sheriff," Kyle said. He stood still, hands half-raised and in plain sight. He had tried to convince G.W. to go back in the house, out of the line of fire, before the sheriff and his men arrived, but as usual G.W. had been stubborn.

"Hello, Bill," G.W. drawled. "You boys look like you're armed for bear."

Jacobs, a horse-faced man with several strands of black hair combed over a mostly bald scalp, grunted and said,

"Can't take chances with anybody who'd attack a federal agent."

"See, the thing is, I didn't do that," Kyle said. "Grayson's the one who jumped me."

"Not my job to figure that out," Jacobs snapped. "Grayson's filed assault charges against you, so you're under arrest."

Kyle smiled faintly and said, "I surrender." He'd already talked more than Miranda told him to, so he guessed he'd better shut up.

"Come down here and turn around," Jacobs ordered.

Kyle went down the steps slowly and carefully, not giving the sheriff or any of the deputies any excuse to over-react and possibly get trigger-happy. He didn't think Slade Grayson had set him up to be killed, using the officers to carry out the execution. It was unlikely that Jacobs would go along with such a thing. But there was no point in being reckless.

That thought made a smile tug at the corners of his mouth. Over the past few years, he'd made a habit of being reckless. Maybe getting caught up in his grandfather's problems was changing him. Maybe he was growing up a little.

He wasn't going to hold his breath waiting for that to happen, though.

At Jacobs's command, he turned around so his back was to the sheriff. Jacobs moved in behind him and fastened plastic restraints around his wrists. Then he took hold of Kyle's upper arm and hauled him around.

"I'll follow you into town," G.W. called from the porch.

Jacobs shoved Kyle toward the closest car. One of the deputies opened a back door. None too gently, they deposited him in the backseat. Once the door was closed behind him, it was only a matter of moments before all the deputies were back in their cars and the convoy was headed toward the county seat, fifteen miles east of Sierra Lobo.

They went into the building that housed the sheriff's department and jail from the rear parking lot, which was surrounded by a high chain-link fence. Kyle had been booked into plenty of jails, so he knew the drill. He cooperated in silence as he was searched, photographed, and fingerprinted. Knowing he was going to be arrested, he didn't have anything in his pockets, so all they had to take away from him were his belt and his boots.

Nobody offered him a phone call, and he didn't ask for one. Who was he going to call? G.W.? Miranda? They already knew he was here. In fact, *they* were probably here by now, too, somewhere out front working to get him released on bail.

The sheriff had disappeared, leaving it to his deputies to get Kyle behind bars. Two of them took the restraints off his wrists and led him down a corridor painted that universal shade of ugly institutional green. He figured they would put him in a holding cell, but instead as they went around a corner, they steered him toward a large area surrounded by iron bars.

They were putting him in the tank, where several other men were already sitting on one of the benches against the wall.

"Wait a minute," Kyle started to say as one of the deputies unlocked the barred door. "I don't think you're supposed to—"

"Shut up, Brannock," the deputy said. "You'll go where we put you."

The other deputy gave Kyle a shove that sent him stumbling through the open door. It clanged shut behind him as he caught his balance.

Kyle tried again, saying, "My lawyer's already here—"

"Well, good for her. Is she just your lawyer, or is she your girlfriend, too?"

Kyle didn't answer that. For one thing, he didn't know the answer. He hadn't known Miranda long enough to consider her anything except an acquaintance, but he had started to hope she might be more than that, even though, as G.W. had pointed out, they weren't really suited for each other.

The deputies turned and walked away, leaving Kyle in the big cell. He turned to look at the other three men in there with him. When the deputies had put him in here, they had been sitting slumped forward with their heads down, but now their heads were raised and Kyle got a good look at their grinning faces.

He recognized one of them. It still had some fading bruises on it . . . bruises Kyle had put there.

He was locked in here with the brutish Vern Hummel, along with two other men who worked with Hummel on the county roads, if their uniform shirts could be believed. One man was Hispanic, with a drooping mustache, and he was even bigger and burlier than Hummel. The third man was short and stocky, seemingly almost as wide as he was tall, but he wasn't fat. His bulk appeared to be mostly muscle. Dark, wiry hair was so thick on his exposed forearms that he looked like an ape.

All of them continued to grin as they stood up and started slowly toward Kyle.

"This is gonna be fun," Hummel said.

Chapter 33

Instinctively, Kyle started to back away from the three men, but he stopped himself as he realized that he didn't want them to trap him against the bars. If they jumped him, he would need some room to move around.

"Take it easy, Vern," he said. "I'm not looking for trouble with you guys. I've got enough already, what with being thrown in here for something I didn't do."

Hummel sneered and said, "I don't know why you're in here and I don't care. I just know I've got a score to settle with you, and I'm gonna enjoy it."

The Hispanic guy laughed and said in a voice that sounded like ten miles of gravel road, "This is the hombre who beat you up, Vern? This scrawny little gringo?"

"Well . . . he's wirier than he looks," Hummel said defensively.

That made both of the other men laugh. Hummel's face darkened with anger.

Yeah, keep it up, fellas, thought Kyle. Make him madder than he already is.

"Three against one isn't exactly fair," Kyle pointed out. "Especially when the one is a scrawny little guy."

"Yeah, well, I don't give a damn about fair," Hummel said. "All I want to do is bring the pain."

They had spread out as they approached, Hummel in the middle, the Hispanic guy to his left, the gorilla to his right. Suddenly, Hummel lunged toward Kyle and looped a punch at his head.

Kyle darted aside, grabbed Hummel's arm, and used the man's own momentum against him to heave him into the bars. Hummel's face crunched against the iron.

Avoiding Hummel's rush brought Kyle within reach of the Hispanic guy, though, and the man's massive fist smashed into the side of his head. Kyle was moving away as much as he could, which made the blow glance off to a certain extent; otherwise, it might have knocked him out. As it was, the punch made him reel against the bars.

Since he was there already, he figured he might as well put them to use. He grabbed the bars, leaped up, and snapped out both legs in a double kick that landed on the Hispanic guy's chest. The man flew backwards toward the benches.

The gorilla swarmed over Kyle as his feet dropped to the floor. He got his long arms around Kyle and rammed him against the bars. Kyle exclaimed in pain and tried to pry the man's arms loose. It was like trying to budge a couple of tree trunks.

The man was several inches shorter than Kyle, so head-butting him wasn't easy. Kyle tried anyway, hunching his shoulders forward and driving his forehead against the top of the man's skull.

He knew right away that was a mistake. He might as well have butted a brick wall.

The man tightened his arms. Kyle's ribs groaned under the pressure. Desperately, he lifted a knee into his opponent's belly, ramming it home as hard as he could.

Still no effect.

Kyle lifted his right leg and reached behind him with it. He got his foot against the bars and shoved with all his strength. That made the gorilla reel backwards across the cell. He lost his balance and fell with Kyle landing on top of him.

Even that wouldn't have done any good if the man's head hadn't clipped one of the benches on the way down. His piggish eyes glazed over and his grip loosened. Kyle writhed an arm loose, planted his outspread hand over the guy's face, and slammed the back of his head against the concrete floor. The man's arms fell away from Kyle, allowing him to breathe freely again.

The respite lasted only a split second. Then, roaring in rage, Hummel grabbed the back of Kyle's shirt and jerked him upright. The Hispanic guy was waiting. He looped a punch into Kyle's belly, burying his fist almost to the wrist.

Kyle would have doubled over from the pain if Hummel hadn't been holding him up. Hummel shoved him forward, into the other man's arms. The man grabbed him, spun him around, and got hold of both arms, jerking them back so they were pinned behind Kyle.

"All right, Vern," the man panted in Kyle's ear. "I'll hang on to him for you."

Hummel waded in.

His big fists battered Kyle again and again, slamming into him from the waist to his shoulders. Even awash in pain, Kyle was thinking straight enough to understand what Hummel was doing. The man wasn't hitting him in the head because he didn't want to kill him or even knock him out. No, Hummel wanted his victim to remain conscious so he could inflict as much punishment as possible on him.

Hummel must have gotten tired after a while. He stepped back with his chest heaving, and the gorillalike man took his place, smashing several punches into Kyle's torso. Then he asked, "You want a turn, Gutierrez?"

"Nah, I'm good," the Hispanic guy said. He let go of Kyle and gave him a shove that sent him sprawling to the floor.

Kyle could tell that he was on the verge of passing out. A part of him still wanted to fight, though. That primitive, animal-like area of his brain forced him to struggle in an attempt to get to his feet.

"Look at him," Gutierrez said with a note of admiration in his voice. "Stubborn bastard won't just give up and lay there."

"Stubborn bastard is right," Hummel said. He stepped in and swung his leg in a kick that crashed into Kyle's side. "Stay down, you stupid son of a bitch."

Kyle's fingers scrabbled at the concrete. He tried to push himself to his hands and knees.

That was when his muscles betrayed him. They all went limp at the same time, and he couldn't fight off the darkness closing in around him.

The last thing he was aware of before oblivion claimed him, though, was a sweet sound.

The sound of Miranda Stephens's voice.

Chapter 34

G.W. was already waiting in the sheriff's office when Miranda got there. The office door was open and they could see her coming. Both men stood up as she walked in.

"Don't bother," she snapped. "I don't give a damn about chivalry right now."

"You may not care," G.W. said gently, "but fellas like us can't just forget the way we were raised."

"Sorry," Miranda muttered. "I didn't mean to sound rude." She fixed Jacobs with a cold stare. "But I'm a little surprised at you, sheriff, doing the Feds' dirty work for them."

"I didn't have a choice," Jacobs said. "Somebody files a complaint with my department, I have to act on it. That fella Grayson is just like any other citizen, as far as the law is concerned."

"Sure," Miranda said, but the scorn in her voice made it clear that she didn't really agree.

The sheriff's face reddened in response. Miranda warned herself to rein it in a little. Bottom line, getting Bill Jacobs mad wouldn't really help Kyle's cause.

"I'd like to see about arranging bail for my client," she said in a more reasonable tone.

"It's kind of late in the day for that. The hearing might have to wait until tomorrow morning—"

"I stopped by Judge Calhoun's office on the way in here. He's willing to set bail, and he's waiting in the Justice of the Peace courtroom right now."

The sheriff stared at her for a second, then chuckled.

"You're right on top of things, aren't you, counselor?"

"I try to be, especially where my clients are concerned," Miranda said.

Jacobs pushed himself to his feet and nodded.

"All right. Let's go get him."

He led Miranda and G.W. through the corridors toward the rear of the building where the drunk tank and the holding cells were located.

Miranda had been back here before to see clients. It was no worse than any other jail, she supposed, but she still didn't like it. The smell of disinfectant and unwashed human flesh hung in the air, and nothing could ever get rid of it completely.

G.W. had called her as soon as Kyle was arrested and told her he would meet her at the sheriff's office in the courthouse. The news of the arrest had come as no surprise, of course. After Kyle's fight with Slade Grayson that morning, Miranda had known the government man would do *something* to retaliate.

Grayson could have filed federal charges against Kyle, but instead he had decided to make the first move at the local level. He was probably holding the other option in reserve, in case Miranda succeeded in getting these charges dropped.

That was what she hoped to do. It was Grayson's word against Kyle's, after all, and Kyle also had his grandfather to testify that Grayson had instigated the trouble. Miranda thought she stood a good chance of persuading the district attorney not to pursue the case. Even if he did, Miranda considered it unlikely that the grand jury would indict Kyle.

Even so, these were just the sort of harassment techniques that an overbearing government used to batter its citizens into submission. An ordinary person, even one in the right, couldn't stand up forever against an enemy with endless, taxpayer-funded resources.

The irony that law-abiding, taxpaying citizens actually paid to have their government abuse them wasn't lost on her.

Despite being taxpaying and law-abiding, the Brannocks weren't exactly ordinary citizens, though. G.W. would fight for what he believed in as long as there was breath in his body, and Miranda was starting to get the sense that Kyle was the same way. He liked to talk about himself as if he were just a shiftless bum, but Miranda's instincts told her there was a lot more to him than that.

She knew he was interested in her, too. After the breakup that had brought her to Texas, it was a little bit soon for her to be getting romantically involved with anyone else, even now, but Kyle Brannock was intriguing, no doubt about that.

The three of them went around a corner, and there to the left was the large, barred area that served as the county's drunk tank. Three men stood inside it, clustered around something on the floor, and Miranda's heart leaped into her throat as she realized the huddled shape was actually Kyle. He looked like he was unconscious—or worse.

"Oh, my God!" Miranda cried as she instinctively lifted a hand to her mouth in shock. "Sheriff, get him out of there!"

"What the hell!" Jacobs rushed forward. "Back off in there! Get away from that man, damn it!"

G.W. hurried up beside the sheriff and grasped the bars.

In a tight, angry voice, he said, "If that boy's hurt bad, Jacobs, you're gonna be sorry."

"I didn't order this." Jacobs turned his head and shouted, "Phillips! Cranston! Somebody get in here and unlock this damned door!"

One of the deputies appeared in another corridor and ran toward them. As he fumbled with a ring of keys, he said, "Sheriff, what happened?"

"That's what I'd like to know," Jacobs snapped. "This man should've been put in a holding cell, not in the tank."

"Sorry, sheriff," the deputy muttered. "We didn't know."

Jacobs glared at the man, who finally managed to unlock the cell door.

"Don't touch him," Miranda said as the three men went into the cell. "He needs medical attention. If he has broken bones or internal injuries, you could make them worse if you move him."

"The lady's right," Jacobs said to the deputy. "Get an ambulance here right away. Move!"

The deputy left the cell on the run.

G.W. dropped to a knee beside his grandson. He studied Kyle intently for a second, then said, "He's breathin', thank the Lord. Looks like he got the hell beat out of him, but Kyle's tough. He'll pull through this."

"He had better," Miranda said grimly. "If he doesn't, I'll see to it that this county is bankrupt and nobody in this department ever has a job in law enforcement again."

Those were bold claims, but at the moment she was angry enough to make them and mean them.

More deputies hurried in from elsewhere in the building and took charge of the three prisoners who had beaten Kyle. They all looked a little sheepish and scared now.

One of the men said, "We didn't mean to really hurt him. Just wanted to teach him a lesson, that's all."

"You have a grudge against this man, Hummel?" the sheriff asked.

G.W. answered the question, saying, "Yeah, he and Kyle tangled a few days ago over in Sierra Lobo. What are these three doin' in here?"

"I'll have to check the log, but my guess is they were brought in for drunk and disorderly or disturbing the peace. It wouldn't be the first time."

"And you expect us to believe that you didn't know about this?" Miranda said caustically. "That you didn't have Kyle put in here on purpose so those men would attack him?"

"I give you my word I didn't," Jacobs said. He rubbed a hand over his face. "And I swear to you that I'll get to the bottom of this."

Somewhere outside, a siren wailed as it came closer. That would be the ambulance coming for Kyle, Miranda thought as she looked down at him.

She prayed that he would be all right, and as she did, she thought she might as well admit to herself that her concern wasn't completely that of an attorney for her client. . . .

Chapter 35

The first thing Kyle was aware of as consciousness seeped back into his brain and body was the feel of crisp, cool sheets against his skin. He was lying in a bed somewhere.

Probably in a hospital, he thought as memories of what had happened in the drunk tank came back to him.

He would have a score to settle with Vern Hummel, Gutierrez, and the apelike man whose name he didn't know.

That would have to wait, though, until he wasn't filled with aches and pains from head to toe.

His eyes were still closed, but he opened them when someone took hold of his hand. He looked up and saw Miranda smiling down at him.

"I saw you move and knew you were awake," she said. Her voice sounded even sweeter to him now than it had earlier.

G.W. moved up on the other side of the bed and rested a hand on Kyle's shoulder.

"How're you feelin', son?" he asked.

"Like I got the sh—the heck kicked out of me," Kyle replied in a raspy whisper. "How bad . . . is it?"

"Bruised ribs, but nothin' broken. The doctors want to keep you here overnight, just to make sure there aren't any internal injuries they don't know about, but mostly you're just gonna be stiff and sore and hobblin' around for a few days."

"Sorry I . . . let you down, G.W."

"How in the hell do you figure you let me down?" G.W. asked with a puzzled frown.

"There were only . . . three of those guys. I should've . . . taken 'em."

Miranda said, "Don't be ridiculous. Nobody would have been able to handle all three of those brutes by himself."

"I wouldn't be so sure about that," G.W. said. "Kyle might've been holdin' back a little."

There was some truth to that, Kyle mused. He hadn't thought about it at the time, but he'd gotten in the habit of not cutting loose with everything he was capable of when he found himself in scrapes like that.

He had come close—too close—to beating a man to death once, and he didn't want that on his conscience unless there was no other alternative.

He looked around the hospital room and didn't see anybody except G.W. and Miranda. He said, "I'm not in jail anymore . . . but I'm guessing there's a deputy outside the door."

"Nope, the judge set bail," G.W. said. "He was pretty upset when he heard about what happened. He set bail at four hundred bucks. I was able to come up with that much cash without any problem."

"So I'm free again."

"For now," Miranda said. "And I'm going to be in the district attorney's face first thing in the morning, letting him know that he needs to decline to prosecute this case.

He's a reasonable man—most of the time—and I think he'll see that he doesn't stand much chance of winning, especially if it goes to a jury."

Kyle muttered, "Grayson got me beaten up anyway. That's probably all he wanted."

G.W. said, "Sheriff Jacobs swears he didn't order you put in there with Hummel and those other fellas, and the deputies claim it was all just a misunderstandin'. There's no way to prove they're lyin'."

"Grayson had something to do with it," Kyle said. "I can feel it in my bones." He winced. "Along with some other things. Where are Hummel and the other two now?"

"Still locked up," Miranda said. "I've filed assault and attempted murder charges against them on your behalf." She shrugged. "The attempted murder charges may not stick, but the assault will. They'll be going to Huntsville."

"Good riddance," G.W. said.

Kyle was starting to have trouble keeping his eyes open. He had an IV needle in the back of each hand, and he suspected one of the lines was feeding painkillers into his veins. That would make him drowsy. He murmured, "I'm all right. . . . Both of you . . . better go on and . . . get some rest."

"I'm not goin' anywhere tonight," G.W. declared. "That chair's not the most comfortable one in the world, but I can sleep in it. You don't need to be alone."

"I'm sure the nurses . . . can take care of me."

"I'm not worried about your medical condition. I'm worried about how that Grayson fella might not stop at anything to settle the score with you. Hospitals are dangerous places, you know. Folks die in 'em all the time."

Miranda frowned and said, "Surely Grayson wouldn't go that far."

G.W. nodded toward Kyle in the hospital bed.

"Take a good look at the boy, then tell me you really believe that."

Miranda didn't say anything. After a moment, though, she squeezed Kyle's hand.

"I can stay, too, if you'd like."

He managed to shake his head and said, "No, you go on home. Just be careful. . . . When you agreed to help us . . . you got on the wrong side of the government, too. . . ."

Chapter 36

Red Mike's Tavern was on the highway about halfway between Sierra Lobo and the county seat. A long, low frame building behind a gravel parking lot, it had been there under various owners and names for more than fifty years. Every time the door opened, cigarette smoke and honky-tonk music drifted out into the night. It was one of the few places left where people could poison themselves with nicotine in public.

Slade Grayson didn't like secondhand smoke, but he could put up with it for a while. He sat in one of the booths, on a bench seat covered in red Naugahyde, and nursed a bitter, watery beer. The lonesome strains of George Strait's "Amarillo by Morning" came from the old-fashioned jukebox in the corner.

Damn rednecks, he thought. In his more gloomy moments, he believed the country really would be better off if most of the area between the two coasts was depopulated.

But then who would grow the food and pay most of the taxes? Sometimes realism trumped idealism, which was a truth that his progressive masters often had trouble grasping.

Grayson checked the door every time it opened. Finally,

the man he was waiting for came into the tavern. The man was about twenty-five, very clean-cut with his dark hair shaved close on the sides. He wore jeans and a short-sleeved shirt with a buttoned-down collar.

The man spotted Grayson and came across the room toward him. He slid into the booth on the other side and glanced around nervously.

"Try not to look like you're about to shit in your pants, Deputy Phillips," Grayson told him.

"I just don't want anybody to see me who knows me," Phillips said as he clasped his hands together on the table.

"You come here often, do you?"

"Never. I've never even answered a call here. That's why I picked it."

"Then you shouldn't have anything to worry about."

A bosomy waitress with hair a shade of red that had never occurred in nature appeared beside the table and asked, "What can I get you, honey?"

Phillips shook his head and said, "I don't want anything."

"Oh, now, don't be like that. I got to eat, too, and my little boy needs braces."

Grayson said, "My friend will have a beer. And I'll take a refill on mine."

"There you go," the redhead said with a crooked smile that revealed no one had gotten braces for her when she was young. "That wasn't so hard, now was it?"

When the waitress was gone, Phillips said, "Kyle Brannock is in the hospital."

"How badly was he hurt?"

"Hummel, Gutierrez, and Johnson gave him a pretty bad beating. Last I heard, though, he was in no real danger."

"Good, good," Grayson said as he nodded slowly. "This

was really just to get his attention. A wake-up call, you could say. Most of my efforts are going to be focused elsewhere."

Phillips leaned forward and said between clenched teeth, "Who the hell are you, mister? How . . . how do you know the things you know?"

"You mean how do I know about the fourteen-year-old girl you've been seeing?" Grayson asked. "The fourteen-year-old girl you don't want your wife or your boss or anybody else to know about?"

Finding out about that had been simple. He had gotten a list of all the deputies who worked for the sheriff's department in this county and checked the NSA logs of their e-mails and cell phone calls.

Grayson knew the chances were he would find plenty of things he could use to pressure one of the officers into doing what he wanted. Phillips's affair with an underage girl was just the first thing Grayson had come across—and he couldn't have asked for better leverage.

"Shut up!" Phillips hissed frantically. "Don't go talking about that in here." He passed a trembling hand over his face. "Anyway, if you saw her you'd think she was twenty. I swear you would. I did at first."

"So all you thought you were doing was cheating on your wife, not committing statutory rape as well. I'm sure no one will have any trouble accepting that excuse."

For a long moment, Phillips didn't say anything. Then, "Look, I did what you asked, mister. I told you we had Hummel and those friends of his locked up, and I saw to it that Brannock went into the drunk tank with them. They jumped him just like you thought they would. What more do you want from me?"

Grayson leaned back, smiled, and said, "Not a damned thing, deputy."

Phillips started to look relieved.

"Not right now, anyway," Graysonsaid, which caused the younger man's expression to drop again. "But if I need to call on you again in the future, I'm sure you'll be more than willing to help."

"You . . . you're not going to say anything about . . ."

"No, that stays between the two of us, for the time being."

"All right, then," Phillips said hollowly. "Sure. Anything you need, I'll be glad to help."

"I thought so." Grayson nodded toward the bar. "Here comes your beer. Drink up. Enjoy."

He laid a twenty-dollar bill on the table as he stood up, favoring the leg Kyle Brannock had wrenched that morning. The waitress had just arrived carrying a tray that had two mugs of beer on it.

"Don't leave now, honey," she said to Grayson. "I got your refill here."

"Leave it for my friend," he told her. "I think he probably needs it more than I do."

Chapter 37

Kyle was discharged from the hospital the next morning with a prescription for painkillers. He planned not to take any more of them than he had to. He had seen guys get addicted to the things and didn't want any part of that.

The nurses insisted on putting him in a wheelchair and wheeling him to the hospital's front door. Several of them gathered around to escort him. G.W. grinned at all the feminine attention his grandson was getting.

Once they were outside and the nurses had reluctantly gone back inside, G.W. said, "You can lean on me if you want. I don't reckon those gals can see."

"I don't care if they can see," Kyle said. "I don't need any help. I can make it."

The steps he took were careful ones, though, as he and G.W. walked out into the parking lot toward G.W.'s old pickup. Kyle didn't feel too bad, but if he moved wrong, his bruised ribs gave him a pretty sharp twinge.

Other than that, he was just stiff and sore, as he'd expected. That would go away in a day or two.

The anger he felt was liable to hang around for a while, though.

"Have you heard anything from Miranda this morning?" he asked.

"Not yet," G.W. replied. "I know she was goin' to see the district attorney. . . . Well, speak of the devil."

Kyle saw Miranda's car turning into the parking lot. He smiled and said, "I wouldn't call her the devil."

"No, that doesn't suit her very well, does it? Come on, let's get you to the pickup so you can sit down."

Stepping up into the pickup's cab caused Kyle to grit his teeth, but he made it. He left the door open. Miranda parked, got out of her car, and came over to join them.

"Good news," she announced. "The DA is dropping all the charges against you, Kyle."

"That won't make Grayson happy," G.W. said.

"I don't think he really cared whether I was convicted or not," Kyle said. "He just wanted to flex his muscles a little. Wanted me to see that he can reach out and make my life a living hell any time he wants." Kyle paused, then continued. "A man like Grayson, the worst thing you can do to him is make him feel like he doesn't have the absolute power he thinks he does."

"You're right," Miranda said. "He thought he would waltz in here and everybody would bow down to him just because he works for the government. He can't stand it when that doesn't happen."

G.W. said, "He'd better get used to it. Not much bowin' and scrapin' to the government's gonna happen in *this* part of Texas." He turned his head and spat. "This isn't *Austin*."

Kyle laughed.

"Come on," he said. "Let's go home."

That was the first time he had used that word in a long time . . . and meant it.

"I'll follow you out there," Miranda said. "We need to talk."

That was good news, thought Kyle. No matter what Miranda had to say, he was glad to have her around.

Roberto Quinones and several of the other hands were waiting for them. The foreman had a rifle in his hands, and a couple of the other men carried shotguns.

"Any trouble while we were gone?" G.W. asked as he got out of the pickup.

"No, señor," Roberto replied, "but we were ready if it visited us. Our families are gone, as you asked. They left this morning."

"I'm glad to hear it, and I'm sorry you folks have to be separated. I'm glad to know they'll be safe, though."

"*Sí*, so are we. Señor Kyle, let me give you a hand."

"I can make it," Kyle said stubbornly as he climbed out of the truck. He held on to the door to steady himself.

"I got a cane inside you can use," G.W. said. "Juan, go get it."

"I don't—" Kyle stopped because one of the hands was already hurrying into the house to fetch the cane. When the man came back with it, Kyle took it, nodded, and said, *"Gracias."*

He had to admit, walking was a little easier with the cane, too.

Miranda drove up a minute or so later. By the time she came in, Kyle was sitting on the old leather sofa in the living room, with a good view of the fireplace and the heads of a couple of bucks and a bighorn sheep mounted above the mantel.

Kyle's great-grandfather had taken those trophies. G.W.

confined his hunting to snakes, coyotes, and the occasional wolf or mountain lion. He had no interest in hunting for sport, but any predator that came after his stock had better watch out.

The same held true for government weasels who wanted to steal the ranch, Kyle suspected.

"Miranda, you sit down there with Kyle," G.W. said. "I'll get iced tea for everybody."

He went out into the kitchen as Miranda sat on the sofa.

"How do you feel this morning?" she asked.

"Like I got kicked by a mule," Kyle said, "but I'm all right. A couple of days and I'll be good as new."

That was probably too optimistic, but it never hurt to think positively. A second after that thought crossed his mind, he told himself that it was another example of how being around G.W. and getting caught up in his grandfather's struggle was changing him. For years now, he had been mired in pessimism.

It was sort of nice to get out of that mental swamp.

"Well, maybe while you're recuperating, it'll keep you out of trouble," Miranda said.

"Hey, it's not like I go looking for fights," he protested. "Well . . . I guess have sometimes, but that was in the past. These days, I'm a peaceable man."

He chuckled, knowing Miranda wouldn't get the joke.

Evidently she didn't, because she said, "Grayson can still bring federal charges against you, you know. US Marshals may show up to take you into custody. If they do, I want you to do the same thing as before: cooperate and keep your mouth shut."

"I tried that." Kyle looked down at himself meaningfully. "It didn't work out too well."

"You didn't get beat up because you did what I said."

"Why *did* I get beat up?" he mused. "Do you think Grayson set the whole thing up somehow?"

"I don't know. It doesn't really seem likely, but I don't suppose we can put it past him."

"I don't plan on putting anything past him," Kyle said. "He struck me as pretty much of a cold-blooded, ruthless son of a . . . gun."

"What is it with you Brannock men always watching your language around me?"

"Just the way we were raised," G.W. said as he came into the room carrying a tray with three glasses of iced tea on it. He set the tray on the coffee table and handed glasses to Kyle and Miranda. "We're old-fashioned, and you might as well get used to it. Isn't that right, Kyle?"

"I'm afraid so," he said with a smile.

"All right, fine," Miranda said. "Let's move on to the problem at hand. I've got a call in to Maria Delgado's office."

Kyle raised his eyebrows.

"The governor?"

"That's right. I don't know if she'll return the call or not, and even if she does, I'm not sure if she can help us, but she's had a number of skirmishes with the federal government already, in the time she's been in office. Remember that business with the prison and the terrorists a while back?"

"It was on all the news," G.W. said dryly. "From what I gather, certain folks in Washington were pretty dang peeved at her for sendin' in soldiers to rescue those people trapped in that prison."

"That's right. I'm hoping she can give us some advice on how to deal with the BLM."

"A private army would be nice," Kyle said.

Miranda shook her head and said, "No, we don't want

that sort of bloodshed here. There has to be a peaceful solution."

Kyle drank some of his iced tea and glanced over at his grandfather. Their eyes met, and Kyle knew that G.W. was thinking the same thing he was.

The longer this oppression by the government went on, the less likely it was that a peaceful solution could be found.

The really frightening thing was that he was no longer sure the other side *wanted* a peaceful solution. The liberals, the so-called "progressives," had been trying to solidify their grip on the country for decades now. Academics and members of the mainstream media constantly beat the Democratic drum and preached that conservatism was dead and the Republicans were nothing more than a minor, regional party. They might as well have been Whigs, to hear certain sectors tell it.

And yet with every national election, a large part of the country voted against the continued growth of government and managed to keep it from being a total runaway to disaster. That had to be frustrating to the statists, the crowd to whom their politics *was* their religion, although they would never admit that. One of these days, the self-styled Washington elite would get tired of being frustrated and decide to crush the opposition once and for all.

It had happened again and again, in Russia, in China, in Cuba. Millions had died, all because a small group of people who thought they were smarter and better than everyone else had seized power and set out to do "good," even if it meant killing or imprisoning anyone who opposed their warped ideas.

Kyle didn't know if that would ever happen in the United States, but he knew that what once might have been unthinkable now lurked in the back of many minds on both sides.

Sooner or later, it might come down to a battle between true freedom and the false freedom of the progressives, which was really nothing more than a dictatorship. No sane person wanted American blood running in the streets of home. . . .

The question was whether or not there were enough sane people left in Washington to prevent that.

And Lord help us all, thought Kyle, they might soon find out the answer.

Maybe it would even be found here in a beautiful valley in West Texas, a veritable paradise. . . .

With Hell lurking right around the corner.

Chapter 38

The next few days provided a lull, a welcome respite from all the trouble. No US Marshals showed up to arrest Kyle, and G.W., Roberto, and the rest of the hands were able to go about the business of running the ranch without anyone bothering them.

There was no sign of Slade Grayson, Warren Finley, Woodrow Todd, or any other intruders from Washington or elsewhere.

Since the women and children were gone, all the men took their meals together in the ranch house's big dining room, with G.W. doing most of the cooking—or rather the grilling, as they ate mostly steaks and hamburgers. One day, Roberto cooked up a big pot of chili so hot Kyle felt like it blistered his insides . . . but that didn't stop him from having a second bowl.

He enjoyed these meals. They gave him a chance to get to know all the hands, and his command of Spanish came back to him as he sat there with the musical language flowing swiftly around him. They were good times, and he was convinced the camaraderie helped him recover from the beating he had received. His strength came back as the soreness in his ribs and elsewhere faded.

It would have been nice to think that this pleasant interval would last—but Kyle knew better than that.

He had gotten out of the hospital and come back to the ranch on Tuesday morning. The next Saturday, he and G.W. were sitting at the table in the kitchen having breakfast when Roberto came in with a worried frown on his face. The sun was up and normally G.W. would have been out on the range already, but he had told Kyle he was moving a little slow this morning.

G.W. had finished his bowl of cornflakes and started on his toast. He set it down and asked his foreman, "What's wrong, Roberto?"

"Benito just came in from checking the waterhole at Barranca Blanco," Roberto reported. "He said there were several dead cows near it."

G.W. sat up straighter as his face settled into angry lines.

"Could he tell what happened to them?" he asked.

Roberto shook his head and said, "He was not sure. He thought they may have been poisoned."

"Damn it!" The flat of G.W.'s hand slammed down on the table, making the dishes and silverware jump. "Did he haze any other stock that were around the place away from it, anyway?"

"He said there were no other cattle nearby, señor."

"That doesn't mean they won't drift that direction before we can get back out there." G.W. scraped his chair back and stood up.

Kyle got to his feet as well and said, "I'm coming with you."

"You're in no shape to—"

"I'm fine," Kyle interrupted his grandfather. "As long

as I don't get into any more of those three-against-one sparring matches."

"There won't be any of that," G.W. declared. "All right, then, come along if you want to." He added grimly, "Grab a rifle on your way out."

All of them were armed as they headed out to the Barranca Blanco waterhole. Kyle and G.W. were in the pickup, Roberto and Benito in the jeep that served as the ranch's second vehicle, and the other hands following on horseback.

G.W. knew where they were going, of course—he knew every foot of the ranch—and handled the pickup expertly as it bounced across country toward the foothills at the edge of the mountains. Most of the ranch's waterholes were located in those foothills.

Kyle peered anxiously through the dusty windshield. As soon as he had heard there were dead cattle, he'd thought of Slade Grayson.

They knew the BLM wasn't interested in the stock. Grayson had made that abundantly clear.

Would the man go so far as to kill some of the animals just to continue his campaign of harassment against G.W.? Kyle didn't really doubt that Grayson was that cruel . . . and that stupid. Striking at G.W. like this would just harden his resolve. Given Grayson's arrogance, he might not understand that.

"There's the waterhole, up yonder in those rocks," G.W. said, pointing.

"I remember it," Kyle said. "Seems like we all rode over here for a picnic, one day when I was a kid."

G.W. glanced over at him and nodded.

"You remember that, do you? You couldn't have been more'n six years old or so."

"I remember it," Kyle said quietly. It was one of the good memories of his parents and his childhood.

And the memory made anger burn even more fiercely inside him when he saw the dark shapes of the dead cattle on the ground near the waterhole.

G.W. brought the pickup to a stop and they climbed out carrying their rifles, as Roberto and Benito pulled up in the jeep. Kyle felt a little sick when he saw that three full-grown cows and two good-sized calves had died here.

G.W. looked around, then said, "You can tell they all went up to the waterhole, had themselves a drink, and then collapsed and died when they started to wander off. There aren't any wounds on them, so they weren't shot. It had to be poison that killed them, and there's no place they could've gotten into it but here."

Roberto hunkered on his heels next to the small pool nestled in the rocks.

"It looks okay," he said. He reached out with a hand, as if he intended to cup some of the water and taste it.

"Don't do that," G.W. said sharply. "We'll leave that to the experts. I want to get Doc Bryan out here from town to have a look at those cows and confirm they were poisoned." His expression was bleak as he went on. "For now, once the other fellas get here on horseback, I want some of 'em to stand guard on this waterhole and turn back any stock that tries to get to it. The cattle may not like it, but there are other waterholes where they can drink. I don't plan on losin' any more of 'em."

"You know Grayson did this," Kyle said. "If not him personally, then somebody he hired. But he's responsible for it."

"I don't know anything yet," G.W. snapped. Then his tone eased a little as he went on. "But you're probably right. Let's take a look around and see if we can find any sign. Chances are, if any of those boys from back East did this, they'll have left some tracks."

Kyle went with his grandfather as G.W. walked a wide circle around the waterhole. About a hundred yards away, they found tire marks that hadn't been left by the two ranch vehicles.

"You were right," Kyle said as G.W. knelt beside the tracks and studied them. "Somebody drove in here last night, and the only reason they'd do that would be to poison the waterhole."

"Well, there might've been another reason," G.W. said, "but all the evidence points to you bein' right."

"So what do we do now?"

G.W. squinted off into the distance and said, "There are other waterholes on the spread. Maybe they'll try to spread their poison again." His lips drew back from his teeth in a savage grimace. "I almost hope the sons o' bitches do . . . because I plan to be waitin' for 'em."

Chapter 39

Barton Devlin had turned his cell phone off several days earlier when he got tired of ignoring the calls from his supervisor. He knew that by now his government employment had probably been terminated, and that left him with an aching emptiness inside.

For more than two decades his life had revolved around the Internal Revenue Service. His entire career had been spent punishing those who tried to get by without paying their fair share. He had gone to sleep at night firm in the conviction of his righteousness.

Now he had to fight off a persistent nausea at the thought that maybe—just maybe—the IRS really was as bad as its critics claimed. That it was nothing more than a bullying, hectoring, strong-arm branch of the administration, intended to punish not tax cheats but political enemies, to weaken conservative organizations and make it more difficult for conservative candidates to win elections. That it was really just a tool of the Democrats in their obsessive need to achieve and maintain power.

And that, Devlin knew in his heart, was not what he had signed on for.

Once he'd been forced to admit that possibility, it was

like floodgates had opened in his mind. If the IRS, never well-liked but once a bastion of neutrality, had been so corrupted by a series of Democrat administrations, what about all the other government agencies? The Bureau of Land Management, for example?

On the surface, there was no more innocuous agency in Washington. The BLM was charged with managing land owned by the federal government. Nothing could be simpler.

But no agency engaged in such innocent activity would have need of a man like Slade Grayson working for them. The man was a piranha . . . no, a shark. Pure, elemental destruction in an expensive suit. If Grayson was trying to seize G.W. Brannock's ranch on behalf of the BLM, then there had to be something fishy about the deal.

Devlin was going to find out what it was.

That was why he was following Grayson's two cohorts at the moment. Finley and Todd had snuck onto the ranch well before dawn. Devlin had no idea what they were up to, but it had to be no good. The sun was up now, and the two BLM men were on their way back to Sierra Lobo.

Devlin was a hundred yards behind them in his rental car. All he knew about tailing someone he had learned from watching hundreds of TV shows in hundreds of motel rooms over the past twenty years, but he seemed to be getting better at it.

It probably helped that Finley and Todd were amateurs just like he was. None of them had any business carrying out this cloak-and-dagger stuff, especially when they were dealing with a professional like Grayson.

Sooner or later, thought Devlin, that shark was going to turn around and consume them.

* * *

"It's done," Warren Finley reported. "I don't like it, and neither does Woody, but it's done."

"Maybe you should let Woody speak for himself," Grayson said. He hadn't put on his coat and tie, but he was dressed otherwise, and even though the hour wasn't much past nine o'clock in the morning, the glass in his hand had a couple of fingers of scotch in it.

Todd frowned and said, "I don't care much for killing animals, even cows."

"Turning vegetarian on me, Woody?" Grayson asked mockingly. "Because all those burgers and steaks and roasts didn't commit suicide, you know."

"I know. But it's different when there's not a good reason for it."

"Not a good reason?" Grayson tossed back the drink and then glared at the two men he had sent on this errand. "What better reason can there be than furthering the cause of the United States government?"

"Are we really doing that?" Finley asked. "Or is there some other agenda at work here?"

Grayson set the empty glass aside and pointed a finger at Finley.

"I'm going to forget I heard you say that, old buddyroo. That sounded pretty freaking disloyal to the Bureau, if you ask me, and I know that's not what you want."

Finley felt himself go pale. Disloyalty to the Bureau meant disloyalty to the administration, and that could be dangerous. Not just to a guy's career, but to his very life.

"No, that's . . . that's not what I mean," Finley said hastily, stumbling over the words.

"I didn't think so," Grayson replied with a superior sneer. His briefcase lay on the dresser. He went to it, opened it, and took out another plastic vial. Negligently, he tossed it to Finley, who turned positively white as a sheet as he caught it. "Empty that in another of Brannock's waterholes tonight. By the time we go out there Monday to take over, he won't have any cattle left."

"Monday?" Finley repeated in confusion. "I thought he had sixty days to vacate the ranch."

"Timetable's been moved up," Grayson said as he reached for the bottle of whiskey next to the briefcase. "We're taking possession of the ranch Monday, and if Brannock resists, he and anybody who takes his side will be placed in federal custody. The gloves, gentlemen, are off."

And it was damned well about time, Grayson thought as he poured himself another drink.

Chapter 40

Miranda had checked in with G.W. every day by phone, but she hadn't been out to the ranch since the day Kyle got out of the hospital. He missed seeing her, but he knew she was probably working hard on his grandfather's behalf.

When she heard about the waterhole being poisoned, though, she came out to see the results for herself.

"I still haven't heard back from the governor's office yet," she said as she took pictures of the dead cows, "but I'm working on something else. It's not going to hurt to have public opinion on our side, and this could help with that."

"I don't reckon I understand," G.W. said.

She turned her phone around so that he and Kyle could see the screen. It displayed a landscape shot that Kyle knew had been taken here on the ranch, and superimposed over the photograph in a brightly colored, easy-to-read font were the words STAND WITH G.W.

"What in blazes is that?" G.W. asked.

"It's a Web page devoted to your efforts to keep the government from stealing your ranch from you," Miranda explained. "I'm posting it on all the different social media platforms and updating it several times a day. You have more than five thousand likes on this one already."

G.W. shook his head and said, "I have no idea what you're talkin' about."

"I do," Kyle said as he felt excitement growing in him, "and I think it's a great idea. People all over the country—shoot, all over the world—are finding out what the government's trying to do to you, G.W., and they don't like it."

"I thought Miranda just said they do like it," G.W. said with a frown.

"No, they like the page—" Miranda began. She stopped and tapped on her phone's screen for a moment. "Just let me post those pictures I took, and we ought to see plenty of comments right away disapproving of what the BLM has done here."

"You mean people are gonna believe us over the BLM?"

"A lot of people will. Sure, there's plenty of craziness on the Internet, but the truth has a way of getting out there, too, and when enough people see it, they realize it."

Kyle said, "So we wage a war for public opinion?"

"It can't hurt," Miranda said.

That was probably true, he thought . . . but now that he thought about it, he couldn't really see how it was going to help much, either. All the Internet outrage in the world wasn't going to bring those dead cows back, and it wouldn't stop Slade Grayson and the BLM, either.

"I suppose the vet confirmed that the cattle were poisoned?" she asked.

"Yeah," G.W. said, "although he couldn't tell exactly what it was."

"He took tissue samples and samples of the water back to town with him to analyze them," Kyle put in. "He said he'd let us know if he found out anything definite."

"I'll add that to the post," Miranda said.

They had come out here in G.W.'s pickup, the three of them crowded into the front seat with Miranda in the middle. Kyle hadn't minded that at all.

Now, as they started back toward the truck, G.W. went on ahead, leaving Kyle and Miranda to follow. She asked quietly, "How are you doing? I haven't talked to you in several days."

"I know," he said.

"I've been busy researching other cases and all the laws regarding the concept of eminent domain. That's not exactly what this is, of course. The government's not condemning the property to take it and use it for the public good. This is a land grab, pure and simple. We have to make sure everyone sees it as such."

"Seems like you've got a good start on that. And to answer your question, I'm all right. Doing better every day. I don't yelp when I climb out of bed in the morning or take a deep breath, and that's a big improvement over the first day or so."

"I'm glad." She changed the subject by asking, "G.W. has a computer, doesn't he?"

"Yeah, and Internet access, although he's never done much with it."

"Then you can take part in this social media campaign."

"Yeah, I suppose," Kyle said.

She looked over at him and said, "You don't sound very enthusiastic."

He hadn't wanted to throw cold water on her ideas, but he had to be honest with her, too.

"You know what social media outrage is like, all sound and fury and not much else. It makes people feel good about themselves and what they believe, but I'm not sure it ever accomplishes anything else."

Miranda shook her head and said, "I disagree. People

all over the world have used it to further their causes. All the Islamic terror groups who hate us use it. There must be something to it, or people wouldn't keep coming back to it."

"We'll see, I guess," Kyle said.

"I suppose so," Miranda said, and now her voice was a little cooler than it had been earlier.

As arguments went, this one was pretty minor, Kyle thought. Even so, he wished it hadn't happened.

He wanted things to bring him and Miranda closer together . . . not drive them farther apart.

Doc Bryan, the veterinarian, called later that afternoon to tell G.W. that he hadn't been able to identify the unusual element that he'd found in the sample from the waterhole. It was some sort of organic compound unknown to him, but he was confident that it was what had killed the cattle, because he had found it in their tissue samples, too.

Having reached the end of his capabilities, the doctor was sending the other samples he had taken to friends of his at the School of Veterinary Medicine at Texas A&M. They would have a better shot at identifying the compound than he would, he explained.

"If the stuff came from Grayson, there's no telling what it might be," Kyle said to G.W. after the phone conversation with Doc Bryan. "From what I hear, the government's developed quite a few biological and chemical weapons that it's kept secret. Wasn't there some big deal a while back about a secret lab in this part of the country . . . ?"

"Casa del Diablo," G.W. said, nodding. "Yeah, that fella who cheated his way into the White House tried to use some sort of nerve gas from there to wipe out a whole town that thumbed their noses at his gun-grabbin' habits. That's what made him go loco and refuse to leave office when Congress impeached and convicted him." G.W. sighed. "I thought that might be enough to make the whole country come to its senses. Didn't last long, though. Before you knew it, half the folks had their hands out again and were promisin' to vote for whoever would fill 'em up. We know which bunch *that* is."

"So if Grayson's some sort of government trouble-shooter, he could have gotten his hands on something very few people know about."

G.W. nodded and said, "That's right, and when you get right down to it, it doesn't really matter what he or his flunkies used to poison that waterhole. What's important is that they're still tryin' to run me off . . . and I'm not gonna go."

After supper, as evening approached, G.W. went out to the barn to saddle one of his horses. Kyle went with him and said, "I've got a pretty good idea what you're up to, and I'm coming with you, G.W."

"I'm not sure you're in any shape to sit a saddle."

"I can ride," Kyle insisted. "My ribs still hurt a little, but the rest of me is fine. Riding isn't going to cause a problem."

"Well, I don't mind tellin' you, it'd be good to have you along, son," G.W. admitted. "There's no way of knowin' what we're gonna run into out there, but if it comes to trouble, you're a good man to have beside me."

Kyle's heart swelled with pride. Those simple words from his grandfather meant a lot to him.

"You want me to fetch a couple of rifles while you're saddling the horses?" he asked.

G.W. nodded and said grimly, "We're liable to need 'em."

Chapter 41

Warren Finley thought of himself as an amateur cartographer, and a good one, at that. One thing he had done while he and Woody Todd were exploring and taking inventory on Brannock's ranch was to map all the waterholes in the valley.

Because of that, he wouldn't have any trouble finding another of them to dump Grayson's poison into. As much as the thought of killing more cattle disturbed him, he knew he would go through with it.

Handling some mysterious biological weapon scared him, but making Slade Grayson angry was an even more frightening prospect.

Finley wasn't the only one worried. From the passenger seat of the jeep, Woody said, "I don't like this, Warren. We're gonna wind up getting in a lot of trouble over this. Mark my words."

"I don't doubt it, but what else can we do?" Finley asked. "We work for Grayson now, and he gave us an order. We have to carry it out."

"You got the stuff?"

Finley's hands were clenched tightly on the steering wheel as he drove across the valley without lights. He said,

"Of course, I have it. What, did you think I was going to forget and leave it in the motel room?"

"Just making sure. If we have to do this, I want to get it done and get the hell outta here." Todd paused. "Those poor cows."

Finley knew what he meant. Neither of them were going to give up eating meat, but somehow this was different. This served no purpose except to make life more difficult for G.W. Brannock and push him closer to either surrendering or going off the deep end and giving Grayson an excuse to use force.

Finley wasn't sure which of those options Grayson preferred, but he was starting to get an idea. He didn't like that idea, either. He thought there was a good chance nothing short of bloodshed was going to satisfy Grayson now.

"There it is, just inside the mouth of that little canyon," he said to his companion. He took one hand off the wheel long enough to point. "We're almost done."

"Grayson will just come up with some other crappy job for us to do."

"Probably. But we'll deal with that when the time comes."

Finley brought the jeep to a stop about fifteen feet from the edge of the waterhole, which was a black, irregular circle in the light from the moon and stars. Both men climbed out.

"I hope this is the last time we have to do this," Todd said.

"If Grayson goes ahead with his plans and makes his move the day after tomorrow, it should be," Finley said.

They walked toward the pool. Finley reached up to the breast pocket of his shirt, which was buttoned closed. He unfastened it, reached inside, took out the plastic vial.

He was about to work the stopper out of its neck—oh,

so carefully—when a voice said somewhere nearby, "I'd think twice before I did whatever you're about to do, mister."

Brannock.

Todd let out a started curse and exclaimed, "Not again!"

"I'm afraid so," Brannock said as he and another man emerged from the shadows deeper in the canyon. There was enough light for Finley to see that both of them were armed. The rifles they pointed at him and Todd were steady, too.

Finley swallowed hard and said, "Please be careful, Mr. Brannock."

"So it's you two again, is it?" Brannock said disgustedly as he stalked forward. "What's the matter, Grayson can't do his own dirty work? He has to send somebody else to handle it for him?"

"Don't get too close to him, G.W.," the other man advised. That would be Brannock's grandson Kyle, the former army ranger in training, thought Finley. "There's no telling what that is he's got in his hand."

"Please, we don't wish either of you any harm—" Finley began.

"Now that's a damned sorry joke," Brannock interrupted. "All you've been tryin' to do is run me off the ranch that's been in my family for generations. Seems like harm to me."

"I understand how you feel," Finley said. "But the situation has changed. This isn't your ranch—"

"Just shut your trap. I don't want to listen to that bull, especially after you varmints killed some of my cattle."

Todd said, "We're sorry about that."

"Then why'd you do it?"

"We didn't have any choice—"

"People always have a choice," Brannock said. "It's just

that sometimes they're hard ones. Now, we're goin' back to the ranch house, and I'm callin' the sheriff. No matter what happens in the future, right now you two are trespassin', and I've got a right to turn you over to the law. I reckon that bottle of devil's brew in your hand will be evidence. I'm lookin' forward to seein' what the law can find out about—"

A brilliant beam of light suddenly shot out and hit both Brannocks, causing them to step back involuntarily and fling up an arm to block the blinding glare.

"Run!" another voice shouted. "Get out of here!"

The waterhole was between the BLM agents and the two Brannocks. That would slow down the pursuit. Finley and Todd turned and sprinted toward the jeep. Finley kept his hand closed tightly around the vial of poison. He didn't want to drop it and leave it behind.

As the light snapped out, Finley expected to hear the rifles roaring and feel bullets smashing into him at any second, but that didn't happen. The Brannocks weren't cold-blooded killers, he supposed, and he was thankful for that. He and Todd piled into the jeep, and Finley's hand found the key in the ignition and twisted it desperately.

The motor caught instantly. One-handed, Finley spun the wheel and tromped down on the gas at the same time. Dirt and gravel flew into the air as the tires slid and then caught. Finley headed the vehicle away from the waterhole as fast as he could.

Long moments went by before he stopped worrying about shots coming after them.

"Who . . . who the hell was that?" Todd panted.

"The man who helped us, you mean?" Finley shook his head and said, "I have no idea."

* * *

Kyle had the butt of the Winchester snug against his shoulder. He knew he could bring down one and possibly both of the fleeing federal agents, but he hesitated as his finger tightened on the trigger.

G.W. must have been feeling the same thing, because he said, "Hold your fire, son. I don't hold with shootin' a man in the back, even if he is a thief."

Kyle lowered the rifle and said, "Yeah, I know what you mean." Bright spots still danced in front of his eyes. "What the hell happened just now?"

"Don't know, but I intend to find out. Come on."

They moved quickly in the direction the unexpected voice had come from, along with the blinding light. Kyle knew his grandfather hoped to catch whoever had been behind that light.

"We could be waltzing right into a trap, you know," he said quietly.

"Yeah, but I don't think so. That didn't sound like a fella who'd be settin' a trap. And it sure as blazes wasn't Grayson."

Kyle agreed with that. The voice of the man who had shouted to Finley and Todd had been totally different from Grayson's smug tones.

They moved quickly along the base of the bluff near the canyon mouth where the waterhole was located. Kyle thought there was a good chance their quarry was gone by now, but then he heard rocks rattle somewhere not far ahead of them. The guy was still up there somewhere, probably trying to get away but not doing a very good job of it.

Suddenly, G.W. lifted his rifle and barked, "Hold it right there, mister! I see you, and if you move again I'll drill you."

Kyle doubted that his grandfather really would shoot—but the man who had been fleeing through the darkness didn't know that.

As his eyes continued to adjust, Kyle spotted the figure, too. The man stood with his arms raised. As Kyle and G.W. approached warily, he said, "Don't shoot. I'm unarmed." He paused, then added, "Well, I have a flashlight, but that doesn't really count, does it?"

"Just stand still and don't make any sudden moves," G.W. told him. "I've got a hunch you're another of those government types, and I'm not overly fond o' you boys right now. Who are you, and what're you doin' out here on my ranch?"

"My name is Barton Devlin," the man replied. Kyle was close enough to him now to see moonlight reflecting off the lenses of Devlin's glasses as he went on. "As for what I'm doing out here . . . I'm not sure that I really know."

"Wait a minute," G.W. said. "Devlin . . . Blast it, I know that name."

"You should. I sent you a letter recently."

"Now I remember!" G.W.'s voice fairly shook with anger. "You're that son of a bitch from the Internal Revenue Service who said he was gonna take my ranch away from me!"

Chapter 42

Kyle and G.W. marched Devlin back to the pickup. As they walked, the IRS agent said, "My car is parked about a quarter of a mile from here."

"Somebody'll come get it later," G.W. told him. Kyle could tell that his grandfather was still furious, but G.W. had his emotions under control, as usual.

"Thank you. It's a rental, you know. I wouldn't want anything to happen to it."

"You may have bigger problems than that," G.W. said ominously. "This is a big ranch. Lots of places where a fella could disappear and never be seen again."

"Your threats don't frighten me, Mr. Brannock. I know you're not a killer."

"Yeah, well, I've never been backed into a corner quite like this before, either."

Kyle heard Devlin swallow hard. The government man might be getting a little nervous.

That was good. It made him more likely to answer questions.

Instead of all three of them crowding into the pickup's seat, Kyle suggested, "Why don't Devlin and I ride in the back? I can keep an eye on him that way, and he can't try anything."

"Good idea," G.W. agreed.

Devlin said, "You don't have to worry about me. I'm not a violent man."

"Let's just make sure of that," Kyle said as they reached the pickup. He lowered the tailgate, then used the rifle barrel to motion to Devlin. "Climb in."

Awkwardly, the government man did so. Kyle told him to go all the way to the front and sit with his back against the cab. When Devlin had done that, Kyle closed the tailgate and climbed in over it. He sat down with his legs crossed and the rifle across his lap.

G.W. got behind the wheel and started the pickup toward the ranch. As they rode, Kyle asked, "Why did you follow Finley and Todd out here, Devlin? You fellas work for different agencies, don't you?"

"Yes, I work for the IRS," Devlin replied. "Worked for it, I should say. I strongly suspect that I don't have a job there anymore."

"Why not?" Kyle asked with a frown.

"Because I was ordered to return to Washington, but I'm still here. The service dropped the case against your grandfather."

"Really? Because of that injunction his lawyer got?"

"What? I don't know anything about an injunction. No, my impression was that we were pressured to step aside in favor of the Bureau of Land Management."

Devlin was being a little more talkative than Kyle had expected, so it might be wise to keep the pump primed. Kyle said, "Pressured by who? Who's more powerful than the IRS?"

Devlin let out a little bark of laughter, but he didn't really sound amused.

"You're joking, aren't you, Brannock?" he asked.

"I'm deadly serious," Kyle assured him.

"There are any number of agencies in Washington equally as powerful, or more powerful, than the IRS. It all depends on how closely they're linked to the seat of ultimate power."

"The White House," Kyle said.

"Exactly. The executive branch has expanded and consolidated its power over the past three decades until the system is no longer equal. With one party controlling the White House and having supermajorities in both houses of Congress and a seven-to-two advantage on the Supreme Court . . ."

Devlin shrugged as his voice trailed off.

"What you're saying is that for all practical purposes, the President is now a dictator," Kyle said.

"That's not necessarily a *bad* thing," Devlin argued. "With the obstructionists dealt with, by and large, the government can actually get its work done—"

"You mean it can grow faster and faster and gobble up more and more of everything people used to own and control more and more of people's lives."

Devlin leaned forward, evidently agitated. He said, "But . . . but that's what government is *supposed* to do, isn't it? Control things? Keep people safe, even from themselves?"

Softly, Kyle said, "There was a time when the government in this country kept people free."

Devlin shook his head and said, "Freedom of the sort you're talking about is . . . messy. It's inefficient and unfair. That's why government has to step in and make things right. I mean . . . the government knows best."

The man was really brainwashed, thought Kyle. Devlin actually believed the drivel he was spouting.

"At least . . . I always thought it did," Devlin added, then he sighed.

Now, that was interesting. The fella sounded a little disillusioned, as if he might be starting to see that the fairy tale he had believed in for so long was nothing but an elitist, statist fantasy that couldn't function in the real world unless the government had plenty of jackboots and "re-education camps" to impose its will. True freedom had to be stamped out before the progressives' warped version of freedom could take hold. That was why they had been trying to take away everyone's guns for so long.

The feel of the Winchester in Kyle's hands was reassuring proof that so far, they hadn't quite succeeded.

But as true believers, the Democrats couldn't give up.

And so the pockets of resistance, the holdouts like Texas where freedom—the real deal—still existed, had to be just as vigilant and stubborn. Otherwise, what was once the true America would someday vanish, never to be seen again.

It was a depressing feeling, but Devlin's words offered a ray of hope. Kyle said, "You're starting to see that everything's not exactly the way you thought it was, aren't you?"

"I was told that your grandfather has been systematically cheating on his taxes for years now—"

"That's a lie," Kyle said. "G.W.'s as honest as the day is long, and a damned good citizen. A better citizen than this government today deserves. He'd never cheat on his taxes or anything else, and his lawyer has the documentation to prove it."

"I've seen the results of the audit," Devlin insisted. "If it's accurate . . ."

Again he didn't continue. Kyle said, "You don't believe that audit is right, though. Or at least you're starting to have some doubts."

"I'd have to see it for myself," Devlin insisted with a note of stubbornness coming back into his voice. "I'd have to see the numbers."

"Maybe that can be arranged," Kyle said. Miranda had all those numbers. If she showed them to Devlin, maybe she could convince him the government's case against G.W. was built on a pack of lies. Kyle didn't know what good it would do in the long run to convince the IRS agent of that, but as far as he could see, it wouldn't hurt anything.

"I'd be willing to look at them with an open mind," Devlin said.

"I'll talk to G.W. Now, what do you know about the BLM trying to take over the ranch? How in the world could they have any use for it?"

"I don't know," Devlin replied with a shake of his head. "I honestly don't."

"Why'd you step in to help Finley and Todd get away?"

"I'm not sure about that, either. There's no real love between their agency and mine, of course . . . my former agency, more than likely . . . but when I saw they were in trouble, I just . . . felt the urge to help them. After all, we're all fellow government employees. Or at least we were. . . ."

They rode in silence for a few minutes, then Kyle asked, "What are you gonna do if you find out everything you thought you knew is wrong, Devlin?"

"I . . . I don't know," Devlin replied, and the hollow tone in the government man's voice told Kyle that he found the prospect horrifying.

Chapter 43

Miranda didn't look quite as put together as she usually did. Her hair was a little tousled and she wasn't wearing much makeup. But it had been late when G.W. called her and asked her to come out here to the ranch, and anyway, Kyle thought the natural look made her even prettier, if such a thing was possible.

She had regarded Barton Devlin with considerable suspicion at first. Kyle could tell that she didn't want to show him all the information she had put together to argue G.W.'s case against the IRS.

"I assure you, Ms. Stephens, I can't use any of this against Mr. Brannock," Devlin had told her. "I doubt very seriously that I even have a job with the Internal Revenue Service anymore."

"You don't know that for sure," Miranda had argued. "What if when you do go back to Washington, they still want to pursue the case against G.W.?"

"If the numbers truly do support his position, then there's nothing I or anyone else can do to harm him."

After thinking it over, Miranda had said, "I suppose that's true." She set the cardboard file box she had brought with her on the kitchen table and took the lid off it, then looked at Kyle and G.W. and went on. "This is going to take a while. You two might as well go and do something else while Mr. Devlin and I go through this paperwork."

That was how they came to find themselves in the living room, watching G.W.'s copy of *Ride the High Country*.

"Reckon I've always liked what Joel McCrea says in this movie," G.W. commented. "I just want to enter my house justified, whatever that takes."

"Hard choices, like you said."

"More than likely."

Kyle glanced toward the kitchen door and then asked quietly, "If it comes down to a fight, G.W., do you really plan to start shooting?"

G.W. sighed and said, "I hope it never goes that far, but if it does, this is my land and I know that, no matter what anybody else says. If somebody tries to take it away from me, I'll defend it."

"Honestly, though, you can't start a shooting war against the United States government and expect to win."

"If I've done what I know is right, then that's winnin' as far as I'm concerned."

That was an admirable attitude, thought Kyle, but it might wind up getting his grandfather killed.

And him, too, because whatever G.W. did, Kyle intended to be right beside him. He had spent enough time wallowing in self-pity and not amounting to anything. Even though he hated what G.W. was going through, the adversity had taught him some valuable lessons. He wished he had come back here to the ranch sooner.

"How do you reckon it's goin' in there?" G.W. asked with a nod toward the kitchen.

"I don't have any idea," Kyle said. "If I was awash in a sea of numbers like that, I'd drown for sure."

* * *

"That's it," Miranda said as she showed Devlin the last of the printouts she had brought with her. "I spent a long time putting all this together with the best tax accountant I could find. Some of it is subject to rules interpretation, of course, but even taking those areas into account, it seems obvious to me that G.W. is so scrupulously honest he actually *overpaid* what he owed. The amount may be uncertain, but it's clear to me that the government owes my client money."

Slowly, Devlin shook his head. Miranda could tell that it was a gesture of amazement, though, not disagreement.

"This . . . this just isn't possible," the man muttered. "There must be some other source of income you're not showing. . . ."

"You've studied the case," Miranda said. "Where is it? What is it? You can look around and see how the man lives. Do you honestly think he has millions stashed away in secret bank accounts in Switzerland or the Cayman Islands?"

"He could," Devlin said stubbornly. "This humble lifestyle he lives could just be a front—"

"He's never been out of the country except to go to Mexico a few times. We can prove that."

"These things can be set up via computer."

Miranda laughed and shook her head.

"Not by G.W. Brannock," she said. "And if I were to put him on the stand in court, a jury wouldn't have any trouble seeing that." She tapped a fingernail on the printout lying on the kitchen table in front of Devlin and went on. "Just look at that for a minute and then tell me the government was right to try to take that man's home away from him."

Devlin sighed and said, "I can't." He looked up at her. "But it's all moot. The case has been dropped."

"It could be reopened."

Devlin shook his head.

"I suppose it's possible, but I doubt if that would ever happen. The focus now is on the BLM. Someone must have decided that we weren't going to win the tax case, so now they're trying something else."

"They?"

"Whoever is pulling the strings on this. Whoever Slade Grayson is really working for."

"Who do you think that is?"

"There can only be one answer to that, can't there?" Devlin scraped his chair back and stood up. "This goes as high as it can go."

He turned and walked toward the living room. Miranda hurried after him. Evidently, Devlin wanted to say something to G.W., and she wanted to be there for that, whatever it was.

"Mr. Brannock," Devlin said as he came into the living room. "I have to talk to you."

G.W. turned the TV off and stood up. Kyle got to his feet as well and stood beside his grandfather.

"Whatever you've got to say, spit it out," G.W. said.

"Ms. Stephens has presented your case to me, just like she would in a hearing. This is all unofficial, of course, but if I had been presiding over such a hearing . . . I would have been forced to rule in your favor."

A grin split G.W.'s rugged face.

"What you're tryin' to say is that I'm right and you were wrong," he declared.

Devlin sighed and nodded.

"Yes, that's what it amounts to," he said. "And one more thing . . . I'm sorry."

This time G.W. looked surprised. He said, "Somebody from the government . . . apologizin'? Did I hear right?"

"There's no need to rub my nose in it," Devlin said peevishly. "I was prepared to do my job, that's all. I just wish . . . what I mean to say is . . ." His expression was bleak now. "To be honest, it appears that much of the government's case against you was . . . fabricated."

"You mean somebody lied and made up a bunch of bullcrap just to get their hands on my ranch."

"That's the way it appears." Abruptly, Devlin brought up a trembling hand and rubbed it over his face in a gesture of utter weariness and desolation. "God help me," he muttered, "how many other lives have I ruined based on falsehoods?"

"I can't answer that question," G.W. said. "I reckon that possibility is just somethin' you're gonna have to live with."

Devlin sank into an armchair without being invited. He put both hands over his face now. He didn't cry, but he seemed shaken to the very core of his being.

"There's probably nothing you can do about anything that happened in the past, Mr. Devlin," Miranda told him. "But there *is* something you can do about this situation."

He looked up at her and asked hollowly, "What's that?"

"Help put it right," she said. "Help us save G.W. Brannock's ranch."

Chapter 44

Slade Grayson kept his temper under control, but it wasn't easy.

"You just let them get the drop on you like that?" he demanded.

"What else were we going to do?" Finley asked. He sounded angry, too. "It's not like we're some sort of Old West gunfighters or anything!"

Grayson narrowed his eyes and asked, "Are you mouthing off to me, Warren? Is that really the tone you want to take after your little screwup?"

Finley had the good sense to swallow hard and look a little nervous. He said, "With all due respect, Mr. Grayson, I just don't see what else Woody and I could have done."

Todd grunted and put in, "We're lucky we were able to get away from those guys. Brannock said he was gonna call the sheriff."

Grayson shook his head and waved a hand dismissively.

"I'm not worried about some Texas yokel sheriff," he said as he began to pace back and forth across the motel room's carpet. "But things might have gotten tricky if Brannock got hold of that stuff I gave you." He glanced at the vial sitting on the dresser. "I'm really glad you didn't lose it, Warren."

"So am I," Finley said. "I made sure to hang on to it as tight as I could."

"Well, another thirty-six hours and none of it will matter anyway. That ranch will belong to us."

"To the government, you mean."

"Yes, of course, that's what I meant, Warren," Grayson said. "It's not like any of this is personal."

But it was, of course, and deep down, Grayson knew that. He didn't like being defied, and that old man had made a habit of it. So had Brannock's grandson. Grayson had scores to settle with both of them, and he had a strong hunch that they would both be behind the bars of a federal penitentiary before this was over—at the very least.

There were black sites that might be better suited to enemies of the country like those two. Places where they would never be seen again, so they couldn't stand up to the government—or even worse, inspire other people to do so.

"What I'm really curious about," Grayson went on, saying, "is who it was that helped you get away. Neither of you recognized the guy's voice?"

Finley shook his head, and so did Todd. Finley said, "We never got a look at him. That light was too bright and blinding. And the voice wasn't familiar to me."

"Me, either," Todd added.

"Well, did he sound like a Texan?" Grayson persisted. "Did he have some stupid drawl?"

Finley frowned in thought, then said, "No, not really. He didn't have much of an accent, but if I had to guess, I'd say he came from . . . well, from somewhere around Washington."

"One of us, eh?" Grayson said. He frowned, too. The

only other recent visitor from Washington to Sierra Lobo he could think of was . . .

No, that didn't make any sense. He had sent that IRS weasel scurrying back to his hole.

Anyway, Barton Devlin didn't possess any real courage except what he got from the backing of the most powerful government in the world, and he didn't have that on his side anymore. The Internal Revenue Service was done here. This was Slade Grayson's job now.

No, he didn't have anything to worry about from Devlin.

The government man looked like an animal caught in a trap, Kyle thought as he, G.W., and Miranda loomed over him.

Devlin glanced around at them nervously.

"I don't see what I can do to help you," he said. "I told you, I've probably lost my position. I don't have any influence in Washington anymore. It . . . it's all out of my hands."

Miranda crossed her arms over her breasts and regarded him coolly. She said, "Maybe you know something about what Grayson is planning. You admitted that you talked to him."

"Yes. He sent me packing. At least, he thought he did. I didn't feel like I could leave yet, though . . . and it's probably cost me everything."

"He didn't say anything about his plans?" Kyle asked.

"No, he just said he was taking over. . . ."

Devlin frowned as his words trailed away. G.W. leaned forward with his hands on the table and said, "You look like somethin' just occurred to you, son."

"Something that Grayson said?" Miranda asked.

Devlin licked his lips and shook his head.

"No, this was something I overheard Finley and Todd

talking about tonight right after they got to that waterhole," he said. He looked at Kyle and G.W. "The two of you might not have been close enough to hear it. Finley said something about how Grayson was planning to go ahead and make his move the day after tomorrow . . . ?"

Miranda's eyes widened as she said, "That's not possible. He told G.W. he had sixty days to vacate the ranch."

"You're sure about what you heard?" Kyle asked. He leaned over and put both hands on the table just like G.W. so he could look directly into Devlin's eyes.

The man didn't flinch under their intense scrutiny. He nodded and said, "I'm absolutely certain. Finley said Grayson has something planned for the day after tomorrow. That's Monday. And it sounded final, too."

Kyle straightened and exchanged looks with G.W. and Miranda. If Devlin was right—and they had no reason to doubt him now—their timetable had been cut very short indeed.

"Maybe we can create a distraction that will cause Grayson to postpone whatever he has planned," Miranda suggested. She tapped the documents spread out on the table in front of Devlin and asked him, "Would you be willing to go public with any of this? Would you tell the media that someone in the IRS falsified the audit reports so that they could try to seize G.W.'s ranch?"

Devlin just stared at her for several heartbeats before he said, "Are you completely insane? If I went to the press with that, I'd be ruined."

"I thought you said you already were," Kyle pointed out.

"I'd be *worse* than ruined. I'd be signing my death warrant. I never would have believed that before now. . . ." Devlin shook his head. "But if they'll deliberately get the math wrong and file false reports based on those numbers . . . my God, there's nothing those monsters won't do."

Kyle managed not to laugh at the absurdity of that statement. This was all deadly serious to Devlin.

Besides, he was probably right. The people in power in Washington didn't like to be crossed. Rumors had floated around for years about mysterious deaths that looked like suicide but might be something else, homicides that appeared random or were committed in the course of a robbery, and outright disappearances that were never solved. The trail of bodies that followed around some Democrat politicians and their families was a long and grisly one.

Crushing a petty bureaucrat like Devlin wouldn't mean anything to those people. To them it would be like swatting a gnat or stepping on an ant.

So maybe he was right to worry.

"We heard you say all of that, you know," Kyle told Devlin. "There's nothing stopping us from going to the media."

"I'll deny it," Devlin responded instantly. "I'll say you made the whole thing up, and it'll be your word against mine."

Kyle started to step around the table as anger welled up inside him. Devlin could help them, and Kyle wasn't going to let him get away with refusing to do so, even if he had to get rough.

G.W. put out a hand to stop him, though.

"Hold on," G.W. said. "I know what you're thinkin', Kyle, and I don't blame you for feelin' that way, but we're not gonna sink to their level. If we've got to be as underhanded as those folks from Washington in order to win, it's just not worth it."

"But you heard him," Kyle argued. "Grayson's making his move in less than forty-eight hours. He might have to back off if it came out that the IRS tried to seize your ranch illegally."

G.W. shook his head and said, "You saw Grayson the other day. He didn't strike me as the sort of fella who'd back off for any reason, once his mind is made up."

"He won't," Devlin said. "Everyone in Washington is afraid of him. He has a reputation for being . . . well . . . ruthless."

"Then we need something not even Slade Grayson can overcome," Miranda said. "We need an army."

"Where do you figure we can find one on such short notice?" G.W. asked.

Miranda took out her phone, smiled, and said, "The old-fashioned ways are fine most of the time, G.W., but sometimes modern technology comes in handy, too."

Chapter 45

Special update for those who follow this page: as you know, Texas rancher G. W. (George Washington) Brannock has been under assault by the federal government in recent months. Basing their case on a fraudulent audit, the Internal Revenue Service has attempted to seize Mr. Brannock's ranch near Sierra Lobo, Texas. With their underhanded tactics about to be revealed, the IRS has been forced to drop their case, but Mr. Brannock's ranch is still in jeopardy. The Bureau of Land Management is acting on an unsubstantiated claim of ownership and planning to take possession of Mr. Brannock's property on Monday. Any of you reading this who are close enough to Sierra Lobo to get here by then, G.W. Brannock desperately needs your help to protest this unlawful seizure of private property. This will be a peaceful demonstration to let the government know that as citizens we will stand up for our rights, and for those of our friends and neighbors.

Please come to Sierra Lobo and stand with G.W.

Miranda posted that message on a dozen different Internet forums and social media platforms on Saturday night. By Sunday morning it had gone viral as those who read it shared it. By the time G.W. got home from church, a couple of dozen cars and pickups had shown up at the ranch, each of them carrying several people who had come to protest the BLM's proposed action. Some of them were from conservative groups located in Texas and promised that more of their members would be showing up before the day was over.

Still wearing his suit and tie and carrying his Bible, G.W. looked at the gathering crowd and muttered, "What the Sam Hill is goin' on here?"

From the porch where he stood with Miranda and Devlin, Kyle grinned and said, "Looks like you've got a lot of friends you didn't know about, G.W."

"Looks like some kind o' fandango."

The gathering did have a festive atmosphere about it. People talked and laughed, some of them reminiscing with old friends while others made new friends. Children ran around playing. Several men had brought grills that they set up by the open tailgates of their pickups, and aromatic smells of burgers, hot dogs, and barbecued ribs rose from them. Ice chests full of beer, soft drinks, and bottled water were in the backs of those pickups as well.

A couple of men approached G.W. and shook hands with him. One said, "It's an honor to meet you, Mr. Brannock. There aren't enough folks like you in this country anymore, folks who are willing to stand up for what's right and take a stand against what's wrong. My name is Dave Sparks, and this is Thad Bowman. We're from the Texas Coalition for Smaller Government."

"I'm pleased to meet you fellas," G.W. said. "Did you really show up out here just to help me?"

From the porch, Miranda said, "I told you we could get the word out, G.W."

"Yes, sir," Dave Sparks said. "We've all been aware of the troubles you've been having with the federal government, but until Ms. Stephens posted what she did last night, we didn't realize they were about to launch a sneak attack on you. As soon as some of our members saw the news, we started e-mailing and calling each other, and everybody knew we had to get out here and give you a hand."

G.W. frowned and said, "I don't expect anybody to get in trouble on my account."

"It's not just on your account, Mr. Brannock," Thad Bowman said. "It's for all of us who believe in freedom. If the government can lie, cheat, and steal your land away from you, what's to stop them from coming after everything we own next?"

Dave said, "You can bet your bottom dollar they've got a list of everybody in our organization, too. They're watchin' us, and sooner or later they'll come after us. They already audit members of conservative groups at a much higher rate than they do with members of liberal and progressive groups."

Kyle glanced over at Barton Devlin. The IRS agent—or former IRS agent, as Devlin insisted he was—had a frown on his face, as if he were hearing things he didn't want to hear—but knew to be true anyway.

"Well, I'm mighty happy to have you here," G.W. said. "You folks make yourselves at home. Anything you need, just let me know."

He went inside the house with Kyle, Miranda, and Devlin. As he looked at Kyle and Miranda, he said, "You young folks knew this was gonna happen, didn't you?"

"I didn't know," Kyle said. "This was all Miranda's idea. I hoped she was right and that people would show up."

"I hoped I was right, too," she said. "We need a big group to block Grayson and his flunkies. We'll fill up the gate and the road, and he won't be able to get to you to serve any papers on you."

"That won't stop him in the long run," G.W. said with a frown.

"Probably not, but the longer we can keep him from taking over the ranch, the better. Has the government ever given back *anything* once they get their hands on it?"

"Not that I recall," G.W. admitted. He sniffed the air. "Do I smell chili?"

"Roberto's out in the kitchen cooking up another pot of his special blend," Kyle said with a grin. "He said he's gonna make enough he can share it with all the folks who show up to help you. And if there's any left over, we'll use it for rocket fuel."

"There won't be any left over," G.W. predicted.

He was right. As the afternoon went on, more supporters poured onto the ranch. The tailgaters kept their grills going all day, and Roberto passed out bowl after bowl of chili. The holiday atmosphere grew even stronger. No one knew what the next day might bring, but for today, these people were going to enjoy each other's company.

Late in the afternoon, while Kyle, Miranda, and G.W. were sitting on the front porch watching the festivities, Miranda's phone rang. She looked at it to see who was calling, then immediately sat up straighter in the rocking chair as she answered it.

"Miranda Stephens . . . Yes . . . Yes, thank you so much for returning my call, governor."

That made Kyle and G.W. perk up, too.

"Yes, I'm here with Mr. Brannock now," Miranda went

on. "Of course." She took the phone away from her ear and told Kyle and G.W., "She wants me to put her on speaker." She touched the screen to do that and said, "Go ahead, governor."

"Mr. Brannock? This is Maria Delgado."

G.W. leaned toward the phone and said, "Hello, ma'am. It's an honor to be talkin' to you."

"And I'm glad to be speaking with you," the governor of Texas said. "I hear you've been having some problems there."

"Yes, ma'am. Not with the state of Texas, though, I'm glad to say."

"I've had my own skirmishes with the federal government, as you may know. I wish there was something I could do to help you, but as far as I can tell, my hands are tied on this matter. You have all the moral support I can give you, though. I think you're completely in the right. I plan to issue a statement to the press saying that very thing."

"Well, I appreciate that, governor. Looks like we've got some help from the common folks today. Quite a few of 'em have shown up to let those fellas from Washington know they're not welcome here."

Governor Delgado laughed and said, "I've heard something about that. If it's all right with you, I'd like to send someone there to keep an eye on the situation for me. That way if things change, I'll know about it right away."

"Sure," G.W. said without hesitation. "Send as many as you want. We've got plenty of food and drink."

"Sounds like a party," the governor said.

"Right now it is," G.W. agreed. "But I reckon the feds are liable to put a damper on things when they show up."

Chapter 46

Miranda was disappointed when Governor Delgado said she couldn't do anything to help, but Kyle told her not to worry about that.

"We didn't really expect much, if anything, from the state," he pointed out. "This is between G.W. and the feds, and the state government doesn't have any jurisdiction in the matter."

"I suppose. At least she's supporting us publicly. That can't hurt."

"Can't hurt us," Kyle said with a smile. "It'll make that fella in the White House hate her even more than he already does, if that's possible."

A short time later, the media began to show up. Kyle was surprised that it had taken them this long to get out here. Usually they were all over anything they could twist and distort to make conservatives look bad.

Some of the people who had gathered came to G.W. and suggested throwing the news crews off the ranch and barricading the gate against them.

"You can't trust these people," Dave Sparks warned.

"They'll make up outright lies to discredit anybody who doesn't agree with their radical leftist agenda."

"Shoot, I know that," G.W. said. "But I'm not in the habit of bein' inhospitable, even to folks who don't like me. Besides, no matter what sort of garbage they spew, people who can think for themselves will just consider the source and move on."

"I hope you're right," Dave said as he shook his head. "They'll do their best to turn public opinion against you, though."

"The only ones who believe the mainstream media are the ones who would never support our cause anyway," Kyle said. "They've been brainwashed by decades of public education and government assistance."

"Suckin' off the government tit, you mean," G.W. said, after glancing around to make sure Miranda wasn't within range of his voice. Kyle noticed that and chuckled. Some things would never change.

Several of the TV reporters approached the porch wanting to ask G.W. questions. Kyle shook his head and said, "My grandfather doesn't have any comment at this time."

"But aren't you afraid that he's inciting a riot with his behavior?" asked a well-groomed female reporter who didn't appear to care for the haze of dust that hung in the air from so many people and vehicles moving around. She waved some of it away from her face.

"What behavior?" Kyle shot back. "He's sitting in a rocking chair and drinking iced tea. How can anybody get inciting a riot out of that?"

The reporter waved an expensively manicured hand and said, "But all these people—"

"Are about as well-behaved a group this size that you'll ever see. They're having a good time and cleaning up after themselves. Compare that to any leftist protest you can find and see which bunch knows how to act like civilized human beings."

The woman glared at him, but didn't press her argument. As she stalked off, Kyle fully expected that she would report what he'd said in some slanted, biased way that would make him look like a lunatic. As long as the media was in the hip pocket of the Democrats, lying was all they had. They couldn't afford to tell the truth.

By the time the sun went down, at least three hundred people had shown up at the ranch. Kyle stopped trying to count them. There were people everywhere he looked, though, and he could tell that G.W. was touched by the outpouring of support.

Dave Sparks and Thad Bowman, who were loosely in charge of the group, came to the house as night was falling and told Kyle, G.W., and Miranda that they had posted guards at the gate to make sure no one from the federal government tried to sneak onto the ranch.

"That's fine," G.W. told them, "but I don't want any shootin' out there."

"We're not planning on any," Dave said, "but a lot of our people are armed and we're going to defend ourselves if we're attacked."

Kyle could tell that Miranda was worried about that very thing. A shoot-out would give the feds the excuse they might be looking for, a reason to come down on the ranch with all their armed might.

"Tell you what," he said, "I'll go out there and stand guard, too. We'll keep the lid on things, G.W."

"I'm coming, too," Miranda said. "It won't hurt to have legal representation on hand."

G.W. looked like he was going to argue, but then he shrugged and said, "Reckon I trust the two of you young folks as much as I trust anybody in the world. Just be careful, all right?"

"We will be," Kyle promised.

"Take the pickup," G.W. said as he tossed the keys to Kyle, who plucked them deftly from the air.

The pickup had a lever-action Winchester on the rack behind the seat in the back window. Miranda gave it a wary look as Kyle held the passenger door open for her and she climbed into the vehicle.

"I assume that's loaded?" she said.

"G.W. always says that an unloaded gun isn't good for anything but a club. It's liable to take more than a club to stop Grayson."

"That's why we have a crowd of witnesses on hand."

"And we hope that'll be enough. I'll do my best to make sure that's the way it works out."

Miranda still looked worried in the light from the dashboard, Kyle thought as he drove toward the distant gate. He didn't blame her.

By now, with the news coverage the informal protest was getting, Slade Grayson had to know what was going on out here. Would that cause the government man to move up his timetable?

Kyle didn't know, but he wasn't going to bet against it.

"Yes, sir," Grayson said into his phone. "I understand. Don't worry about a thing, sir. I have it all under control."

As Grayson broke the connection, Todd said, "Was that . . . you know?"

"Yes, that was him," Grayson confirmed. "He's been watching the news coverage of what's going on at Brannock's ranch."

Finley said, "This is turning into a complete disaster."

Grayson made a scoffing sound and said, "What the hell makes you think that? Haven't you been paying attention, Finley?"

He picked up the remote control and turned on the motel room TV, which was already tuned to one of the cable news networks known to be sympathetic to whatever the administration wanted to do.

An attractive female reporter whose hair looked a little the worse for wear because of dust and wind was looking into the camera in footage obviously shot earlier because the sun was still up.

"In a situation that seems rife with the potential for domestic terrorism, a group of dangerous right-wing extremists have gathered here in Texas in support of rancher G.W. Brannock's lawless defiance of the federal government. These heavily armed radicals have sworn to prevent agents of the Bureau of Land Management from entering property that Brannock has claimed as his own, despite the fact that it has always belonged to the federal government. For more than a century, Brannock's ancestors have been illegally squatting on this land."

Finley said, "But no one even knew that until recently. There's never been any question until now about who owns that land."

Grayson laughed and said, "You think the people watching this know any of that, or would care if they did? For some of them, the government can do no wrong if it's in the hands of the Democrats, and the only thing the rest give a damn about is getting their check every month. They'll believe whatever they're told." His voice hardened. "And they're right to do so, aren't they? I mean, our elected leaders wouldn't *lie* to us, would they?"

"Of course not," Finley said, his voice betraying the

nervousness he felt. "I didn't mean that, Mr. Grayson. You know I didn't."

Grayson shrugged. Keeping the others toeing the party line didn't really mean anything to him except that it made them more useful that way. A scared bureaucrat was an obedient bureaucrat.

"What did *he* want?" Finley went on.

"He was asking if I thought we should go ahead and make our move tonight," Grayson explained.

"But you think that would be a mistake."

"Of course, I do. Let those right-wing crazies sit out there and stew in their own juices overnight. We'll go in tomorrow morning, just like we planned, in broad daylight so the whole world can see what happens."

Todd said, "It looked on TV like there are hundreds of them. What if they won't let us in?"

"They will if they know what's good for them," Grayson snapped.

But some of that was bravado, and he knew it. But the thing was, it didn't really matter. When the time came, Brannock and his friends would back down, or they wouldn't.

Either way, in the long run Grayson and the people he worked for would win.

It was just that one way, a lot more people probably would die.

And that didn't matter, either. . . .

Chapter 47

There were other ways onto the ranch besides the main gate where the road to the house turned off from the highway. The area up in the mountains wasn't even fenced. Kyle thought it was unlikely the government agents would try to come in that way, but G.W. had sent some of the hands up there on horseback to patrol the area anyway.

Kyle's instincts told him that Slade Grayson would want the inevitable confrontation to take place at the gate, though. That would provide the maximum amount of drama and also would be easier for the news media to cover.

Several cameramen were already out here tonight, just waiting like the rest of them. Kyle was confident that if anything happened, they would call the reporters in the vans parked at the ranch headquarters, who would then race out to the gate to cover the event as if they had been there all along.

He and Miranda sat in the back of G.W.'s pickup on some folded blankets that Kyle had thrown in for this purpose. There was another blanket that they could spread over them if it got too chilly before morning, which was possible at this elevation and in this dry climate. So far, though, he was quite comfortable.

A dozen cars and pickups were parked along the road and near the fence. Men sat in the cars or stretched out in the backs of the pickups to doze as they waited for trouble to arrive.

When Kyle and Miranda had gotten there, Kyle had gone around and talked to all the men, making sure they understood that G.W. didn't want any shooting unless it absolutely couldn't be avoided.

He had also checked to be certain that nobody had any kids out here at the gate. All the children were safe back at the ranch headquarters.

As he and Miranda sat in the back of the pickup, they talked quietly about G.W.'s troubles at first, but after everything they had been through the past week, it didn't take long to exhaust that subject.

Then Kyle said, "You know, I don't know much about you, Miranda. You're G.W.'s lawyer, and I can tell from the way you talk that you're not from around here, but that's about it."

"You can tell that, can you?" she asked.

"Well, yeah. I'm pretty sure you're not a Yankee, anyway. But I don't know where in the South you're from."

"Florida," she said. "I grew up in the Panhandle there, in a little fishing and tourist town on the Gulf. What else can you figure out about me?"

Kyle laughed and said, "I never claimed to be a detective. But I'm pretty sure you're not married."

"Oh? What makes you think that?"

He felt a moment of alarm. If she had a husband, he didn't need to be feeling about her the way he did.

"You don't wear a wedding ring," he said.

"Some women don't."

"That's true, I guess. But you've never mentioned having a husband. Seems like as much as we've talked, you would have."

"Maybe the subject just never came up."

"Well . . . uh . . ."

As if she took pity on him, she laughed and said, "I'm just messing with you, Kyle. I'm not married. Never have been. In fact, me *not* being married is why I'm in Texas right now."

"How's that?" he asked.

"I was engaged, back there in Florida. High school romance that lasted all the way through college and law school. But he met somebody else. Maybe he'd gotten tired of me because we were together for so long, or maybe he just thought the two of them were a better match. Anyway, he backed out a month before the wedding."

"Or maybe he was just a damned fool," Kyle said with some heat in his voice. "That's what it sounds like to me."

"Maybe so. I can't really argue with that. But after that happened, I didn't feel like staying around there where there were so many memories of all our time together. So I packed up and left. Headed west until I got to Sierra Lobo."

"What made you stop there?"

She looked over at him and said, "I'm starting to think it was fate."

Their heads were close together, and her blond hair shone silvery in the moonlight. Kyle didn't think about what he was doing. He just let his instincts take over, and his mouth found hers as he slid an arm around her shoulders and pulled her closer.

His heart hammered in his chest as he kissed her, and he held her close enough that he could feel hers beating, too. Her lips tasted incredible. He thought that he could sit here like this with her all night, until the sun rose in the morning.

But something made him pull back, and he said quietly, "Look, Miranda, I'm sorry. You deserve to be with somebody better than me—"

"Oh, shut up," she said as she slipped her hand up to the back of his neck. She held him there as she pressed her mouth to his again. She pulled away just enough to whisper, "I'm right where I want to be."

So was Kyle, and they stayed there in each other's arms until she dozed off with her head resting on his shoulder and he pulled the extra blanket over her so she wouldn't get cold.

They were still there like that in the morning when trouble arrived with the dawn.

Chapter 48

Shouts from the men standing along the fence, watching the highway where it came from town, roused Kyle from sleep.

His left arm was numb from the weight of Miranda leaning against it as she slept. He eased himself out from under her as gently as he could, but the movement was still enough to wake her as well.

"What is it?" she asked as she sat up and pushed the hair back out of her face.

"Don't know," Kyle said. He flexed his arm a couple of times to get some feeling back into it, then stood up, put a hand on the side of the pickup bed, and vaulted over it to the ground. He went to the tailgate and lowered it so Miranda could climb out.

Men were gathering along the fence, and several of them were holding rifles or shotguns. That worried Kyle, but he didn't see what he could do about it other than warn them not to overreact. He hurried along the fence doing so, then asked one of them, "What's going on?"

"Headlights coming fast from the direction of town," the man replied. Kyle recognized him as one of the members of the Texas Coalition for Smaller Government. "Cars have been going by every now and then all night without stopping, but this one seems different."

Kyle agreed. The sun hadn't quite peeked over the eastern horizon, so it was still dark enough for the approaching headlights to be seen. Whoever was driving was in a hurry.

Miranda came up beside Kyle. He looked over at her, took the pickup keys from his pocket, and pressed them into her hand.

"Go back to the house and get G.W.," he told her.

"You're just trying to get me out of the way because you think it might be dangerous," she objected. "I can call G.W. and tell him to get out here."

"We've got his pickup, remember?"

"There are plenty of other vehicles there. He can get a ride with somebody."

"Just go, all right?"

She looked at him with narrowed, angry eyes and said, "All right, but later we're going to have a talk about this. I don't like being shunted aside."

"Fine," he said. "We'll talk about it later."

She glared at him for a second longer, then turned and walked quickly toward the pickup.

Kyle relaxed a little when she was on her way back to the ranch house . . . but not much.

Trouble was still coming fast.

Of course, maybe it was just somebody in a hurry to be somewhere else, he thought. They would all feel a little foolish if the vehicle streaked on past and disappeared into the new morning without ever slowing down.

That wasn't what happened. Brakes squealed as the car came closer to the gate. Kyle recognized the old rattletrap as its driver slowed down to turn off the highway.

He knew who was at the wheel, too. It was easy to

recognize Stella Lopez as she brought the old car to a stop, threw the door open, and leaped out. In cut-off jean shorts and a tank top, she was spectacular.

"Let me in," she told the men at the gate, most of whom had momentarily forgotten about politics and oppressive governments at the breathtaking sight of Stella dressed like that.

They remembered why they were here as she went on, saying, "Those government guys, they're on the way."

"Open the gate," Kyle told the men. While they were unfastening the chain one of them had looped around the gate and one of the posts, he asked Stella, "How do you know about that?"

"That's all everybody in town is talking about," she said. "I was working the early shift at the store, and quite a few people came in to get coffee. They said they were gonna come out here and back up your grandfather. But then one of the guys from the BLM—the big, dumb-looking one— he came in, too, and bought a dozen coffees to take back over to the motel with him. He wouldn't be doing that unless they were getting ready to come out here, would he?"

"Not likely," Kyle admitted. "Did you just run off and leave the store unattended?"

"No, I called Mr. Charlton and told him what was going on. He told me to lock up and let you know. So that's what I did. I got here as fast as I could. Some of the people from town, they'll probably be along, too, but they may not beat the government men out here."

"More headlights coming!" one of the men along the fence called excitedly.

"Get your car inside so we can lock up again," Kyle told Stella. He touched her arm to stop her as she started to turn away. "And thanks for coming to warn us."

"That's okay," she said with a dazzling smile. "I know

there's nothing between us anymore. You're in love with that lawyer lady."

"Hey—"

"Oh, don't bother arguing. Everybody in Sierra Lobo knows about it. They've seen the way you look at her. But I still think you're a good guy, and I *know* G.W. is. We're not gonna let the government steal his land."

"No, we're not," Kyle agreed.

Stella drove onto the ranch, and the men swung the gate closed behind her and fastened the lock on the chain again. If any more of the townspeople showed up in time, they could come in, too. Otherwise the gate was staying locked.

The upper edge of the sun appeared, an orange hemisphere that spilled its garish light across the landscape. It was bright enough that the headlights of the approaching vehicles were washed out almost to the point of disappearing, but the SUVs themselves were visible in the growing light.

There were three of them, Kyle noted. Grayson had called in some reinforcements. Even so, there couldn't be enough men in the SUVs to overpower the fifty or so defenders gathered at the gate. Stella had said Woodrow Todd bought a dozen cups of coffee. That was a reasonable number of men to be in the vehicles.

"Keep those guns pointed at the ground," Kyle called to the men. "We're here to talk, if they'll listen to reason."

"They're from the government," one of the men said scornfully. "Do you really think they're gonna be reasonable?"

"We can hope," Kyle said under his breath. He turned to Stella, who had gotten out of her car again, and told her, "Go on up to the ranch house."

She gave a defiant toss of her head that threw her long black hair back.

"And miss all the excitement? No way!"

"Then at least stay back behind the cars and trucks. Please. I don't want you getting shot full of holes."

"You still got some feelings for me, don't you? For old time's sake?"

"Of course, I do," Kyle said. "Now go."

Stella moved behind some of the parked vehicles. Kyle didn't really expect her to stay there if trouble broke out, but he hoped she would.

The men crowded up to the gate and along the fence were visibly tense as the SUVs slowed and then stopped along the side of the highway. The vehicles were black and their windows were tinted, so Kyle couldn't see into them.

For a long moment, nothing happened. It was like the SUVs didn't have anybody in them, Kyle thought crazily. Like they were sentient beings that had come out here on their own.

Then the front passenger door of the first one opened, and Slade Grayson stepped out, complete with sunglasses, expensive suit, arrogant demeanor, and everything else about him that was so infuriating.

Chapter 49

Grayson stood there next to the SUV, blatantly posing for the news cameras shooting from the other side of the fence.

Kyle heard engines and looked over his shoulder to see several vehicles headed his way from the ranch headquarters. Some of them were news vans, but he spotted G.W.'s pickup, too. He hoped that Miranda had stayed behind at the ranch house, but then he saw her in the passenger seat as G.W. drove. The fact that she had returned to the site of confrontation with the government surprised him not one little bit.

Grayson took off his sunglasses and swaggered forward, coming straight toward the gate. He stopped about fifteen feet away and looked at Kyle over the bars of iron pipe.

The government man's face was smooth and unperturbed. It didn't seem to bother him that fifty obviously angry men, some of them armed, stood on the other side of the fence. He said to Kyle, "You know why we're here, Brannock. Open up."

Behind Grayson, the other doors on the SUVs had

opened, and men climbed out. Kyle saw Finley and Todd, both of whom looked like they would have rather been somewhere else. The other men all looked similar to Grayson in that they wore suits and sunglasses. Hired muscle here to intimidate the ranch's defenders, thought Kyle.

"This is private property, Grayson," Kyle said. "If you set foot on it, you'll be trespassing."

Grayson shook his head and said, "We both know better than that. I have an emergency injunction giving possession of this ranch to the Bureau of Land Management. This is now federal property."

The crowd along the fence opened to let G.W. through. He stepped up beside Kyle and said, "That's a damned lie, mister, and you know it. This is Brannock range and has been for more than a century."

Kyle glanced around and saw Miranda hanging back a little. Barton Devlin was with her, looking upset but very interested in what was going on.

Grayson spotted the former IRS agent, too. He exclaimed, "Devlin! Is that really you? You're supposed to be back in Washington." A wolfish smile spread across his face. "Damn, Barton, you haven't gone over to the enemy, have you? I didn't think you had enough guts to do that."

Devlin looked extremely nervous as he glanced toward the news crews. Kyle knew he had wanted to stay out of this, but evidently something was compelling him to speak up despite his fear.

Maybe years of working for the government hadn't completely eroded his sense of right and wrong.

"American citizens are *not* our enemies, Grayson," Devlin said.

"They are if they oppose the will of the government," Grayson snapped. "They're worse than that. They're traitors."

"Damn you," G.W. said. "You can't call me that."

"I just did, old man," Grayson replied with a sneer. "Now, are you gonna unfasten that chain, or do I have my men get the bolt cutters?"

All along the fence, the defenders stiffened at that threat. Rifle and shotgun barrels came up a little higher.

"Blast it, this is wrong!" Devlin said in the tense silence. "I know the IRS case against this man was false, and I'm starting to think the BLM claim may be as well!"

"You're a damned fool," Grayson told him. "The press is here, and you've just gone on record as supporting these . . . these domestic terrorists. You know you just threw away your career, don't you, Devlin?"

"Maybe it wasn't a career worth having."

Grayson shook his head in dismissal, as if Devlin wasn't worth bothering with. He turned back to G.W. and Kyle and said, "What's it gonna be? Do you open up, or do we arrest you for being in violation of federal law?"

Before either of the Brannocks could respond, a new sound intruded on the morning air. The *whup-whup-whup* made everyone turn to look as it steadily grew louder.

The helicopter seemed to fly out of the sun. It swooped over the vehicles and people on both sides of the fence, made a circle, and then began to descend about a hundred yards inside the ranch. The downdraft from its rotors kicked up a huge cloud of dust.

"What the hell?" G.W. muttered.

The chopper settled to the ground, barely visible because of the dust that surrounded it. But as that cloud began to settle, everyone saw a man climb out of the passenger seat and start toward them. He was tall and lean, dressed in camo fatigues, and also wore sunglasses. His short, curly fair hair was starting to turn gray, and his close-cropped beard was the same shade.

Several of the ranch's defenders swung up rifles and shotguns to cover him. He never broke stride as he made a curt gesture and barked in an unmistakable tone of command, "Put those guns down, boys. I'm just here to observe."

G.W. stepped forward to meet the newcomer. He said, "Who in blazes are you, mister?"

The man stopped to meet G.W.'s level stare and said, "Colonel Thomas Atkinson, retired, sir." He put out his right hand. "It's an honor and a pleasure to meet you, Mr. Brannock. Governor Delgado sent me."

Something was vaguely familiar about Atkinson's name, thought Kyle, but he couldn't place it. Clearly, though, the man wasn't from the federal government, and that was a mark in his favor.

G.W.'s instincts must have told him him that Atkinson was all right, because he didn't hesitate in gripping the newcomer's hand. He said, "If that fine lady sent you, then you're welcome on my ranch, colonel."

From the other side of the fence, Grayson shouted, "This isn't your ranch, damn it! It belongs to the federal government, old man!"

Kyle smiled. Grayson didn't like it that the cameras had turned away from him and were pointing toward the impressive figure of Colonel Atkinson now.

Grayson went on. "The state of Texas doesn't have any jurisdiction here, and the governor knows it!"

"Didn't say that it does," Atkinson drawled. He took a stub of a cigar from his shirt pocket, stuck it in the corner of his mouth, and clamped his teeth on it, leaving it unlit. "Like I said, I'm just here to observe."

Grayson continued to fume. He said, "I want this gate open *right now!"*

Miranda stepped up to it. Kyle didn't like her getting in the middle of the confrontation, but he knew there was nothing he could do about it.

"I'm Mr. Brannock's legal counsel, Mr. Grayson," she said, "and if you have an injunction to serve, I have a right to see it."

Grayson's lip curled. He said, "All right, blondie." He half-turned and snapped his fingers. Warren Finley hurried forward, carrying a document. Grayson took it from Finley and extended it through the bars to Miranda. "Go ahead and look at it. You'll see that it's signed by a federal judge."

Miranda took the injunction, then reached inside the lightweight jacket she wore and brought out a folded paper.

"And I have here a temporary restraining order signed by a judge blocking any attempt by the federal government to take possession of my client's lawful property."

Grayson's eyes widened. Kyle was shocked by this development, too. Obviously, Miranda had been holding this trump card in reserve.

"Let me see that," Grayson demanded.

"Of course," Miranda said. She passed the document through the bars of the gate.

Grayson studied the paper for a couple of seconds, then snapped a finger against it and exclaimed, "This is signed by a damned justice of the peace!"

"A legally elected judicial official," Miranda said.

"Federal law supersedes state and local law!"

"I suppose we'll have to let the courts work that out, won't we? In the meantime, until the case is heard and ruled on, you're not welcome on this property, and you have no right to force your way onto it. If you do, you'll be in violation of state statutes and county ordinances, and as an attorney and officer of the court, I'll place *you* under a citizen's arrest."

As Grayson glared at her, clearly flabbergasted, Kyle had never liked and admired Miranda more.

Maybe Stella was right. Maybe he did love Miranda.

He could try to figure that out later. Right now there was a little matter of keeping Grayson from taking over the ranch. . . .

Shaking with rage at the way he was being defied, Grayson crumpled the paper he held and flung it to the ground at his feet. Kyle was a little surprised he didn't stomp on it like a kid throwing a tantrum.

Miranda slid the federal injunction back through the gate and dropped it. It floated gently down to the ground.

"Open the gate," Grayson said.

"No," G.W. said. "This is my land."

Grayson looked at the grim-faced defenders lined up along the fence and the cars and pickup blocking the dirt road. He rubbed a hand over his face, then put on his sunglasses and squared his shoulders.

"One more chance," he said coldly. "Open up and relinquish this property, or I'll come back with armed federal agents."

"This is my land," G.W. said again. It was a simple, yet eloquent, statement.

"All right. You've made your choice. I gave you a chance to comply, Brannock. When I come back, you'll either open the gate . . . or there'll be a bloodbath here. And it'll be on your head, old man."

With that, he turned, stalked toward the SUVs, and waved his men back into the vehicles. Finley and Todd looked relieved. The other agents were as expressionless as the automatons they resembled.

Once everyone was back in the SUVs, they turned around and started toward Sierra Lobo. The defenders along the fence seemed to all let out pent-up breaths.

But this wasn't over, thought Kyle.

Unfortunately, it might be just beginning.

Chapter 50

"That was a gutsy move, Ms. Stephens," Colonel Atkinson said to Miranda. "That fed could have arrested you."

"He could have tried," Miranda said.

Kyle had to grin at that. They were back at G.W.'s house, sitting around the table in the kitchen eating a belated breakfast and drinking coffee. Miranda and Stella were at opposite ends of the table, keeping a discreet distance from each other but otherwise being cordial.

"I remember how come I've heard of you," Kyle said to the colonel. "You were involved in that prison riot a while back. What was the place called? Hell's Gate?"

"That's right, but it wasn't exactly a riot," Atkinson said. "It was a terrorist attack that the federal government did nothing to deal with. They left it up to state forces to take care of the problem." Atkinson sipped his coffee and added, "In fact, there's pretty good evidence that some members of the federal government helped instigate the whole thing."

"Good Lord!" Barton Devlin exclaimed. "You can't be serious. The federal government would . . . would never cooperate with Islamic terrorists! That's insane!"

Quietly, Atkinson said, "Yes, it would be insane for our own government to do that . . . unless the people running the country at the highest levels actually hate America and everything it stands for and would like to destroy it."

As Devlin sputtered, the colonel added, "You can't elect people who promise to transform America and then be surprised when they try to do it. We've been dealing with that for a couple of decades now . . . and God help us, they're winning more than they're losing."

"Not here," G.W. snapped. "Not in Texas."

"Not yet," Atkinson acknowledged. "And they'll never succeed in turning Texas into the sort of socialist state they want without spilling a lot of blood on both sides." He smiled. "Who knows? Maybe we'll beat 'em."

An air of gloom settled over the table momentarily. Devlin broke it by asking, "Is all this you're saying really true, Colonel Atkinson?"

"About the federal government being riddled with people whose real goal is to bring the country to its knees? I believe it is, Mr. Devlin. I hate to say it, but with all my heart, I believe it. I've seen too much evidence proving it."

Devlin took a deep breath and said, "Then someone has to stop them. We have to stop them. We have to fight them."

G.W. grinned and reached over to slap the former IRS agent on the back.

"Never thought I'd say this to somebody who used to be in your line of work, Bart, but I like the way you think."

"Well, I . . . I believe maybe I actually *am* thinking for the first time in ages. Maybe ever."

"So what do we do now?" Kyle asked. "You know Grayson's not going to back down."

G.W. shrugged and said, "There's not much we can do

except keep on with what we've been doin'. I'm not lettin'
that varmint on my ranch."

"He's going to bring back armed agents," Miranda said
worriedly.

"They'll be well-armed, too," Atkinson said. "The
federal agencies and bureaus have been militarizing themselves for years now, stockpiling weapons and ammunition
and assault vehicles. They're almost as prepared to go to
war as the real military." He paused. "The big difference is
that they've been getting ready to go to war against American citizens, instead of foreign enemies. This may be the
first real test of that."

"So you're saying people are going to be hurt or killed,"
Miranda said.

Atkinson said, "I'm sure someone as well-educated as
you are has to have run across the quote about the tree of
liberty and the blood of patriots, Ms. Stephens."

That made everyone around the table fall silent again.
While they were sitting there, one of the men who had
showed up to back G.W. came into the kitchen and said,
"More folks from town are out there, Mr. Brannock."

G.W. scraped his chair back.

"Reckon I'd better go talk to 'em."

Kyle got up, too, and said, "I'll come with you."

"Why don't we all go?" Atkinson suggested.

G.W. led the way onto the front porch. A group of people
stood in front of the house, including Chief of Police Ernie
Rodriguez and several of his officers.

"Ernie, what are you doing here?" G.W. asked. "What
if there's a crime wave in Sierra Lobo?"

Ernie grinned and said, "The only real crime in these
parts right now is what's happening out here. Grand lar-
ceny, if you ask me. That's what it'll be if the government
succeeds in stealing your ranch, G.W."

"I agree with you about that, but you've got a duty to the folks in town you work for. You don't have any legal jurisdiction out here, either. You'll just get yourself in trouble if you take on the feds."

"How about Bill Jacobs?" Ernie asked. "I talked to him on the phone earlier. He has jurisdiction in the county, and he's thinking about coming out and making a stand with you."

"I'd rather he didn't. In fact," G.W. said, "I sort of wish everybody would just go home!"

Most of the people within earshot frowned, including Kyle. He said, "I don't think you really mean that, G.W."

"Yeah, I do," G.W. insisted, "but probably not for the reason you're thinkin'. I'm touched by the way so many folks want to take my side in this. I appreciate it, I really do. But after listenin' to the things the colonel had to say, I'm startin' to worry that too many innocent people are gonna be hurt."

"You're afraid there's going to be a bloodbath, like Grayson threatened."

G.W. grimaced and said, "The more I talk to that man, the less I'd put past him. There's just no tellin' what he might do or who he might hurt in order to get his way."

Atkinson said, "I think you're right about that, Mr. Brannock, but we're all in agreement that Grayson and the federal government have to be stopped. As a matter of fact, Governor Delgado didn't mention this when she was talking to you yesterday, but she got her hands on a copy of that so-called Spanish land grant, and she's got every expert who works in the state archives going over it, along with some pretty high-powered professors from the university. If it's a phony, they'll be able to prove it."

"That's exactly what I wanted to do," Miranda said.

Atkinson nodded and said, "Maria got the idea from the

message you left for her, Ms. Stephens. No offense, but she's got a little more clout when it comes to things like this, so she went ahead."

"No offense taken," Miranda assured him. "The sooner and the more definitively we prove that the government is lying about the land grant, the better."

G.W. said, "Could be Grayson's bosses have gotten wind of what the governor's doin', and they're afraid the whole thing's about to be exposed and blow up in their faces. That's why they've hurried him up. They figure that once they've gotten me out of here, they won't ever have to give up the ranch, no matter what comes out about the whole land grant thing." He ran a thumbnail along his jawline and frowned. "But that still leaves one mighty troublin' question. . . ."

"Why do they want this ranch so bad in the first place?" Kyle said.

None of the others had an answer.

Chapter 51

Kyle really expected Slade Grayson to return with armed agents and try once again to take possession of the ranch that day, but by sundown there had been no sign of the man or any of his Bureau of Land Management cohorts.

The cameramen and technicians from the news crews remained on the ranch with their vans and satellite uplinks, but the on-camera talent all went back to Sierra Lobo for the night. The motel rooms there were nothing fancy, but they beat sleeping in a van.

Ernie Rodriguez and his police officers returned to Sierra Lobo as well, once G.W. persuaded them that they might be needed more back in town. Many of the other locals had returned home, too, as had some of the people who had come in from nearby towns.

Everyone promised to be back the next morning, but Kyle suspected that some of them wouldn't be. It was easy for people to get all worked up about something they regarded as injustice, but no matter how sincere they were in their feelings, it was difficult to maintain that sort of fervor.

Stella Lopez was one of the townspeople who remained on the ranch. Kyle worried that her presence might cause some friction with Miranda, but on the contrary, the two women seemed to warm up to each other slightly as the day went on. They had something in common, after all— Kyle.

And when he saw them with their heads together, talking quietly, that *really* worried him. If she wanted to, Stella could probably tell Miranda some things that would lower her opinion of him.

Whatever had been between him and Stella was years in the past, though, Kyle told himself. He'd been a different person then. Surely Miranda would be able to see that and understand that he had changed.

What he really wished, more than anything else, was that both Miranda and Stella would go back to town where they would be safe. Even though Grayson seemed to be taking his time about returning, he would be back sooner or later, and he would bring more trouble with him than ever before. Kyle was certain of that.

In fact, he wished all the men who had brought their wives and children with them would leave. He understood what G.W. had been talking about. No matter how much G.W. loved the ranch, he didn't want the blood of innocents on his hands.

Kyle loved the place, too, now more than ever after spending this time here with G.W., and he felt the same way. He would die to defend it, but he wasn't sure anyone else should.

During the afternoon, Colonel Thomas Atkinson had checked in with Governor Delgado by phone, then told the others that she didn't have any news to report on the effort to uncover the truth about the land grant.

"She wants me to fly back to Austin to brief her in person on the situation here, though," he'd told the others.

"There's nothing else she can do to help us, is there?" Miranda asked.

"Oh, you never know. Maria's a clever lady. No telling what she might come up with."

A short time after that, Atkinson had chomped down on a cigar, climbed back into the helicopter, and nodded to the pilot to crank up the whirlybird. With the usual racket and cloud of dust, the helicopter rose into the air and flew off to the east, rapidly disappearing into the blue sky.

Now night had settled down over the West Texas landscape, bringing with it a deceptive peace and quiet that Kyle knew could be shattered at any time, with no warning.

He was standing on the front porch, gazing out at the darkness, when he heard a soft step behind him. He looked over his shoulder to see Miranda standing there. The two of them were alone on the porch, so when she moved closer to him, Kyle put his arms around her and kissed her again. She responded by putting her arms around his neck.

After a moment, he drew back a little and said, "I wish all this trouble would go away so you and I could spend a lot more time getting to know each other."

"And doing this," Miranda said.

"Definitely and doing this," he agreed with a grin.

"Well," she said, "it'll be over sooner or later, and with any luck we won't both be in prison or dead."

Kyle's forehead creased. He said, "If you were trying to lighten the mood, I'd say you failed."

"Yeah, I guess so." She sighed. "But we have to be realistic. This could end badly. For G.W., for you and me . . . for everybody."

"That's true. But I guess there have never been any guarantees in life, have there? And people still . . . fall in love anyway."

"Yes," Miranda whispered. "In the worst possible circumstances . . . people still fall in love."

He bent his head down and kissed her again, and they were both so caught up in each other that neither of them noticed the shadowy form moving from the corner of the house toward the road leading to the gate.

The crowd at the fence had remained fairly large most of the day, but as evening approached more of the defenders had gone back to the ranch headquarters to be with their families. Half a dozen men remained on guard at the gate, all of them armed. If anyone approached, they would alert the others at the ranch house by phone.

G.W. Brannock walked warily as he approached the gate. He didn't want to startle any of the sentries. They weren't professionals; there was no telling what they might do if they got spooked. So when he was close enough, Brannock called, "Howdy, boys! It's just me."

A man Brannock recognized as Thad Bowman came up to him and asked, "Is anything wrong, sir? I mean, beyond the obvious?"

"Nope, I just wanted to come out here and spend a little time with you fellas. You've all gone out of your way to give me a hand, and I appreciate it."

"You're welcome, Mr. Brannock," another man said as he approached. "It's an honor for us to help you."

A third man came up and said, "It's not often everyday folks like us get to take a stand and do something as important as this. I sort of feel like . . . well, like the freedom of the whole country might be at stake here."

"That's right," Bowman said. "If the government can get away with stealing your ranch from you, what will they try next? Who will they come after and try to ruin?"

"Somebody who's not a Democrat, you can bet on that!" another man responded with a laugh. The rest of them joined in. Even Brannock chuckled.

He said, "You know, when I was a young man, I never put much stock in which political party somebody belonged to. The way I figured, there were good and bad folks and good and bad ideas on both sides. That's the way it ought to be. Maybe that's the way it really was back then, or maybe I just didn't know any better. But over the past forty or fifty years, it's sure changed. There might still be a few good people over there on the other side, but they're fightin' for bad ideas. Evil ideas that are gonna wind up ruinin' this country. I don't care how misguided you are, when you set out to destroy America, you've got to be stopped."

"Amen," several of the men said.

Brannock grinned and said, "Well, I didn't mean to go to preachin'. It's liable to be pretty chilly out here by mornin'. Might be a good idea to build a little fire. Plenty of mesquite around to use for firewood."

It wasn't long before the men had a small but cheerful blaze going at the side of the road. As they hunkered around it, including Brannock, one of the men said, "You know, this is sort of like the old days, like the night before a battle like Gettysburg or Bull Run, and we're sitting here with General Lee himself."

Brannock laughed and said, "Lord, don't go comparin' me to Robert E. Lee. I never commanded an army in my life, or much of anything else. Never had any ambition to. But I've studied enough history to know that if there's a battle, I sure hope it turns out more like Bull Run for our side. The damn Yankees won at Gettysburg!"

Despite their determination to remain vigilant, by the wee hours of the morning all the guards were stretched out on the ground, asleep. Brannock still sat beside what was left of the fire, which had burned down to embers. He remained there all night, his mind full of thoughts.

Because of that, he was awake and alert when vehicles running without lights slid to a stop on the highway outside the gate. Brannock heard the hiss of their broad tires on asphalt as they approached. He reached over, picked up a shotgun one of the sleeping men had set aside before dozing off, and rolled away from the embers into deeper shadows.

He moved through the blackness like a phantom as he went toward the gate, sticking to the low brush that provided a little cover. A dozen armored vehicles had stopped on the shoulder of the highway. Men were getting out quietly. Brannock felt confident that Slade Grayson was among them.

He slipped his cell phone from his pocket and turned so that his body would shield the glow of the screen as he turned it on. The phone came on, all right, but it blinked NO SERVICE at him.

Brannock frowned. That didn't make any sense. Sure, West Texas was isolated, but cell service in this area was good. He'd never had any trouble making calls before.

Suddenly, he had a hunch that none of the phones belonging to the other men would work, either. With the resources of the government at his beck and call, Grayson would have been able to persuade the carriers in this area to shut down their towers and kill all the service. He wouldn't want civilian calls going in or out.

Knock out the enemy's communications, Brannock thought, and you've taken a vital step in winning a battle.

But not the only step, he thought. Not by a long shot.

Several men were approaching the gate. Brannock was close enough to hear one of them give a whispered order.

"Blow the damned thing down."

That was Grayson's voice. Brannock was able to tell which of the shadowy figures it belonged to, so he leveled the shotgun at that one as he stepped into the open and said in a loud, clear voice, "The only thing that's gonna get blown down is you, Grayson, if you don't back off."

Chapter 52

Grayson let out a startled curse, then yelled, "It's Brannock! Shoot him! Shoot the old fool!"

The other men hesitated, though, instead of blindly following Grayson's order, and that gave Brannock time to warn again, "If anybody opens fire, I'm gonna blow your head off, mister."

Grayson must have heard the sincere threat in Brannock's voice, because he said hastily, "Hold on, hold on."

One of the other men said, "There's no need for anybody to start shooting. Mr. Brannock, you've been legally served with the paperwork giving possession of this ranch to the Bureau of Land Management. I'm asking you to comply with this order and vacate the property peacefully."

"This is my land," Brannock said, "and the state of Texas is workin' on provin' that."

"We're federal agents," the man said. He carried a rifle and wore body armor and a helmet, as did the other men. "We're not required to follow the laws of the individual states."

"Yeah, well, that's one of the things that's wrong with this country today," snapped Brannock. "Used to be the states had some rights, and that meant somethin'. You fellas have stolen that away. And I do mean stolen—just like Grayson here is tryin' to steal my land for some reason."

"We're wasting time here," Grayson said. "Put down the gun, old man, or people are going to die."

From behind Brannock, Thad Bowman said, "You're sure right about that, you son of a bitch."

The confrontation at the fence must have awakened the other defenders, thought Brannock as Bowman and the other men stepped up on either side of them, rifles and shotguns at the ready.

"None of our phones work," Bowman said, confirming Brannock's suspicions of a few minutes earlier, "but I told one of the guys to get back to the ranch as quick as he can and let the others know what's happening."

As if to punctuate Bowman's words, a pickup engine roared to life, and the vehicle took off with a spurt of dirt and gravel from the tires as the driver floored the gas.

"We need to get in there *now!*" Grayson told the man who seemed to be in command of the other agents. "Come on, Lassiter! Do something!"

The agent called Lassiter said, "Mr. Brannock, you know we're coming in there one way or the other, so you might as well stand down and let us do this peacefully. There's no need for anyone's blood to be spilled."

The eastern sky was turning gray with the approach of dawn. There was already enough light for Brannock to make out the figures on both sides of the fence. The defenders were outnumbered, but their guns were up.

So were the rifles of the federal agents. All it would take was a single shot to set off a storm of gunfire that would probably leave everyone on this side of the fence dead. But some of the government men would die, too.

More men would arrive from the ranch headquarters in

a matter of minutes, Brannock knew. That would tip the odds in their favor, although there was no telling what sort of armament those federal agents might have in those armored vehicles. They might cut loose with machine guns that would mow down Brannock and all his allies.

The idea that popped into Brannock's head just then would accomplish two things, he realized: It would allow him to stall for time, and there was just the faintest chance that it would bring this confrontation to an end without dozens of people dying.

"All right," Brannock said. "Grayson can come in."

"What!" Thad Bowman cried. "No, G.W.! Don't give in to them!"

"Grayson can come in," Brannock repeated, "but *only* Grayson."

The government man gave a little jerk of surprise. He said, "What the hell are you talking about, Brannock?"

"The fence is electrified, but the gate's not. There's nothin' stoppin' you from climbin' over, Grayson. We'll back off and let you do it."

"This is some kind of trick," Grayson snapped. "You'll let me climb over, and then you'll shoot me and claim self-defense."

"Nope," Brannock said. He lowered the shotgun he held. "Nobody'll lift a hand against you . . . except me."

Grayson frowned at him and asked, "What the hell are you talking about?"

"We're gonna settle this," Brannock said. "You and me. Man-to-man."

Grayson stared at him for a couple of heartbeats, then let out a bark of laughter.

"You're offering to *fight* me?" he asked in disbelief. "Some sort of trial by combat thing? You're crazier than I thought you were, old man! I've got thirty years on you, and I've trained for years. You won't stand a chance."

"Then you don't have any reason to be afraid of me, do you?"

Brannock knew that veiled taunt would strike home. Sure enough, Grayson stiffened. After a moment, he reached up and unsnapped the helmet he wore.

Lassiter said, "Grayson, what are you doing?"

"Giving this old fool what he wants." Grayson tossed the helmet aside and started removing his body armor. "He thinks he's making some sort of grandiose statement, but all he's really going to get is a beat-down."

"He's an old man," Lassiter said tightly, disapproval obvious in his voice.

"He called the tune."

Grayson stood there wearing boots and tight-fitting black trousers and shirt now. He didn't appear to be armed.

"I can't order you not to do this—" Lassiter began as Grayson started toward the gate.

"Then don't try to," Grayson interrupted. He grabbed the iron pipe at the top of the gate, put a foot on the bottom rail, and started climbing.

"G.W., are you sure about this?" Bowman asked as they all moved back to give Grayson some room to jump down inside the fence. "Kyle and the others will be here soon."

"I'm sure," Brannock said. "This showdown has been a long time comin'."

"I hate to say it, but . . . this isn't the Old West. And you're not John Wayne or Randolph Scott."

Brannock grinned and said, "Actually, I've always thought I look a mite like Ben Johnson when he was older."

Grayson threw a leg over the top of the fence, climbed on over, and then dropped lithely the rest of the way to the ground. He stood there in a slight crouch, waiting.

Brannock handed the shotgun to Bowman, then turned to face the government man.

"Just so everybody's got the terms of this deal straight here, Grayson," he said, "if I whip you, you and your friends pack up and go away and forget about stealin' my ranch from me."

"Sure," Grayson said.

His scornful tone of voice made it clear he didn't expect any such thing to happen, and even if it did, Brannock knew good and well the man would renege on any deal they made. He didn't trust Grayson's word for a second.

But he pressed on anyway, saying, "And if you win, we'll all step aside so you can come in and do whatever you want."

Bowman said, "I don't know if we can go along with that."

"I'm askin' you to, Thad," Brannock said solemnly.

Bowman grimaced, but then he jerked his head in a nod and said, "If that's what you want, G.W."

Grayson said, "What I want is to get this farce over with."

Brannock took off his hat, handed it to Bowman as well, and said, "Hold this for me, will you?"

Then he turned toward Grayson, and as he did, the government man suddenly lunged at him, striking before Brannock could set himself.

Chapter 53

Kyle was asleep in one of the rocking chairs on the front porch with a Winchester across his lap. Miranda was using the bed in his room tonight, and as much as he would have liked to join her there, he knew they weren't at that point in their relationship yet and would have been a gentleman about it even if there hadn't been so many other people around.

As he had dozed off out here on the porch, he had thought wryly that a month earlier, nobody in the world would have considered him a gentleman, least of all himself.

Life had a way of changing in a hurry, usually for the worse, in Kyle's experience. But sometimes good things happened, too, and at least partially balanced out the bad.

Because of that, his dreams were of kissing Miranda instead of battling against a brutal, oppressive federal government. It was a peaceful respite. . . .

So of course, it was doomed not to last long.

The roar of an engine jolted Kyle out of sleep. He snatched up the rifle and leaped to his feet. As he glanced around, he could tell that dawn wasn't far off. He was able to see the pickup that came skidding up to the house with its headlights off.

The driver didn't turn off the engine. He shouted through the open window, "Grayson and a bunch of government men with guns are out at the gate trying to get in!"

Kyle didn't hesitate. He turned and pounded on the door with the flat of his hand, making quite a racket as he shouted, "Everybody up! Get to the gate! Get to the gate!"

Then he stepped up onto the porch railing and made a flying leap from there to the bed of the pickup.

"Head back out there now!" he called to the man who had brought the warning.

The guy spun the wheel and gunned it. Kyle hung on to the Winchester with one hand while he used the other to grab the top of the cab and brace himself. He stood there peering over the cab roof toward the distant gate as the pickup rocketed away from the ranch house. The chilly early morning air ruffled Kyle's fair hair and made him narrow his eyes.

He wondered where G.W. was, but then instinct made something inside him tighten.

He would have bet money that his grandfather was already out there, confronting the men who wanted to steal his land.

The impact of Grayson's sneaky tackle drove Brannock backwards, but he managed to stay on his feet. Grayson's arms locked around Brannock's waist, and he butted his head against the older man's sternum.

Brannock clubbed his hands together and brought them down with smashing force on Grayson's back. That made Grayson's grip loosen slightly, and the punch that Brannock slammed to the side of the man's head knocked him to the side. Brannock backpedaled quickly to put a little distance between them.

Not enough, because Grayson instantly launched into a spinning kick that sent his boot at Brannock's head. Brannock knew if the kick connected, the fight was over.

He twisted away and raised his shoulder. Grayson's boot thudded into it, staggering Brannock, who had to drop to one knee to keep from falling down completely.

Grayson landed agilely and came at Brannock with a flurry of martial arts blows too swift for the eye to follow, especially in the dim light. Brannock surged to his feet as he tried to block the punches, but most of them got through and thudded against his head and chest. He had to give ground again.

Grayson came after him, grinning, and now the government man's overconfidence backfired against him. He was concentrating on his attack so much that he forgot to defend himself. Brannock took an unexpected step forward and shot out a straight right that landed squarely on Grayson's nose.

Decades of hard physical work had given Brannock plenty of strength. Cartilage crunched and blood spurted under his knobby fist. Grayson's head rocked back as he let out a grunt of pain. He was so startled that he didn't even try to block the punch as Brannock hooked a left to his belly.

The biggest advantage Grayson's relative youth gave him was stamina, Brannock knew. Already, the old rancher's heart was pounding and his breath was coming shorter and faster. He couldn't keep this up for long.

So he seized the momentary advantage he had and threw another punch, this one a looping right that found Grayson's jaw. Grayson staggered to the side, and for a second Brannock thought he was going to go down.

But then the government man caught himself and leaped in the air for another kick. Brannock couldn't get out of the way of this one, either, although he tried. It caught him on the left hip and spun him halfway around.

Grayson chopped a blow against his right shoulder where the arm met it, and that side of Brannock's body went numb. He felt himself on the verge of collapse, so he tried to use that to his advantage.

As Grayson crowded in on him, he grabbed the front of the man's shirt with his left hand and threw himself over backwards, heaving as hard as he could and using Grayson's own momentum against him.

Grayson hit the ground hard and rolled over, and a scream suddenly ripped out from him. Brannock didn't know what had happened. Maybe Grayson had landed wrong and broken something.

Brannock's right arm hung limply at his side, but he got his left hand underneath him and levered himself upright. He called on his reserves of strength and staggered to his feet.

Grayson got up, too, clawing at his face and continuing to howl in pain. Brannock saw what had happened. Grayson had rolled right into a bed of cactus, and dozens of needles were embedded in the left side of his face and neck. Some of them were probably sticking through his shirt into his shoulder, too.

While Grayson was distracted by that, Brannock hauled in a deep breath, stepped forward, and swung his left fist, putting every bit of strength he had into the blow.

The punch exploded against Grayson's jaw and lifted the man off his feet. He slammed down on the ground, luckily for him not on cactus this time. With a groan, he tried to get up, then slumped back, apparently only half-conscious, if that much.

With his pulse pounding in his head like a wild summer thunderstorm, Brannock turned toward the gate and the armed federal agents on the other side of it. He glanced to his right and saw that Kyle had arrived and was standing in the back of a pickup, leveling a Winchester over the cab. More vehicles were racing up and spilling armed defenders from them.

Brannock took a few unsteady steps toward the gate and looked over it at the grim face of the agent called Lassiter, who stood there unmoving.

"Looks like . . . I won," he panted. "You and your boys . . . can clear out . . . mister."

"You may outnumber us now, Mr. Brannock," Lassiter said, "but I assure you, you're still outgunned."

Behind Brannock, Grayson regained enough of his senses to push himself up on an elbow.

"Shoot him!" Grayson screamed. "Shoot the old bastard! Shoot all of them!"

"What's it gonna be?" Brannock asked Lassiter. "You gonna do what he says and murder American citizens . . . or you gonna honor the deal that was made?"

"I don't give a damn about any deal," Lassiter snapped. "Grayson's the one who agreed to that, not me."

"Then go ahead and shoot," Brannock told him. "And you can start with me."

For a couple of long, tense seconds, everyone stood there frozen. Then Lassiter said, "I didn't come out here to spill American blood." He turned his head and called to the men with him, "Stand down!"

Grayson climbed to his feet. He was shaky and stumbled as he came toward them, but he managed to remain upright as he screeched, "What are you doing? I ordered you to shoot these traitors! Kill them! Kill them all!"

"Mr. Grayson, you need medical attention," Lassiter said. "Let's go."

"No! No, damn it! They're defying the government! You have to shoot them!"

Lassiter asked Brannock, "Can I come in and get him?"

"Sure," Brannock said. "We'll even open the gate for that."

He nodded to his allies. One of the men, with obvious reluctance, went to the gate and unlocked the padlock on the chain holding it closed.

"Leave that rifle on the other side," Brannock told Lassiter.

The agent nodded and handed the weapon to one of his companions. Several of them looked like they thought Lassiter was making a mistake, but he was in charge and they weren't going to go against his orders.

"Stop it! Get away from me!" Grayson cried as Lassiter approached him. "I'm in charge here! I told you to shoot those bastards!"

"You need to get those cactus needles removed as soon as you can, Grayson," Lassiter said. "Otherwise, your face is liable to swell up like a basketball." His tone hardened slightly. "And we're in joint command of this mission, remember?"

"I'll get you for this," Grayson threatened. "I'll get all of you! You'll be sorry!"

Brannock drawled, "Sounds to me like he's gettin' a mite delirious from the pain."

Lassiter took hold of Grayson's arm and steered him toward the gate. Grayson resisted, but he wasn't in good enough shape at the moment to stop Lassiter from leading him off the ranch. As soon as they were on the other side, the gate was closed and locked again.

Lassiter turned Grayson over to a couple of his men and

told them, "Put him in one of the vehicles. Then the rest of you load up. We're withdrawing." He turned to the gate and said through it, "Don't think you've gotten away with anything, Brannock. Just because I'm not willing to massacre American citizens doesn't mean the next man to come out here won't do it. You'd be smart to go along with what the government wants."

"I don't reckon I can do that," Brannock said. "Not when what they want is to steal my ranch."

Lassiter just pursed his lips for a second, and then he got in the lead vehicle. A moment later, it pulled away, turning wide across the highway to start back toward Sierra Lobo. One by one, the other armored vehicles followed.

Cheers went up from the defenders inside the fence. Men whooped and pumped their rifles and shotguns above their heads in sheer exuberance. Thad Bowman said, "We won, G.W.! You won!"

Brannock looked over at Kyle, saw the grim cast to his grandson's features, and knew that Kyle understood the same thing he did.

As much as they might wish it was, this trouble was probably far from over.

Washington, D.C.

The man seated behind the desk in the Oval Office hung up the phone and sat back in the comfortable swivel chair. If anyone else had been in the room, they wouldn't have been able to tell anything from the unreadable expression on his face.

Slowly, though, his features began to darken as his anger grew and more blood flowed into his face. His jaw clenched, and his breath hissed between his teeth. The hands resting on the desk in front of him closed into fists and began to tremble.

Suddenly, without warning, his left arm shot out and swept the desk clean. Everything that was on it crashed to the floor as the man bolted to his feet and let out a strident, incoherent shout.

Less than a heartbeat later, several Secret Service agents were in the room, guns drawn, ready to defend their charge against any danger.

Clearly, though, the President was alone and unharmed, other than the now bright red face that indicated he might be about to have a stroke from sheer rage.

"Get out!" he screamed at the Secret Service agents. "Get out! Find Jessup!"

By the time White House Chief of Staff Angela Jessup entered the Oval Office three minutes later, the President was sitting down again, and although he was still breathing hard, he seemed to have his emotions under control again.

Jessup, as attractive and sleekly groomed as always, showed no sign that the hour was as early as it really was.

"I suppose you've heard from Grayson, sir," she said in a voice honed by years of lecturing at one of the most prestigious East Coast universities. She had doctorates in gender studies, racial studies, economics, and public policy. She was married to one of the lead anchors at a major cable news network. She also had the ear of the President and was accused by many of being the puppet-master who pulled his strings.

In reality, that wasn't true. He was radical enough in his beliefs without any urging from her. The fact that he was a raging narcissist and megalomaniac didn't hurt anything.

"He failed," the President said. "Grayson failed. I thought he was ruthless enough to take care of anything.

But that old man is still on his ranch, defying the will of the American people."

What he meant by that was G.W. Brannock was defying the federal government in general and the executive branch in particular, but to the President it was all one and the same.

"I saw a little about it on the news," Jessup said. "Evidently, the cameramen were asleep on the job. They didn't get any footage of the fight between Brannock and Grayson." She shook her head slightly. "It's amazing an old man like that was able to beat Grayson. That seems to be what happened, though."

"Brannock was lucky," snapped the President. "And Lassiter refused to open fire on those traitors. Well, he's through at the BLM. He's through, period. In fact, I want him behind bars for the rest of his life."

"I'm not sure if that's possible, sir—"

"Of course, it's possible! It's what I want, isn't it?"

"I'll see what I can do," Jessup promised.

The President snorted and said, "See to it. And I want to see Milburn right away."

"General Milburn is standing by, sir." As the head of the Joint Chiefs, Milburn had an office here in the White House, as well as at the Pentagon, and was on call 24-7.

"Get him here. I have an important question to ask him."

Jessup thought she knew what that question was.

Unfortunately, she didn't know what the answer would be.

General Thurgood Milburn walked into the Oval Office ten minutes later, his cap tucked under his left arm. His grandfather, a great admirer of Thurgood Marshall, had asked the general's father to name him after the famous jurist and Supreme Court justice. Of course, at the time Thurgood Milburn had been just a little black baby in Alabama, with very little to indicate that sixty years later he would be the top brass in the American military.

He came to attention and saluted. The man behind the desk was the Commander-in-Chief, after all, even though he despised the military and everything about it except the power it gave him. The President waved a hand negligently, which was as close as he ever came to acknowledging a salute from a soldier, let alone returning one.

"Sit down," he snapped, then grudgingly added Milburn's rank, "general."

Milburn thought about saying that he was all right standing, but he couldn't quite bring himself to be that insubordinate. Instead, he said, "Thank you, sir," and took a seat in one of the comfortable leather chairs in front of the desk.

It didn't feel so comfortable at the moment, however.

"You know what I brought you here to ask you," the President said.

Milburn had a pretty good idea—he had seen the news reports from Texas, too—but he wasn't going to admit that.

No, if the son of a bitch behind the desk had something to say, he was going to have to come right out with it.

"No, sir, I'm afraid not."

The President's lips twisted in a snarl as he leaned forward.

"What question have we been asking officers for twenty years now?" he demanded.

"You mean whether or not we we'd be willing to give the order to fire on American citizens in the case of insurrection or other national emergency."

"That's right. You said you were, or else you wouldn't

be where you are now. You wouldn't even be in the service anymore."

"Yes, sir, I said that." Milburn took a deep breath. "But I'm very glad that I've never been put in that position, as are all the other officers I know."

"Well, that's where we are now," the President snapped.

Milburn shook his head slowly and said, "There's not any insurrection or national emergency that I'm aware of, sir."

"Those bastards in Texas!" the man behind the desk yelled. "That old man who won't get the hell off his ranch!"

"I was under the impression that case hadn't been settled yet. Anyway, with all due respect, sir, it seems to me that a property dispute doesn't really rise to the level of—"

"The man is defying the federal government! That's treason!"

"Not technically."

Milburn's mouth was dry. He knew that if he wanted to save his career—if he had any sense of self-preservation at all—he'd be agreeing with the President and falling all over himself to promise to do whatever was necessary to give the man what he wanted.

Unfortunately, a tiny but maddeningly persistent voice in the back of Milburn's head kept telling him that if he did that, he might as well be shuffling bare feet in the dirt and saying, *Yassuh, bossman*.

Deep down, that was the way most Democratic politicians saw members of his race anyway, he knew. Even the ones who shared that heritage with him.

The President was on his feet now, leaning forward and resting his hands on the big desk as he glared at Milburn.

"If I say something is a national emergency, then it's a goddamn national emergency, is that clear, general?"

"Most of the time, yes, sir. But not if it involves killing American citizens. That's not what the armed forces are for."

As you'd know if you had any clue to what we're really like, thought Milburn.

"So, if I tell you I want the army to go in and clean out everybody who's on that ranch, are you saying you won't give the order?"

Milburn took a deep breath. This man was the Commander-in-Chief. The Constitution said so.

But that same Constitution had been willfully, even gleefully, ignored by the past four presidents, he recalled.

"No, sir," he whispered. "I won't give that order. Not so you can get your hands on some old man's ranch."

The President stared at him for several seconds, then exploded in a barrage of racial slurs and curses. A man's true colors always came out when he was under enough stress. Finally, he calmed down enough to say, "You're done, Milburn. You're relieved of command. You're not a general anymore. You're not even a soldier anymore."

On the contrary, thought Milburn, he actually felt more like a soldier than he had for quite a while.

He got to his feet and said, "That's fine, sir. I assume I'm dismissed?"

"Get your black ass out of here!"

Milburn started to turn away, but then the President stopped him.

"What about all the other officers below you? Are they going to say the same thing?"

"I don't know, sir," Milburn answered honestly. "I'd like to think most of them would. I believe most of them will, if you back them into a corner over something like this." He paused. "It takes a lot to get an American soldier to spill his countrymen's blood."

The President slumped back into the chair behind the desk.

"Fine. Get out."

Milburn's step was brisk and his back was straight as he left the Oval Office. He was even smiling a little. He didn't know what the future held for him, but he was almost looking forward to it for a change.

When Angela Jessup came back into the Oval Office a few minutes later, she said, "I take it the general didn't tell you what you wanted to hear."

"Take care of him," the President growled. "Make him sorry he was ever born."

"Of course."

The President sighed and said, "The worst of it is, he's got me worried that no matter who I promote to replace him, the answer is going to be the same. Those damned soldiers only want to follow orders when they agree with them."

Jessup weighed her options and decided to go with the truth.

"If you push them too hard, sir . . . they might decide to push back."

For a second, the President's eyes went wide with fear. He had to be aware of how tenuous his hold on power really was. Despite the effort to militarize the agencies, bureaus, and departments under his direct control, and the ongoing program to weaken the actual military, if it came down to a fight he knew which side would probably win . . . and it wasn't his. A military coup was so far outside the main currents of American thought that it had never been regarded as a serious threat to any administration . . . but it wasn't impossible.

"All right," he muttered. "If we can't use the military to get what we want, then we'll just have to do something else." He seemed to relax slightly. He even leaned back in his chair as he went on. "Luckily, we have other options. Get me the Secretary-General of the UN on the phone." He thumped a fist on the desk. "We'll teach those damned Texans to act like they still have rights!"

Chapter 54

For the rest of the day Monday, the news media was clogged with coverage of the showdown at the entrance to G.W. Brannock's ranch. Reporters stood in front of the now-famous gate and intoned solemnly about the unlawful defiance of the federal government's edicts and the potential for domestic terrorism by the right-wing extremists who supported Brannock's position. The White House press secretary issued a statement saying that the President was deeply disturbed by the clash and hoped that it could be brought to a peaceful conclusion. One network did a special report called *STANDOFF IN TEXAS!*, while another ran a special with the ominous title *A SECOND AMERICAN REVOLUTION?*

All the pundits agreed that eventually Brannock and his supporters would back down. Otherwise, the government would have no choice but to send in troops to clean them out, no matter how bloody that might turn out to be.

There were only a few dissenting voices crying out in the wilderness and warning that graphic, bloody images of American citizens gunned down by American troops might in fact *cause* the very uprising that everyone seemed to fear.

But Monday slid into Tuesday with nothing else happening, then Wednesday, and still peace prevailed over the Brannock ranch. More of the defenders drifted away and headed back to their homes, but enough remained on hand to maintain a constant vigil at the gate and patrols along the fence that bordered the highway.

The world held its breath. If nothing happened soon, the news cycle would move along and there would be something else for the cable networks to yammer about twenty-four hours a day.

"Governor Delgado wants me to come to Austin," Miranda told Kyle Wednesday evening as they sat on the porch with G.W. "She didn't say exactly what it's about, but I'm pretty sure it's something to do with the land grant."

"Maybe they've found something that proves it's a phony," Kyle said.

"That's what I'm hoping," Miranda said with a nod. "If it is, then maybe this long nightmare will be over."

G.W. rocked back and forth slowly as he said, "They'll just come up with somethin' else."

Kyle and Miranda turned to look at him. Kyle said, "You mean some other excuse to try to seize the ranch?"

"Yep. It's pretty obvious by now that they want it—danged if I know why—and they're not gonna stop at anything to get their hands on it. Anyway, even if the governor's got proof the land grant is fake, what're you gonna do with it?"

"Shout it from the rooftops," Miranda said. "Spread the news as far and wide as I can through the media."

G.W. grunted.

"The government'll claim it was all a misunderstandin'," he said, "and the press will downplay the whole thing until everybody forgets about it. Then they'll spring some new claim, and the whole thing'll start over again."

"Well, you're sure a pessimist this evening," Kyle said.

"Just tryin' to be realistic," G.W. insisted. "But I could be wrong. Lord knows, I have been plenty of times before. And don't think I don't appreciate what you're doin', Miranda. I know that if there's really a way out of this, you're more likely to find it than anybody else."

"I'm glad you have that much faith in me, G.W.," she said. "I hope I can justify it." She turned to Kyle. "Do you want to come to Austin with me?"

"Of course, I do," he answered without hesitation. They had become closer than ever the past couple of days as they spent most of their time together. "But I can't."

"Don't stay on my account," G.W. told him.

"I'm not." Kyle grinned. "I just want to be here to see it when Grayson gets his butt handed to him again. I missed it the last time."

"And it's a good thing," G.W. said. "If you'd been there, you might've jumped right in."

"Dang right I would have."

"That wasn't the deal I made with Grayson."

Miranda said, "You're lucky those other agents honored that deal. They could have opened fire."

G.W. sighed and said, "Yeah, I know. There's a part of me that still wishes everybody else would just clear out and leave me here to face this by myself. It's my ranch, after all. At least it is until I'm gone." He looked over at Kyle. "Then it'll be your spread, son. I don't have anybody else to leave it to."

"Now, don't start talking like that," Kyle told him. "You're gonna be around for a long time yet."

That brought a laugh from G.W. He said, "In case you hadn't noticed, I'm old. No matter what happens with the government, I don't have that many more years left in this world. I don't plan on dwellin' on the fact, but there's no point in denyin' it, either."

"Right now let's just concentrate on keeping the BLM off your land," Miranda suggested. "Governor Delgado's sending a helicopter for me in the morning. I'll call you as soon as I find out anything."

"Sounds like a good plan," G.W. said as he got to his feet. "Right now I'm sorta tired. Reckon I'll go on in and let you young people enjoy the rest of the evenin' out here."

Kyle knew his grandfather was going inside so he and Miranda could be alone. He appreciated that consideration, too, and wasn't going to argue with G.W. about it.

There was no telling how long Miranda was going to be gone—or what might happen while she was in Austin—so he wanted to enjoy the time they had together.

The helicopter arrived a little before nine o'clock the next morning, setting down not far from the ranch house. Miranda, who had gone back to her apartment in Sierra Lobo several days earlier and packed up enough things for an extended stay at the ranch, waited until the dust had settled and then left the house carrying an overnight bag.

Kyle and G.W. stood on the porch watching her go. Kyle had already said his good-byes to her and still seemed to taste her kiss on his lips. Both men waved as she paused in the chopper's doorway and lifted a hand in farewell to them.

The rotors began to turn again, and a moment later the helicopter lifted off and zoomed to the east. Kyle had a lump in his throat as he watched while it dwindled to a tiny dot in the sky and then disappeared.

"She'll be back, son," G.W. said. "Don't worry."

"I know," Kyle said. "But will we still be here?"

"One way or another, I will be," G.W. said with grim determination.

They went back in the house, and a short time later G.W. announced that he was going out to check on his stock.

"Those cows don't know a damned thing about politics," he said, "and if they did, they wouldn't care. Somebody's still got to look out for 'em."

"Roberto and the regular hands have been doing that," Kyle pointed out.

"Yeah, and I trust those fellas completely. But I like to lay my own eyes on things, too. Want to come with me?"

"Sure," Kyle said. "There's nothing going on here."

Less than a minute later, he had reason to regret saying that. He figured he must have jinxed things.

He and G.W. had just stepped outside to go get in the pickup when they saw dust boiling up from the road. Somebody was coming from the direction of the gate, and in a hurry, too.

"Damn it," G.W. said. "That looks like trouble."

Kyle knew that prediction had to be right.

A moment later one of the jeeps used by the defenders raced up to the ranch house. The driver called to them, "Somebody's coming! Lots of somebodies!"

"Let's get out there," G.W. told Kyle. They ran to the pickup.

When they were in the truck, speeding toward the gate, G.W. took his phone from his pocket and handed it to Kyle.

"See if that gizmo's workin'," he said.

"No service," Kyle reported. "Just like before."

Cell phone service had mysteriously reappeared after the confrontation with Grayson, but now it was gone again and that was yet another indication of bad trouble on the way, thought Kyle.

Men were crowded up to the gate and fence when they got there. They jumped out of the pickup and hurried to join the others. Kyle peered along the road to town and saw a dark mass of vehicles rumbling toward them.

"Those look like trucks of some sort," G.W. said.

"They're troop transports," Kyle said, remembering his days in the army, relatively brief though they had been. "They're going to war against us, G.W."

With a sigh, G.W. said, "Never thought I'd see the day when American troops would be used like this."

"Wait a minute," Kyle said, frowning. "I'm not sure they are. Something's not right about those trucks. . . ."

As the vehicles came closer, he thought he realized what it was. He asked for a pair of binoculars, and one of the men thrust some into his hands. He raised the glasses to his eyes and peered through them.

"Those aren't American trucks," Kyle reported a moment later. "They've got the United Nations insignia on them, and they're flying United Nations flags."

"Good Lord," G.W. muttered.

The trucks, more than a dozen of them, didn't pull up on the side of the highway next to the fence. Instead, they circled out into the open country on the other side of the road, swinging around wide so that they came to a stop pointed toward the fence where Kyle, G.W., and another six or seven men stood tensely.

Troops began to pour from the backs of the trucks. They wore fatigues and bright blue helmets.

"Son . . . of . . . a . . . bitch," G.W. said slowly with heart-felt passion. "That fella in the White House did it. He sicced the damn UN on us."

"That's sure what it looks like," Kyle agreed. He focused the binoculars on the uniformed men scurrying around and got another shock. "That's not all, G.W. It looks to me like every one of those soldiers is Chinese."

Chapter 55

The troop transports weren't the only UN vehicles on their way to the ranch. Over the next hour, armored assault vehicles arrived and moved into position across the highway. G.W. watched in astonishment and asked, "What the hell's next? Tanks?"

"I wouldn't be surprised," Kyle said.

No tanks showed up, though. Kyle supposed they should be thankful for small favors. He estimated that at least two hundred Chinese troops in United Nations uniforms were on hand. A number of them armed with automatic weapons formed a picket line along the front of the UN position and stood there staring impassively across the highway at the defenders.

"Hold your fire," G.W. told the men with him. "Whatever those varmints are plannin' to do, we don't want to jump-start it. Let's see how the hand plays out."

Once all the Chinese troops were in position, a tense, expectant silence settled over the landscape. Kyle figured something else was bound to happen, and a short time later, it did.

A black SUV appeared on the highway, coming toward the ranch. Kyle said, "They're bound to have the road closed off in both directions to move that many troops around, not to mention they wouldn't want any witnesses to this. So whoever that is, the UN forces let them through."

"You know who it is," G.W. said. "Only one son of a bitch it could be."

Kyle nodded.

No one along the fence was the least bit surprised when the SUV came to a stop in front of the gate and Slade Grayson stepped out of it.

Grayson was back in his sunglasses and expensive suit. As he sauntered toward the fence with his usual arrogance, Kyle thought that what he could see of the man's face looked a little puffy, no doubt from all the cactus needles that had been stuck in it a few days earlier.

If the wounds still bothered Grayson, though, he didn't show any signs of it as he stopped a few feet on the other side of the gate and rocked back and forth a little on his toes, obviously quite pleased with himself.

"I told you I'd be back, Brannock," he said.

"I never doubted it for a second," G.W. told him.

"As you can see, I've brought some men with me this time who won't hesitate to open fire on you if you keep defying the government." Grayson gestured toward the Chinese troops, then turned his head and called, "Colonel Ling!"

One of the blue-helmeted soldiers approached. His spine appeared to be as stiff as a steel rod, and his face was set in hard, flat lines, like stone.

"Colonel, please explain your mission to Mr. Brannock and his friends," Grayson said.

"Certainly," Ling replied in unaccented tones. "The president of your country has requested assistance from the United Nations in quelling domestic terrorism. This peacekeeping force is here to assure that international law is followed and that dangerous, terroristic activities will be put to an end in this region."

"You see us engagin' in any terroristic activities, old son?" G.W. drawled. "We're just standin' here . . . on my private property, I might add."

"By defying a lawful order of your government, you are in violation of international law," Ling said. "I call upon you to cease this illegal behavior and surrender to Mr. Grayson."

G.W. shook his head and said, "That's not gonna happen."

As if Ling hadn't even heard what G.W. said, the colonel went on. "You will be given a grace period in which to comply with this order. If you fail to do so, all appropriate action will be taken to ensure that you do."

Grinning, Grayson said, "What the colonel means, Brannock, is that you've got until tomorrow morning to get the hell off this ranch . . . and if you don't, we'll blast you and all your friends right off the face of the earth."

Miranda was impressed when she was ushered into the office of Governor Maria Delgado. Not with the office itself, which was furnished rather functionally, but with the grace and strength of the woman who occupied it. The governor shook hands warmly with Miranda and waved her into a comfortable brown leather chair in front of some bookshelves.

A stocky, middle-aged man with salt-and-pepper hair sat in another chair like the one where Miranda took a seat, and Governor Delgado settled down in a third one. She smiled and said, "Ms. Stephens, this is Dr. Anthony Zara. He's been heading up the team that examined the land grant at the heart of the federal government's attempt to seize Mr. Brannock's ranch."

"Hello," Miranda said to Dr. Zara. "I'm familiar with your work, doctor. I would have approached you to enlist your expertise, if Governor Delgado hadn't beaten me to it."

Zara nodded. He seemed a little stuffy, thought Miranda, but that was to be expected in a university professor with a worldwide reputation as a historian and archeologist.

"I'm glad I was consulted," he said. "This has been a fascinating experience. I knew as soon as I examined the document that we were dealing either with a previously unknown land grant—or an absolutely top-notch forgery. The challenge lay in determining which it was."

"And what did you find out?" Miranda asked. She was anxious to hear the verdict.

Zara wasn't going to be rushed, however. He said, "We couldn't examine the paper on which the actual document is written. Determining the age of it would not have been too difficult. But the federal government refused to turn over even a small sample to us."

"Well, that's pretty suspicious."

"Indeed. Nor would they share a sample of the ink with us. All we had to go by was a digital reproduction of the document. So we began by concentrating on the language itself, to see if there were any anachronistic words or terms included in it. That would have been a determining factor in and of itself." Zara shook his head. "But the language was authentic. It read just as an eighteenth-century Spanish land grant should read."

Miranda felt her heart begin to sink a little. She said, "So if you couldn't prove the paper or the ink weren't old enough, or that the language was wrong, what was left?"

"A question we asked ourselves at great length, I assure

you," Zara said. "The answer came from a member of our team I didn't really expect to contribute much, to be honest. A young man who's a computer expert. He was able to blow up sections of the document in fine detail and extremely high resolution. He's the one who came upon the key to the whole thing."

"Go ahead, doctor," Governor Delgado urged. From the look on her face, she already knew what was coming and didn't want Miranda tortured by waiting any longer.

"A document such as this one purported to be, in order to have been produced in the eighteenth century, would have been written with a quill pen," Zara said. "The tip of every quill, as you might expect, is different and produces tiny irregularities in the edges of the letters that are unique to that pen. These irregularities are invisible to the naked eye, but if the image is enlarged enough, you can see them."

Now Miranda's heart beat faster instead of sinking. She said, "The lettering on the land grant didn't have those irregularities, did it?"

Zara shook his head and said, "No. The edges of the letters are smooth. That document was made to look as much like an authentic Spanish land grant as it could, and whoever did that has a fine hand . . . but he used a modern writing instrument. There's no doubt of that." Zara sat back in his chair and looked satisfied. "The document is fake. Conclusively. And that will stand up as evidence in any court of law in the land, I assure you."

Miranda's pulse pounded. She said, "Then it's over. The government doesn't have any right to take G.W.'s land. No right at all."

"Yes," Delgado said, nodding solemnly. "But the question still remains . . . will they back off once we make this public? Or will they stonewall, deny that Dr. Zara's team is correct, and continue with what they've been doing?"

"But how can they do that?" Miranda asked.

"They're the federal government—and they're Democrats. They've come to believe that with ninety-five percent of the media and more than half the country on their side, they can do whatever they want. They don't think the rule of law applies to them anymore. And for all practical purposes they're right." The older woman smiled. "But we've got more ammunition now. We can keep fighting. I don't intend to give up, Ms. Stephens. Do you?"

"No, ma'am," Miranda said without hesitation. "And I know G.W. and Kyle won't give up, either."

Before any of them could say anything else, one of the governor's aides came into the office. He went over to Delgado and said something quietly into her ear. She frowned and told the man, "Send him in."

A moment later, Colonel Thomas Atkinson came into the office. He wore a suit today instead of fatigues, but Miranda recognized him instantly. The grim look on the retired soldier's face made fear spring up inside her.

"Something's happened, hasn't it?" she burst out before the governor could say anything.

Atkinson looked at Delgado and said, "Your call, Maria."

"I don't think we need to worry about sharing information with Ms. Stephens, Thomas," she said. "What is it?"

"Somebody at Brannock's ranch got a message out via ham radio a little while ago. Evidently, the feds have shut down cell phone communication again, but they didn't think to block the ham frequencies. If what we've been told is true . . . Chinese troops wearing the uniform of the United Nations have moved in, closed off all access to the ranch, and laid siege to those defending the place."

Chapter 56

"Our top story tonight . . . Although there has been no official statement on the matter from the White House, we have learned that the United Nations, acting on a request from the President, has sent peacekeeping troops to Texas to deal with the growing unrest there as right-wing extremists attempt to block the Bureau of Land Management from taking possession of federally owned property.

"The land in question is being squatted on by domestic terrorist G.W. Brannock, who has barricaded himself there along with a number of armed, fanatical supporters. For more on this, let's go over to our White House correspondent, Jack Rosen . . . Jack, why do you think the President took the unusual step of calling in the UN, rather than leaving the matter to local law enforcement or even the National Guard?"

"Thanks, Pamela. As for why the President took this action, the rumor around Washington tonight is that he wanted to demonstrate that this was not a mere criminal matter but rather a dangerous precedent in which ultra-right-wing partisans are attempting to foment open rebellion against the government. The UN agreeing to come in and quash this trouble shows that the entire world community is in agreement: Such radical behavior cannot be tolerated in a progressive society."

"What about those who object to foreign troops operating on American soil with the consent, even the encouragement, of the United States government?"

"Well, I can't speak for the President, Pamela, but I think he's trying to show that we're part of a community of nations now and that in times of trouble we won't hesitate to look to those outside our own borders for assistance and advice. America is no longer too proud to ask for help with our problems."

"Thank you, Jack . . . Now let's turn to our political experts, and also to our top military correspondent, retired Admiral Andrew Shelton. Admiral, we've heard that General Thurgood Milburn, the Chairman of the Joint Chiefs of Staff, has been removed from his position because he refused to commit American troops for the job of ousting G.W. Brannock from his stronghold. Do you know anything about that?"

"Not for a fact, no, I don't. But I do know for a fact that no American commander worth his salt is going to tell his troops to start shooting American citizens unless there's a damned good reason—"

"Thank you, admiral. Peter Henderson, former national security advisor, what do you think?"

"I think the President is in a bad position and is doing the only thing he can. He can't allow dangerous extremists to defy the law of the land. He's trying to be sensitive to the situation, though, and that's why he's brought in outside assistance. There's no more trusted body in the world than the United Nations, and if the UN agrees that something must be done about Brannock and his followers, then it stands to reason the rest of the country will see that the President is right."

"But is he running a political risk by doing this? Sanford Dowling, what do you think?"

"Well, Pamela, I'm told that both houses of Congress will meet tomorrow in emergency session and take up resolutions of support for the President's actions. After all, this is quite a dramatic thing to have happen, to have foreign troops on our soil, as you put it. But those resolutions are expected to pass in both the House and the Senate, so I think the President has the political capital to do this. And from a personal standpoint, what choice did he have? Somebody's got to teach those Texans a lesson!"

G.W. and Kyle stood behind G.W.'s pickup and kept an eye on the gate. The Chinese forces were still lined up on the other side of the highway, about a hundred and fifty yards away, apparently in no hurry to do anything. They had been sitting over there all day, and now it wasn't long until dusk would settle over the West Texas landscape.

Kyle thumped a fist against the truck's fender and said in frustration, "Why are they doing this? What does Grayson hope to gain? They could overrun us any time they want to. Why is he waiting?"

"Ever see a little kid torment an insect with a magnifyin' glass?" G.W. asked. "He's not really interested in killin' the thing. He just wants to cause it as much pain and misery as he can and make it last as long as possible. That's what Grayson is. He's a mean little kid. A bully. No matter why the damn government wanted the ranch in the first place, it's gone long past that point for him. He just wants to make us suffer, and he doesn't want it to be over too soon."

Kyle grunted and said, "A man like that ought to be put down like a mad dog."

"You won't get any argument from me."

"So what are we going to do? Just sit here and wait for them to wipe us out?"

"Nope." G.W. rubbed his chin, his fingertips rasping over the silvery stubble growing there. "Before mornin', you and everybody else are gonna load up and go back yonder to the mountains. You traipsed all over those canyons when you were a kid. You know how rugged they are. Find a good place for all of you to hole up and wait it out."

Kyle frowned and asked, "What the hell are you gonna be doing while we're doing that?"

"I thought I'd take a Winchester and go out there to the gate and make those fifteen rounds count as much as I can."

"You're gonna let them shoot you to pieces, in other words!" Kyle shook his head stubbornly. "Look, G.W., I can't give you any orders—"

"Darned right you can't."

"But I can tell you, none of us are gonna let you just throw away your life like that. Either you come with us to the mountains—we'll hide out up there and wage a guerrilla war against those bastards—or else we're staying here and fighting them with you."

"A guerrilla war . . ." G.W. said slowly. "The idea's intriguin', I'll say that much. But you know, son, that's not really my style. When trouble comes at me, I've always met it head-on. Reckon I'm too old to change my ways now."

"All right. But don't get upset when the rest of us back your play."

"I suppose in the end, that's the sort of thing that every man has to figure out for himself."

They were silent for a few minutes, and then Kyle said, "At least Dave was able to get the word out on that ham radio in his truck before they blocked his broadcast. The rest of the world knows what's going on, anyway."

"The rest of the world only knows what the press tells 'em," G.W. said skeptically. "How much truth you reckon is gonna be in that?"

"Not much," Kyle admitted. "But Miranda's out there, too, thank God. I'm glad she didn't get trapped here. I know she'll do what she can, and so will the governor. Who knows? Maybe they proved that land grant is phony, and now the feds won't have any choice but to back off."

"In a perfect world, that's the way it'd work," G.W. said. "Too bad it's never been a perfect world . . . and it's gotten a lot less so since that bunch in Washington took over."

Governor Delgado set up a command post in the governor's mansion, rather than in the capitol, and Miranda was there that evening along with Delgado and Colonel Atkinson, who was monitoring the situation through law enforcement contacts in the area.

"UN forces have placed the town of Sierra Lobo under martial law and established a strict curfew they're enforcing with armed patrols," Atkinson reported to Delgado and Miranda. "They've also established a no-fly zone from Pecos to El Paso."

"That's several hundred miles!" Delgado exclaimed.

"Yeah, but they're enforcing that, too. They've shut down all the civilian airports and have troops posted on them to make sure nothing takes off. The military fields are shut down, too, per orders directly from the Pentagon."

Delgado snorted disgustedly and said, "From the White House, you mean."

Atkinson shrugged.

"We know that and so does anybody with half a brain in their head, but that lets out most of the media and all the people who voted for the son of a bitch to start with. To a big part of the country, the whole thing is being passed off as a tempest in a teacup, to use an old-fashioned expression. It doesn't matter to them. They're still gonna get their check next month, so what do they care what happens to some old rancher in Texas?"

Miranda said, "They don't care that they've lost all their freedom?"

Atkinson looked squarely at her and shook his head. He said, "No. They don't. They'd rather have the government take care of them their entire lives than be free."

"Slavery," Delgado muttered. "That's what it is, pure and simple."

"Yes, ma'am," Atkinson said. "You're right about that, but to the people who go along with it willing, that doesn't make any difference."

"Has there been any more word from inside the ranch?" Miranda asked.

"I'm afraid not. They're jamming all the radio frequencies now. Brannock and the others . . . they're on their own."

"Against overwhelming odds," Miranda whispered. Suddenly, she couldn't stay there anymore. She grabbed her purse and headed for the door.

"Where are you going?" Governor Delgado asked.

"Back to my hotel," Miranda said. She couldn't keep the despair out of her voice as she added, "There's nothing I can do here."

"If we get any news, I'll let you know right away," Delgado promised.

"Thank you."

One of the governor's aides showed Miranda out of the mansion. Her hotel was here in downtown Austin, only a few blocks away. It was a pleasant evening, and she could make the walk without any trouble. She hoped the exercise would clear her head a little and help her figure out what she needed to do next.

But that was just the problem, she thought.

There wasn't anything she could do to help Kyle. Not a damned thing.

She had covered about half the distance to the hotel when a figure stepped from the shadows under some live oak trees growing next to a building. He shocked Miranda by saying, "Ms. Stephens?"

Fear shot through her as she turned her head to look at him, but she relaxed slightly as she saw a man in his thirties, wearing a rumpled but decent suit. He didn't look the least bit threatening, but she slipped her hand into her bag anyway and closed her fingers around the stun gun she carried.

"Yes, what is it?" she asked. He was probably a reporter looking for a quote, she told herself.

"My name is Gardner—" he began.

That was when a gunshot roared and a garish orange flash of muzzle flame split the darkness.

Chapter 57

Something must have warned the man who called himself Gardner, because he moved at the same instant the gun blasted, diving at Miranda and tackling her off her feet. She cried out in shock and pain as she fell heavily to the sidewalk.

Gardner rolled off her and came up in a blur of motion. Another shot rang out, but this one went up at a sharp angle because Gardner kicked the wrist of the man who came out of the shadows for another try at him.

Before the would-be killer could lower the gun and trigger it again, Gardner crowded in on him, hands flying too fast to follow even if the light had been better. The assassin made a gagging sound as Miranda sat up. Gardner must have struck him across the throat, she thought. The man sounded like his larynx was crushed.

He fell to his knees, making it even easier for Gardner to kick him in the head and send him sprawling across the sidewalk. Then Gardner whirled and leaped to Miranda's side. He held out a hand to her.

"Come on. There are probably more of them close by."

She had no idea of what was going on here. She didn't know if the gunman had been aiming at her or Gardner.

But some instinct compelled her to trust him. She reached up and grasped his hand. He lifted her to her feet as if she were weightless and hustled her along the sidewalk.

"My hotel is up there—" she gasped as he turned into a side street.

"They probably know where you're staying," he said with a quiet intensity. "Chances are they've been following you ever since you left the ranch. They don't want you to find out anything about what's really going on."

"Were they after you or me?" she asked.

A grim chuckle came from him, then he said, "I don't think they'd mind seeing both of us dead. But I've been dodging hit men ever since I got back in the country, so I'm probably their primary target. I've got the proof they don't want to get out."

"The proof of what?" Miranda asked. She had a wild thought that she might already know the answer.

"Of why the government wants G.W. Brannock's ranch so badly," he said as he steered her into a dimly lit beer joint. The place was noisy inside, filled with students from the university that wasn't too far away.

Gardner sat her down in a booth, told her to stay put, and went to the bar for a pitcher of beer and a couple of mugs. Miranda didn't have the least bit of interest in sitting here and getting drunk, but she figured Gardner was doing that for appearance's sake. As long as they were in this crowd and looked like they belonged, they were probably safe.

But they would have to leave sooner or later, she thought. And then what?

He came back, set the pitcher on the table, and slid into the booth across from her. As he poured beer in the mugs, he said, "You're probably completely confused by now."

The place was noisy enough that if they kept their voices low, no one could eavesdrop on them. Miranda leaned forward and said, "I'm confused, and I'm scared, and I'm angry."

"I'd say you have every reason to be."

"Mr. Gardner, if that's really your name, I think you'd better tell me what's going on here. Otherwise, I'm going to have to call the police."

He nodded and said, "You might be all right if you called the cops. Most of them are honest, I'd say. But how would you ever know if there was one who wasn't? One who's working for the people who want to see me dead?"

"And who are those people?"

"The President of the United States, for one," Gardner said. "Senator Charles Rutland, for another."

Miranda felt her eyes widening. She couldn't help it. For all the distrust of the federal government she felt, to hear it stated so baldly that the President and the Senate majority leader would sanction attempted murder . . . it was almost more than she could grasp.

"What are you talking about?" she asked. "Senator Rutland—"

"Is going to get the Democratic nomination and be the next president, I know," Gardner said. "Drink some of that beer, why don't you? Let's try to look like we're having a pleasant conversation."

Miranda forced herself to pick up the mug and sip the beer. It was good, and under other circumstances she would have enjoyed it. Right now, though, her mind was whirling too much.

Gardner swallowed some of his beer, leaned back, and looked like a young businessman relaxing after a hard day's work. He smiled faintly and said, "I work for the CIA—"

"Oh, come on!" Miranda exclaimed, unable to suppress the impulse.

"No, it's true, I swear. Although, maybe I should say I *worked* for the CIA. The administration may well have convinced my bosses by now that I've gone rogue. I'm sure they've been trying to discredit me in advance, ever since I got my hands on the intel they don't want to get out."

"What . . . intel?"

"There's a USB drive in my pocket," Gardner said. "On it are all the details of a deal between an American company and the Chinese government. The American company is owned by a man named Stuart McCauley. He's Charles Rutland's brother-in-law. His company has contracted with the Chinese to dispose of nuclear waste from their reactors. They're going to put the stuff in that valley where Brannock's ranch is, once the US government has taken it over and then sold it to McCauley in a sweetheart deal."

As Gardner fell silent, Miranda stared across the table at him for a long moment. Finally, she said, "That's it? That's why they want to steal G.W.'s ranch? This whole thing has been over graft and corruption and a shady land deal?"

"A shady land deal worth billions of dollars to McCauley. Senator Rutland and the President are in line for a share of that payoff, too." Gardner drank some more beer. "But that's not quite all of it. That Chinese nuclear waste . . . it's incredibly toxic, more so than any we've ever seen before. I got that info straight from a scientist who worked in the Chinese nuclear energy program. He was just one of many involved in the program who were dying of cancer. That's what's going to happen here, too. The stuff will contaminate the environment and in the long run will kill thousands of people. Maybe hundreds of thousands, or even more. Any sort of accident at the containment facility McCauley plans to build on Brannock's land would eventually render the western half of Texas unlivable."

"That's insane," Miranda said. "The government would never risk . . . I mean . . . all those people . . ."

"People in Texas," Gardner reminded her. "The place that the administration in Washington hates for standing up to them over and over. Anyway, when there's this much money involved . . ."

His voice trailed off as his shoulders rose and fell in an eloquent shrug.

Miranda thought about it some more, then said, "You got this information from a Chinese scientist?"

"A terminally ill one who had no reason to lie about it."

"What happened to him? Could he testify—"

"The cancer didn't have a chance to kill him," Gardner said. "A rocket from a Chinese drone got him first, right after he'd passed the USB drive to me. They'd been trying to track him down ever since he slipped out of China, and they caught up to him in Manila. The explosion nearly killed me, as well. But I got out and made it back here. There have been half a dozen attempts on my life since then. You saw the latest one a little while ago. They know who I am, they know what I've got."

"You have to go public with that information! The country has a right to know what's going on."

"That sounds good, but who am I going to tell? The press isn't going to report anything that might make a Democrat look bad, especially not the one who's in the White House now and the one who's next in line to take over. Sure, there are still a few conservative news outlets, but for the most part they're preaching to the choir, the thirty-five percent of the country that still works and pays taxes to take care of the other sixty-five percent."

"If that's true, then why do they care enough to try to kill you?"

"Because sometimes the wind blows in the other direction," Gardner replied. "If something's big enough, and bad enough, like that nerve gas business a few years ago, people might wake up, look around, and see what's really happening in this country. The Democrats are scared to death that'll happen and weaken their grip on power." He shrugged. "Freedom's a funny thing. Once it takes root, you never can tell what'll happen. Demographics say the Democrats can never be beaten again, but they're still running scared anyway. They don't want to take any chances."

Miranda's head was still spinning. She said, "Shouldn't you at least upload what's on that drive to a secure server somewhere?"

"A secure server?" Gardner laughed. "What makes you think such a thing even exists anymore, Ms. Stephens? It's been years since the average citizen or business had any privacy in this country. They see everything. They have programs that monitor billions of e-mails and Web postings a day, and those programs are the closest thing to artificial intelligences that have been come up with yet. They flag anything that looks the least bit like a threat to the administration. Then before you know it, some guy who runs an auto repair shop in Idaho who bitches about the government in an e-mail to a buddy is facing years of harassment from the IRS. A woman who posts something the least bit critical of the President on her blog has her ISP shut her down because she supposedly violated their terms of service. Some poor sucker who writes a magazine article the administration doesn't like is arrested, and the cops find kiddie porn on his computer that he never put there, so he goes to prison and gets shanked the second week he's there. We're one step away from American gulags, Ms. Stephens. One step." Gardner sighed. "Sorry. Didn't mean to get wound up like that. I didn't really realize all this stuff until recently. It's been quite a blow to a guy who always believed in his country." He sat up straighter. "All of which still leaves us with the question of what we're going to do about your client's problem."

Miranda's crazy thoughts had settled down to what seemed to her like the one chance they had.

"Let me make a call," she said. "I think I know someone who might be able to help."

Gardner grunted and said, "He'd better be ready for trouble if he gets mixed up in this."

"I think he's capable of handling it," Miranda said.

Chapter 58

If what Ben Gardner had said was true, somebody somewhere who wished them harm was probably monitoring Miranda's phone calls.

But there was only so much the enemy could do in the middle of busy downtown Austin. It was a little ironic, she thought. Austin was one of the most liberal places in Texas. Most of the other people in the bar were probably staunch supporters of progressive icons like the President and Senator Rutland.

Yet their presence was one of the things that kept killers who worked for those icons from sweeping in here and murdering a couple of their heroes' political enemies.

Twenty minutes later, while Miranda was still nursing her first mug of beer, Colonel Thomas Atkinson and four other men came into the bar. Atkinson was thirty or forty years older than most of the people in here, but somehow he didn't look out of place.

The men with him were all much younger, clean-cut, friendly looking but somehow with an air of danger about them. Miranda suspected that all of them were heavily armed, although you couldn't tell it from their casual outfits.

Atkinson spotted Miranda and Gardner right away and came across the room toward them. One of the men accompanied him while the other three spread out a little to form a perimeter.

Miranda slid over and patted the bench beside her. Atkinson sat down. The other man moved into the other side of the booth next to Gardner, who regarded both of the newcomers warily. Miranda thought Gardner probably didn't like being hemmed in like this.

"I'm glad to see you, colonel," Miranda told Atkinson.

"I wasn't sure we'd hear from you again quite this soon," he said. "When you called our mutual friend's private line, you didn't explain to her what had happened."

"I think it's best we wait until we get back to her place to talk about that," Miranda said.

Even in the governor's mansion, she thought, there might be listening ears—but the likelihood was a lot lower.

"I'm Tom Atkinson," the colonel said as he extended a hand across the table to Gardner.

Gardner shook hands with him and said, "You can call me Ben."

"All right, Ben." Atkinson nodded to his dark-haired, handsome companion. "This is my buddy Dave Flannery."

"Good to meet you, Ben," Flannery said as he shook hands with Gardner, too.

"You have a vehicle outside?" Miranda asked.

"Oh, yeah," Atkinson said. "Armor-plated. Bulletproof glass. You wouldn't know it to look at it, but it'll stand up to anything short of a rocket attack."

"Funny you should mention that," Gardner said. "That's actually one of the things we have to worry about."

Atkinson raised an eyebrow quizzically and said, "Really?"

"I had to dodge one a week or so back in Manila. If it happens here, though, it'll be an American drone launching it."

Atkinson frowned.

"You're not saying that one of our drones would fire a missile into the heart of an American city and kill hundreds of civilians?"

"I think they stopped being *our* drones a while back," Gardner said. "Whoever's sitting in the Oval Office seems to think they belong to him, and he can do whatever he damned well pleases with them."

"As long as he's a Democrat, he's probably right, for all practical purposes," Atkinson said.

Flannery suggested, "Maybe we'd better not waste any time getting out of here."

"Good idea," Atkinson agreed with a nod. "Just so you two know, I've got five more men outside keeping things clean around here. You ready?"

"More than ready," Miranda said. "There are things that the—our mutual friend needs to know."

The governor's mansion was free of bugs, Atkinson assured them.

"We sweep the place every day, top to bottom," he said. "When your enemy has the resources of the entire country at his disposal, you've got to stay on your toes."

"How sad," Miranda murmured, "that we have to regard the President of the United States as the enemy."

"That's what you get when you keep electing people who can't figure out if they want to turn us into a communist nation, or an Islamic one, or some other radical flavor of the month that's supposed to usher in some sort of progressive paradise," Atkinson said. "What they never seem to remember is that the communists have murdered more people than anybody else over the past century and a half. They make the Nazis look like amateurs. And if the radical Islamists ever take over, the first thing they'll do is chop off the heads of about half the people who like to whine about how Islam is a religion of peace. And yet the Democrats are unwavering in their support of those types."

From behind the desk in her private office here in the mansion, Governor Delgado said, "I want to hear what Mr. Gardner has to say about this information he's brought to us."

Gardner, who seemed to have relaxed once he finally realized that he was safe among allies and didn't have to run for his life anymore, held up the little metal rectangle.

"If you want to open these files, governor, they'll tell you the whole story."

Delgado took the USB drive from him and plugged it into a port on her computer.

"Why did you head for Texas when you got back to the states, Mr. Gardner?" she asked as the files were loading.

"I'd looked at those documents you're about to see enough to know that the whole thing centered around Mr. Brannock's ranch. I did a little research, found that you'd had your own squabbles with the Feds—"

"Squabbles," Atkinson said. "I like that."

"Anyway," Gardner said, "I found out as much as I could about what's been going on, and then I figured I would try to get in here and dump the whole thing in your lap. That's why I was outside tonight. I saw Ms. Stephens leaving and recognized her, so I decided on the spur of the moment to approach her first." He looked at Miranda, smiled, and shook his head. "I owe you an apology. I almost got you killed when that assassin came after me."

"What's important is that you're here now," Miranda told him. "And between all of us, we're going to figure out what to do to help G.W. and Kyle."

Delgado leaned forward in her chair to frown at the monitor in front of her. In a stunned voice, she said, "I know what you told us, Mr. Gardner, but to see it all laid out like this in black-and-white . . ."

"Yes, it's pretty sickening that our country's leaders would get mixed up in something like that, isn't it? To put so many people at risk, just to make money—"

"It's not just the money," Delgado snapped. "That man hates Texas and everything about it."

No one had to ask her who she was talking about.

"I'm sure Senator Rutland is more interested in the profit that he and his brother-in-law will make," the governor went on. "But the President, what he wants is to dump millions of tons of poison on us and see what happens. He wants to ruin our air and our water and sit back and laugh while we die of cancer and radiation sickness."

"Why would that surprise you, Maria?" Atkinson asked. "Remember when there was a chance a hurricane would strike the city where the Republican National Convention was being held, and one of the Democrats said he hoped all of them washed out to sea. How many times has some Democrat politician gone on record as wanting Republicans to get cancer and die? Remember the Ebola scare? A Democrat said she wished all gun-rights supporters would get Ebola and die. They say things like that all the time. The so-called party of peace, love, and diversity is just stewing in their own bitter hatred for everybody who doesn't agree with them a hundred percent."

"I know!" Delgado shouted angrily as she slammed a fist down on her desk. "But it shouldn't be that way!"

"No, it shouldn't," Atkinson agreed in a quiet voice. "But we have to deal with the world the way it is, not the way we wish it could be. So what are we going to do about this? Are we going to stand by and let those so-called UN *peacekeepers* sweep over G.W. Brannock's ranch like a Mongol horde? You know good and well the Chinese government insisted that they would provide the troops for this mission."

"Of course, they did," Gardner put in. "They don't want that toxic nightmare in their country, and they've got to have somewhere to put it."

Governor Delgado sat there breathing a little heavily while Miranda, Atkinson, and Gardner watched her. Finally, she gave a little nod, almost to herself, and looked up at them.

"They're not going to get away with it," she said. "Not in Texas."

"We don't know how those crooked bastards in Washington will react if we step in," Atkinson said, but the grin on his face made the statement sound like anticipation, rather than a warning.

"Not in Texas," Governor Delgado repeated.

Chapter 59

It was sort of like they were in a fort surrounded by hostile Comanches in one of those old Western movies G.W. loved so much, thought Kyle as he stood on the ranch house porch watching the stars begin to fade while the ebony sky overhead slowly turned gray. Dawn wasn't far off now.

Slade Grayson hadn't pinned down the hour on the deadline he'd given them. He'd just said that they had until morning to surrender.

Knowing Grayson, he'd tell the Chinese to attack at the crack of dawn. More dramatic that way, and the man loved his drama, even though there were no TV news cameras around to record it this time.

Kyle was sure that after the fact . . . after he and G.W. and all their allies had been wiped out in a bloody slaughter . . . camera crews would come in and broadcast a carefully staged scenario to the rest of the world. They would make it look like the ranch's defenders were the bad guys, the aggressors, the radical, violent right-wing extremists who had caused the whole thing.

And too many people would just nod solemnly and

think that, yes, those awful, evil conservatives are just like that, then go on eagerly lining up at the trough of their masters, never giving a thought to the fact that one of these days, the same sort of hammer inevitably would fall on them, too.

G.W. came out onto the porch behind him, carrying a cup of coffee.

"Thinkin' deep thoughts?"

"Thinking sad thoughts. What we do here isn't going to change anything, you know that, don't you, G.W.?"

G.W. sipped his coffee and said, "Do you recall me sayin' anything about wantin' to change the world?"

"Well, no . . ."

"I'm doin' this because I won't be put off land that rightfully belongs to me. I'm not doin' it to make a statement or to open anybody's eyes. I'm doin' it because I'm a stubborn old bastard who won't be pushed around by the government or anybody else. As for the rest of you . . . well, I reckon you got your own reasons. I'm not sure any of those reasons are good enough to be dyin' over, but I reckon that's up to you." G.W. paused. "I still wish you'd light out for the mountains, all of you. Scatter and go back to your lives."

"My life is here now," Kyle said quietly. "I don't really care about making a statement, either. You're my granddad and I love you. That's enough of a statement for me."

G.W. put his free hand on Kyle's shoulder and squeezed.

"Son, you've made this old man proud."

"It's about time, I suppose."

G.W. shook his head and said, "See, that's where you're wrong. I've *always* been proud of you, even when it looked like you'd lost your way, because I knew the sort of stuff you had inside you. I knew you'd come around and figure things out."

"If that's true, you had a lot more faith in me than I ever had."

"More than likely. That's what family's for, isn't it?"

A grin spread across Kyle's face. He reached down to the Winchester that was leaning against the porch railing and picked it up.

"Let's go kick some Chinese ass," he said.

"Go get you some coffee first," G.W. said. "We want to be good and awake for this."

The Chinese positions had been ablaze with light all night. Generators chugged constantly. The so-called UN forces were trying to intimidate the ranch's defenders and make Kyle, G.W., and the others realize just how hopeless their cause was.

That was wasted effort. The men on the other side of the fence knew exactly how hopeless things looked for them. Each man had searched his own heart, realized that he was going to die, probably not long after the sun came up, and accepted that fact as necessary.

Nearly two hundred years earlier, a small group of rough men had stood together inside an old mission in San Antonio and come to that same conclusion. A lot of things had changed in Texas since then.

But not the hearts and spirits of true Texans. That same love of liberty burned just as brightly inside G.W. and Kyle Brannock, Thad Bowman, Dave Sparks, and all the others. That had never changed and, God willing, never would.

Texan to the bone. Texan to the blood.

Bring it, you sons of bitches, thought Kyle as he stood

behind one of the pickups parked near the fence and watched the Chinese troops moving around on the other side of the highway.

The sun wasn't up yet, but there was enough light for the defenders to see the enemy getting ready to launch their attack. There was nothing secretive about it. With such a huge advantage in numbers and firepower, there was no reason for the Chinese to sneak around and try to hide what they were doing.

The orange glow on the eastern horizon brightened even more. In a matter of minutes, that fiery orb would appear, a sliver at first, then rising steadily higher as its light spread across the West Texas landscape.

Before that happened, Slade Grayson walked out alone into the middle of the deserted highway.

"Brannock!" he shouted. "G.W. Brannock!"

"I hear you!" G.W. called from where he stood beside Kyle.

"Last chance, old man! You've defied the federal government long enough. Your time's up! Open that gate, and you and all the others come out with your hands up. You won't be hurt. You won't ever see the outside of a federal prison again, I can promise you that, but we won't cut you down like you deserve."

"You know, Grayson, I reckon I was a little wrong about you," G.W. said.

Even from this distance, Kyle could see the puzzled frown on Grayson's face. The government man asked, "How do you figure that?"

"I had you pegged as a bully, and most bullies are cowards at heart. But you're not yellow, Grayson. You're standin' right out there in the open, and you've got to know that I could put a bullet through your head before you could get back to cover if I wanted to."

Grayson laughed and said, "You wouldn't do that. I'm a pretty good judge of character. I could tell right away that you think of yourself as an honorable man. You're not a murderer."

"How about you?" G.W. asked. "Have you deluded yourself into thinkin' that *you're* an honorable man?"

That brought another laugh from Grayson. He said, "I'm a man who gets things done. That's all. And I'm getting you off that ranch."

"Not alive, you're not."

"So be it, then," Grayson said with a shrug. He turned and walked at an easy, deliberate pace back toward the Chinese lines. As he went, he raised his right hand above his head and revolved it in a slow, "wind 'em up" motion.

The engines of the Chinese armored fighting vehicles rumbled to life.

Kyle took a deep breath. His heart slugged heavily in his chest. He was scared, no doubt about that. He didn't want to die, and that seemed inevitable.

Yet at the same time a great calmness spread through him. He knew he was exactly where he was meant to be, doing exactly what he was meant to be doing. There really was such a thing as destiny, after all, and this was his.

Still, there was a part of him that wished he could see Miranda one more time, take her into his arms and kiss her and tell her just how much she had come to mean to him over the past couple of weeks. Could people really fall in love that fast?

Damn right they could, he thought.

He turned to look at G.W., grinned, and said, "Here they come."

"Yep." G.W. raised his rifle to his shoulder. "They may take this ranch, but they're not gonna steal it. They're gonna pay for it . . . in blood."

Red-gold sunlight burst over the land.

A thunderous, earthshaking roar of gunfire shattered the early morning quiet.

Chapter 60

A volley of rifle fire crashed out from the Chinese forces in the front ranks. That deadly storm of lead raked the vehicles that the ranch's defenders had arranged in a skirmish line. Kyle and the other men got off a few shots in return, but for the most part the barrage forced them to duck for cover.

As they did that, the Chinese vehicles surged forward through gaps in the line of troops and roared across the highway toward the fence. They would batter through the wire with no trouble at all.

Kyle crouched at the front of the pickup where he had taken cover and fired past its grille at one of the armored vehicles. He aimed at the tires, knowing the rifle slugs would bounce off the armor plating. The windshield was probably bulletproof, too.

Unfortunately, his shots didn't seem to have any effect on the tires. They were probably solid rubber, unable to go flat.

Machine guns mounted on the vehicles opened up, tongues of flame flickering from their muzzles. These weapons were firing armor-piercing rounds, and they ripped through the pickups, SUVs, and jeeps the defenders were using for shelter. Several men were thrown off their feet as those rounds shredded them into bloody husks.

Just before the first of the armored vehicles struck the fence, a high-pitched whine sounded. Something streaked through the air, and the Chinese vehicle exploded in a huge ball of fire. More streaks flashed in, and eye-searing blasts engulfed another pair of attackers. Explosions threw dirt and gravel high in the air and knocked over two more of the vehicles. That left just one of them untouched, and it slewed to a halt as its driver didn't know what to do.

Three helicopter gunships swooped over the highway. Their missile racks were empty now, but they were still armed with automatic weapons that scythed lead through the Chinese ground troops. With an ear-pounding *whup-whup-whup*, a pair of Hueys appeared and lowered toward the highway. Before they ever touched down, armored and helmeted men were leaping through open doors and charging into the fight with automatic weapons blazing.

Behind the bullet-battered pickup, Kyle and G.W. watched in stunned astonishment as the reinforcements took the fight to the enemy. Kyle's mouth opened and closed a couple of times before he was able to say, "Who . . . who . . ."

"Look there," G.W. said, pointing.

Kyle looked where his grandfather indicated and saw the flag painted on the side of the nearest Huey.

It was the familiar red, white, and blue Lone Star flag.

The flag of the state of Texas.

"The governor must have sent those fellas," G.W. said over the cacophony of battle.

"I'll bet Miranda had something to do with this," Kyle said.

"I wouldn't doubt it a bit."

The gunships had done an effective job of softening up the Chinese position, but the Texan troops were still outnumbered. G.W. finished thumbing fresh rounds through his Winchester's loading gate, then stood up and waved the rifle over his head.

"Let's go give those boys a hand!" he shouted to his allies.

Yelling at the top of their lungs, the surviving defenders charged out from behind the vehicles and ran to the gate. They didn't bother unlocking the chain holding it closed. They just swarmed over, leaped to the ground, and raced across the highway to join the battle.

The Chinese discipline had evaporated in the face of the sudden, unexpected attack. Now it was a wild melee that spread across the mesquite-dotted landscape, scores of individual battles or clashes between small groups. The chatter of gunfire, the bursts of explosions, the screams of dying men, all blended together in a nightmarish melody of war.

Kyle was in the middle of it, blasting away at the Chinese troops. Those bright blue helmets made it easy to find targets. He aimed not for the helmets themselves but for the visors of hard, clear plastic covering the faces of the men who wore them. If struck at an angle, those visors would cause a bullet to glance off, but a direct hit would sometimes shatter them and plow into the face behind them.

Kyle felt a moment's sympathy for the men who were dying here, but no more than that. It was entirely possible their communist masters had forced them to come over here, but they and their countrymen had embraced that destructive, insidious, blood-drenched philosophy in the first place.

Kyle was going to kill as many of them as he could.

In the chaos, he lost track of his grandfather. G.W. was somewhere in the ruckus, Kyle knew, but he didn't have time to look for him. Instead, he reloaded until he ran out of ammunition, and then he used the rifle as a club, wading in and downing one of the Chinese soldiers with a butt stroke that knocked the man's helmet off. Kyle kicked him in the head and rendered him unconscious, then moved on in search of another enemy to fight.

He had barely started looking when someone came out of the confusion and tackled him from the side. Kyle and his attacker both sprawled on the ground and rolled over a couple of times. Kyle found himself on the bottom, with Slade Grayson looming over him. Grayson's face was twisted in lines of hate as he locked his hands around Kyle's throat.

Kyle knew he had only seconds to act before Grayson's powerful thumbs crushed his windpipe. He bucked up off the ground and swung his right hand in a brutal chop against the side of Grayson's neck. That loosened the government man's grip, but didn't knock it loose.

Kyle splayed his left hand over Grayson's face and tried to dig his fingers into the man's eyes. Grayson jerked his head back. Kyle shot a short punch into his solar plexus that made Grayson gasp for breath.

Kyle was a lot shorter on air than Grayson was, though. His head spun crazily, and a red haze was beginning to drip down over his vision. He arched his back again and swung both open hands against Grayson's ears.

That finally did it. Grayson's fingers spasmed and came open. Kyle bucked like a bronco for the third time, and

Grayson toppled off to the side. Kyle rolled the other way to put some distance between them as he dragged in desperate lungfuls of air—mixed, of course, with a considerable amount of dust since a huge cloud of it hung over the battlefield.

Elsewhere, not far away, guns continued to chatter and roar. Explosions threw even more dirt and grit into the air.

None of that mattered to Kyle and Grayson. To the two of them, the whole world had narrowed down to the few square yards where they staggered to their feet and resumed their battle.

Elemental, primitive fury gripped both men now as they stood toe-to-toe and slugged at each other. No fancy martial arts moves, no jumping and whirling and spinning, just brute strength and determination as they tried to batter each other into submission.

Grayson was taller and heavier, but Kyle was a little quicker. He landed three punches for every two of Grayson's. And slowly but surely, he began to force Grayson back. The government man gave ground grudgingly, but the tide had turned against him and both of them knew it.

Kyle sank a left to the wrist in Grayson's belly. As Grayson started to double over, Kyle's right first was there to meet his jaw. The blow landed solidly, with a sound like an ax cleaving a block of wood. Grayson's head slewed to the side, and his knees buckled.

He went down on those knees and stayed there as Kyle backed off a step. Slowly, Grayson shook his head as he tried to gather his wits. Kyle expected him to collapse the rest of the way.

Somehow, Grayson stayed upright. He wobbled and swayed to his feet. Fists ready, Kyle moved in to finish him off.

But before Kyle could reach him, Grayson reached under his suit jacket and brought out a small, flat automatic pistol. Through broken teeth and swollen, bloody lips, he rasped, "I wanted to . . . finish you off . . . with my bare hands . . . but you'll be just as dead . . . if I kill you this way."

From behind Kyle, G.W. said, "Go to hell," and a rifle blasted. Kyle felt the hot wind-rip of the bullet as it whipped past his ear. The slug struck Grayson in the center of the forehead and jolted his head back as his skull exploded outward in a grisly spray of blood and bone fragments and diseased brain matter.

This time when Grayson thudded to the ground with the pistol still unfired in his hand, there would be no getting up.

Kyle turned to see his grandfather limping toward him, old lever-action Winchester in hand. Crimson stains dotted G.W.'s work clothes here and there, but he didn't seem to be seriously injured. In fact, there was a big grin on the rancher's rugged face.

Behind G.W. came a tall, equally tough-looking man in some sort of fatigue uniform, flanked by several more soldiers. The patch on the tall man's uniform was a Lone Star flag.

Kyle realized that except for sporadic shots, the battlefield had fallen silent. He looked around and saw that the Chinese troops who were still alive had withdrawn a couple of hundred yards and formed up again, but they weren't attacking, just waiting to see what was going to happen. Kyle estimated that there were fifty or sixty of them left.

The tall man came up to Kyle and said, "I'm Colonel Thomas Atkinson. The governor sent me to give you folks a hand. It took some fancy work from our pilots to get through that no-fly zone, but I'm glad to see that we got here in time."

Kyle was still having a little trouble catching his breath. He said, "Me, too . . . colonel. But isn't the governor . . . gonna get in a lot of trouble . . . over this?"

Atkinson grinned and said, "The mood we're all in, I don't think any of us particularly care right now."

Kyle looked around at the bodies littering the field, the burning Chinese assault vehicles, the gunships hovering not far away, the men who had come to defend the ranch standing ready along the highway, and knew that if the UN forces wanted to resume the battle, they would have one hell of a fight on their hands.

"By the way," Atkinson said, "a certain blond lawyer sends her regards."

"Miranda?" Kyle asked, then realized a second later what a stupid question that was.

"That's right," Atkinson responded with a grin. "She's a pretty determined lady. It was all we could do to make her stay in Austin with the governor."

"Yeah," Kyle said with a smile of his own. "I can see that." He grew more serious. "What made the governor decide to send in troops? And . . . who are you guys?"

"Just some fellas ready to stand up for Texas, and for what's right. Maria's been putting together a force for emergencies such as this, when somebody has to stop the federal government from running roughshod over the people's rights."

"But you're not fightin' just the federal government," G.W. pointed out. He nodded toward the Chinese forces. "You're takin' on the UN. The whole dang world, in other words."

"Texas versus the world," Atkinson said. He took an unlit stub of a cigar from the pocket of his fatigues, stuck it in his mouth, and clamped his teeth down it. "Sounds like pretty fair odds to me!"

Washington, D.C.

Angela Jessup hated to go into the Oval Office right now. The President had been getting reports from Texas all morning, and he was upset.

That was putting it mildly. He was on the verge of a stroke, or declaring martial law, whichever came first.

He wouldn't like hearing what Jessup had to tell him. Earlier, it had seemed impossible that the news could get any worse, but then other bulletins had started breaking. So far, only on the one cable news network the White House couldn't control, but those bastards at the other networks, in their never-ending quest for ratings, would soon start nipping at the story as well. Corporate greed would trump partisanship, at least for a little while.

Jessup took a deep breath and went in.

The President was pacing back and forth, hands behind his back, face mottled with fury. He swung toward her and snapped, "What is it? Have the UN forces wiped out those traitors yet?"

"Not exactly, sir," Jessup replied. "The Secretary-General has ordered General Ling to hold his position."

"Hold his position!" The President stared at her. "That's insane! The damn Chinaman still has enough troops to wipe out Brannock and his friends *and* the rebels that Mexican bitch sent in!"

"That's just it. The Secretary-General says that the actions by Governor Delgado this morning place this incident in the category of an internal problem for the United

States and plans to tell the UN forces to withdraw." Jessup grimaced as the President stared at her. "To put it bluntly, sir, things have gone too far and he's hanging you out to dry." She paused, then added, "He wasn't too happy about the UN being dragged into a situation caused by a phony land grant and a deal with the Chinese government that stinks of graft and corruption, not to mention posing a grave threat to the health and well-being of American citizens."

The President bared his teeth and said, "What. The. Hell. Are. You. Talking. About?"

"The land grant was a fake," Jessup said softly. "You must have known that. And you and Senator Rutland are in bed with the Chinese to the tune of billions of dollars and millions of tons of toxic radioactive waste. I don't really *care* about any of that, Mr. President . . . but you could have told me about it so I wouldn't be operating in the dark."

The President's breath panted between his teeth. He asked, "How did you hear about any of that?"

"The story is breaking on TV. Our friends at the networks will sweep it under the rug as much as possible, of course, but it's out on the Internet, too. Something like that . . . it never goes away. Some people will never look at you the same way again."

His lip curled in a sneer as he said, "Our supporters won't care. Not enough of them, anyway. As long as we keep giving them what they want, they'll keep voting for us. Hell, we're above the law, Angela! You know that."

"Today we are," Jessup said quietly. "What about tomorrow?"

The President clenched a hand into a fist and said, "Tomorrow people will believe what we tell them to believe. They'll do what we tell them to do. They'll blame the goddamn Republicans for anything and everything that's wrong in their lives! Just like we tell them. . . ."

Silence hung in the Oval Office air for a moment, silence broken only by the President's harsh breathing. Finally, Jessup asked, "What are you going to do about the situation in Texas?"

"The UN is definitely withdrawing?"

"Yes, sir. The Secretary-General said something about not doing your dirty work for you."

"Well, then, I guess that the army—"

"With all due respect, sir, if you force your military commanders to give the order to kill American civilians, you run the risk of the front-line troops turning around and firing in the other direction. You don't want to take even the slightest chance of that happening. Once it did . . ."

The President blanched. He knew exactly what his chief of staff meant.

Visions of soldiers bursting into this very office played out in his head. Visions of him being dragged out of the White House, hauled over to one of the trees on the lawn outside, a tree with a rope thrown over a branch, and then . . .

Jessup knew what he was thinking as she saw the fight go out of him. Power meant everything to him—except when it came to saving his own skin.

He said, "It's over, Angela. We made a bet, and we lost. Simple as that." He shook his head. "Lost to a damned old codger and a kid. Who would have thought it?"

"Strange things happen in this country, sir. They always have." She hesitated. "What about Governor Delgado?"

The President's eyes narrowed as hatred blazed in them. He said, "She's drawn the battle lines. We'll let this mess fade for a while. But one of these days soon . . . Texas is going to find out what it's like to go to war against the United States."

West Texas

The bodies, the burned-out assault vehicles, most of the signs of battle were gone by the time the sun set that evening, along with the surviving Chinese troops. The bullet-riddled pickups and SUVs by the fence had been towed away. Wounded men were in the hospital. The ones who had been killed were in the morgue. In the days to come, there would be heroes' burials for them.

The country was deeply shaken. The problems here in West Texas in the past had been characterized by the news media as terrorist attacks or blamed on the Mexican drug cartels or a combination of both. That wasn't the case this time. No matter how much the media tried to shield the Democrat politicians involved, people were starting to talk about how maybe what the President had done wasn't right. He had been mixed up in a clandestine deal with the Chinese that could have done major damage to the country, and he had manipulated events so that troops of a foreign nation had ventured onto American soil and killed American citizens, all with the administration's blessing.

The outrage people felt tonight probably wouldn't be enough to change anything . . . but at least for once it was being pointed in the right direction.

At the moment Kyle didn't care about any of that. The only thing that mattered to him this evening was that he was sitting on the swing on G.W.'s front porch with Miranda next to him. His arm was around her, and her head rested on his shoulder.

They sat there in silence for a long time and let the cool, peaceful night air drift over them, but then Miranda sighed and said, "We're going to have to talk about this sooner or later, you know."

"I don't see why," Kyle said. "We're both alive, G.W.'s a tough old coot who's gonna be fine, and everybody in the whole dang world knows this ranch is really his, thanks to you. I don't see why we have to talk about a blessed thing right now."

"It's not thanks to me that the world knows. It was Governor Delgado and the team she put together that proved the land grant was a fake."

"After you got her started on the idea."

"And it was Ben Gardner, or whatever his name really is, who exposed the reason behind it. Without the information he brought us . . ."

"What happened to him, anyway?" Kyle asked, curious in spite of himself.

"He dropped out of sight again. I think he's worried that someone will come after him in retaliation for what he did. The Chinese or . . ."

"Or the Democrats," Kyle said when she didn't finish.

"The President is a vengeful man, Governor Delgado says. Sooner or later he'll do something about what happened today."

"Texas versus the world, as Colonel Atkinson says." Kyle chuckled. "I like our odds."

After a moment, Miranda asked, "What about you, Kyle? What are you going to do?"

"I'm not going back to being a bum, if that's what you're asking. I'm staying right here on this ranch."

With the clump of the cane he was using because of the minor wound in his leg, G.W. came onto the porch and said, "Darn right you're stayin' here. This'll be your place one of these days, and I've only got so much time left to make sure you know how to take care of it."

"As long as one of these days doesn't come too soon, G.W.," Kyle said.

The old rancher grinned and said, "Oh, I reckon I've got a few years of kickin' and fussin' left. Time enough to enjoy playin' with some grandkids."

"G.W.," Miranda said, sounding slightly embarrassed. "You're getting a little ahead of yourself, aren't you?"

"I don't think so. I know the real thing when I see it, and that's what I see when I look at you two." He leaned a hand on the porch railing as he peered out across the moonlit range and said, "That's what I see out there, too. Somethin' real, somethin' worth fightin' for. It's been ours for a hundred and fifty years, and we're not gonna give it up." He turned and started back toward the door. "Sorry I interrupted you young folks. I'll let you get back to whatever you were doin'."

"Talking about the future," Kyle said. "That's what we were doing."

"It's out there waitin' for us all," G.W. said. "No tellin' what it'll bring."

The screen door banged behind him as he went in the house.